An Impression of Murder

Gerard Gilbert

Published by New Generation Publishing in 2024

Copyright © Gerard Gilbert 2024

First Edition

The author asserts the moral right under the Copyright, Designs and Patents Act 1988 to be identified as the author of this work.

All Rights reserved. No part of this publication may be reproduced, stored in a retrieval system or transmitted, in any form or by any means without the prior consent of the author, nor be otherwise circulated in any form of binding or cover other than that which it is published and without a similar condition being imposed on the subsequent purchaser.

ISBN: 978-1-83563-415-8

www.newgeneration-publishing.com

New Generation Publishing

For Lizzie

First when we see them painted, things we have passed
Perhaps a hundred times nor cared to see;
And so they are better, painted – better to us.
Which is the same thing. Art was given for that.
Robert Browning

BEFOREHAND: MAY 1897

It was while crossing Paris that he first suspected he was being followed. He had taken a one-horse carriage from the Gare de Lyon to the Gare Saint-Lazare when, peering behind him, he had noticed a similar cab on his tail. Nothing extraordinary in that. But when he had told his driver to pull up as they passed the Place Vendome, he noticed that, having overtaken them, the other cab had stopped about fifty metres further on. Nobody climbed in or out.

He had tried to catch a glimpse of any passengers as the cab had passed, but the curtain had been drawn. Having waited five minutes and not wanting to miss his train, he had told the driver to carry on. Pulling up outside the station, he noted that the other cab was again upon their heels. He would have waited for the mysterious passenger or passengers to alight, but his train was about to depart.

Until then, the journey had been long but uneventful. Captain Khaled Ayari of the 4th Tunisian Tirailleurs Regiment had sailed out of the Bay of Tunis the previous morning. Passing the ancient ruins of Carthage, Khaled had raised his hand to feel the packet that was stitched into his undershirt. He would repeat this action on countless occasions during the voyage to Marseille. To an onlooker, the compulsive touching the breast of his gold-braided Zouave jacket might have looked devotional.

He had fought against sleep as the train from Marseille rocked and swayed through the Provencal countryside and its red-roofed villages, past Avignon and the Rhone and then...

He had jerked awake and observed his fellow passengers. None of them appeared unusually interested in him, except for a small boy whose guileless gaze yo-yoed between Khaled's face and the fez that lay on Khaled's lap.

Again, he had felt for the packet sewn into his undershirt and, thus comforted, he was soon once more asleep.

He was familiar with France, one of the reasons that he had been selected for this mission. That and the fact that he was trusted by his commander, a man who confided in very few others. Especially within the army. And now the first inkling that he was being followed as he took the cab to the Gare Saint-Lazare.

Shrouded in steam, the train to Rouen was preparing to depart as he hurried down the platform, the guard urgently ushering him into the last open door. It was a third-class carriage and he had a second-class ticket, but no matter. At least he had caught the train.

The door slammed shut behind him only to be re-opened as another latecomer bundled himself into the carriage. He wore a fashionable Homburg hat which he doffed to the ladies, revealing a large, square and totally bald head. The man passed down the carriage and they set off.

At Rouen, Khaled had to change trains for Dieppe. There was an hour's wait so he sought the refreshment room, ordering coffee and a tart. A coal fire had been lit in here for which he was grateful, for the springtime air in Normandy was noticeably fresher than in Paris.

Finally, the train to Dieppe. In the late afternoon sunshine the countryside was fecund with small grassy meadows, tumbling hedgerows and ancient orchards decked in blossom. The bedecked trees reminded him of the almond blooms back home in Tunisia, but these were apple trees. The square-headed fellow with the fashionable Homburg sat unseen two carriages down.

End of the line. As he left Dieppe station and its swirling miasma of wet steam and black grit, seagulls swooped and cried and taxi cab drivers eyed him uncertainly, caught between a desire for business and confusion at his unusual attire.

He had to find a hotel. A hotel that accepted Arabs because he knew from experience that some wouldn't; not even officers of the French Army of Africa. They would be conveniently "full". *Je suis désolé, monsieur, mais…* And then he had another idea and made his way towards the port. He had been paid well for this mission, with plenty of cash for expenses, and perhaps he could find a lady to entertain him for a while.

He was certain now that he was being followed. On two occasions he found himself wandering down a dead-end street and had been forced to double back on himself. And both times he heard the same footsteps stop and start, not quite in tandem with his own. An echo but not an echo. Turning to look, he couldn't see anybody either on the street or lurking in the shadows of doorways.

He reached the port, where café tables were thronged beneath brick arcades, while fishing boats bobbed on the oily water. To his left were grander buildings while to his right, more humble dwellings rose upon a hill towards the cliffs. He headed in that direction.

Khaled stopped at a waterfront pension that had a board outside advertising vacancies. Peering through the open doorway he saw that it looked clean but not too smart. A concierge beckoned him over and Khaled agreed to take a room, paying in advance. He said he would return in one hour, leaving his valise behind the front desk.

Stepping back out onto the street he waited and listened, breathing in the sea air mingling with the coal fumes of a passing harbour tug. And then he turned and headed towards the red lantern that he had noticed earlier.

Removing his fez, he knocked on the door next to the red lamp. A tall, stern-looking matron opened it almost immediately and looked him up and down. Finally, she nodded and stepped aside.

An hour later, as he dressed, Khaled peeked out from behind the dirty, tattered lace curtain of the bedroom. The young woman was sitting on the edge of her bed with her naked back to him, counting the bundle of notes with which she had been paid. He couldn't exactly say why, but he trusted her to do what he had asked.

The street lamps had been lit and nobody appeared to be around. Stepping outside again, he shuddered at the drop in temperature. A light mist now coated the water, but his mind was on the girl whose room he had just left. Had he been foolish to have trusted her? Her name was Jeanne, she had said, as she tucked the package - the papers that had been sewn into his undershirt - beneath her mattress. She had seemed sweet and honest. She lived a few doors down but would be sleeping here tonight because her husband was a fisherman and wouldn't be back before dawn. She then mimed someone taking a drink and Khaled reckoned she meant that the husband would be drunk. Return after breakfast, she had said, and for some reason he had trusted her – a trust reinforced with the promise of a generous tip.

His commander in Tunis would have been furious, but the conviction of being followed had made Khaled uneasy. If, as he feared, he was being shadowed by the military police, they could easily arrest him and search his uniform. A night's rest should make it clear whether or not he was really being followed.

He was hungry now and hoped that the pension would still be serving an evening meal. As he neared the front steps, he noticed a familiar figure sitting on an iron mooring. It was the man with the square head and the Homburg hat, the one from the Paris train, and he appeared to be smiling. At his feet was the valise that Khaled had left at the pension. What was this stranger doing with his valise?

'*Bonsoir Capitaine Ayari*,' this stranger said. He was not so much smiling as smirking, Khaled realised – his final thought because someone then punched him in the back, hard between his shoulder blades. At least that's what it felt like. If a sharp knock to his temple had not then made him lose consciousness, he might have realised that he had been stabbed and not punched. He did not feel the water rise up to meet him.

CHAPTER ONE

DIEPPE, MAY 1897: THE ENGLISH

'Huzzah! Off with their heads… huzzah!'

Colonel Marsden took another swipe at the long grass with his golf club. A veteran of the Crimean War, he was often heard to utter such martial exclamations.

The Reverend Henry Gibson sighed as he watched his opponent, attired in Norfolk jacket, knickerbockers and blue worsted stockings, flattening the grass. His own garb felt dowdy in comparison, although the clerical collar covered a multitude of sartorial sins.

This was his first visit to Dieppe's newly opened golf course, which was already quite the fashion with the town's English colony. And it would probably be his last, reckoned Henry, who was feeling guilty because today was a Sunday. There were some in his flock who would have disapproved of his engaging in sporting activities on the sabbath.

But Mr Chapman, the British vice-consul, had earlier reassured him. Since there were no servants involved in this particular endeavour, golf was permissible. 'I have your dispensation then,' Henry had thought with unbecoming scorn. The vice-consul was a pompous man who treated the town as his personal fiefdom.

In all his 56 years Henry had never really indulged in any what might be called 'sporting' activities. There had been croquet on the vicarage lawn back in Surrey – an admission that the colonel had seized upon following his invitation to the golf course. 'It's like croquet combined with a pleasant stroll in the countryside,' he had promised, loaning Henry a spare set of clubs so that the vicar now felt under an obligation to join in this fruitless pursuit.

More immediately bothersome, however, was the difficulty of making any meaningful contact between clubface and ball. The colonel was no more successful in this regard and his ball had sliced off towards the cliff edge, where two men stood before an artist's easel. They were gazing out to sea and paying no attention to the golfers.

'Ahoy there!' the colonel bellowed in English at the men, whose attention he instantly captured. 'Did you happen to notice a small white ball come bounding this way?'. Henry, who strongly suspected that the ball had flown over the cliff edge, stifled a yawn.

The men shook their heads and shrugged, either because they hadn't seen his ball or because they didn't understand English. But then Henry recognised one of them as the British painter who was forever parking his easel around town, crowds of onlookers gathering to admire or sometimes to mock.

For the artist was of the Impressionist persuasion – all rough-and-ready daubs and none of the photographic precision and noble historical and religious scenes that Henry so admired. But it was a younger man who actually appeared to be doing the painting, brush poised as he looked out across the sea; a spectacular vista that contained at its bottom the wide beach and village of Pourville-sur-Mer. The glistening sea, frigid blue turning chalky green as the water approached the shore, didn't require an artist's hand to mimic its perfection, thought Henry. God as the supreme artist.

Both men were tall and lean, the younger one clean-shaven and with dark curly hair, the older man with golden hair and a beard. He seemed to be giving instruction to his young companion.

'Oh, the devil,' growled the colonel to no one in particular. "That's the third ball I've mislaid this afternoon. Do you suppose they come out at night and find all the lost balls and then resell them in the clubhouse? I wouldn't put it past the French, you know.'

Henry was about to reply that the clubhouse was, in fact, run by the English, but the colonel's interest had been diverted by the sight of the artists. He had strong views about this exhibitionist fashion for painting outdoors.

If he had only been familiar with the older of the two men standing in front of the easel, he may have been reassured to learn that Walter Sickert shared many of the colonel's misgivings about painting landscapes out-of-doors. For Walter always had in mind his friend and mentor Degas's dismissive words: "Come off it, painting isn't sport".

"If I were the government," Degas had once written to Walter. "I would have a special brigade of gendarmes to keep an eye on artists who paint landscapes from nature… just a little dose of bird-shot now and then as a warning."

Not that Walter was averse to painting *en plein air*, but he preferred to capture the streets of Dieppe, especially when shadows created pleasing darker tones. But his companion was a beginner, and the view here, with its brilliant greens and blues, would be more instantly pleasing to the novice.

As he came nearer, the colonel overheard the older man, who was wearing a deplorable floppy felt hat, say: 'If you start with a grey mid-tone, then you can add darks and lights to establish the extremes.' An art lesson of sorts, thought the colonel peering at the canvas.

'Very picturesque, young man,' he said, although in truth there was very little to look at; a blue wash for the sky and a few daubs of green for the grass, somewhere in which lay, he was convinced, his golf ball.

'An admirer of the Impressionist landscape?' inquired Walter with a mischievous glint.

'Oh, ho, ho… ah, now…I wouldn't say… I don't know,' blustered the old soldier. 'I judge each painting as it comes.'

'Rightly so,' said Walter. "May I introduce my pupil, Emile Blanchet, otherwise known as Agent Blanchet of the Dieppe police?'

The young man turned his face towards the two golfers. He was clean-shaven in the modern manner, noted the colonel with irritation. The old man, like his comrades in arms, had first grown his beard to keep warm during the Crimean winters. He had been flattered when others back home had emulated the style. These days no respectable gentleman in Dieppe, or in his previous home town of Aldershot, went without a healthy growth of facial hair. The vicar's mutton-chop whiskers he dismissed as half-hearted, noting that the clergyman was now sucking meditatively at one end of a sideburn.

Henry now stepped forward and thrust a long, pale hand towards the young policeman. 'Pleased to make your acquaintance, Agent Blanchet. The Reverend Henry Gibson of the Anglican church in Dieppe.'

Henry believed in maintaining good relations with the French authorities, unlike his congregation. They mostly viewed the locals as either a source of cheap and unusually hard-working domestic labour or an utter irrelevance. The unregarded cogs that eased their incestuous lives of gossiping and social one-upmanship.

Emile shook Henry's soft and unexpectedly limp hand and briefly surveyed his face. He had been training himself to take careful note of people's appearances ever since Walter, on one such painting excursion as this, had chided him for being unobservant. It would be useful for Emile as both a painter and a policeman, his friend had said.

So, the vicar's head was shaped like a boiled egg, Emile decided. A high forehead was exaggerated by a bald pate over which lengths of hair has been combed and greased into place. Wispy sideburns spouted from his cheeks.

Emile then turned his attention to the bearded old Englishman in the knickerbockers and blue stockings. He noticed the blood-shot eyes and broken veins on the small patch of face that wasn't covered in facial hair. The man's lack of manners in not introducing himself had riled the young policeman. He knew the police were regularly met with such a lack of respect – in fact they were known locally as *mouchards*, or snitches.

'Yes, indeed, pleased to meet you,' blustered the old man, reluctantly proffering Emile his hand at last. 'Colonel Aubrey Marsden, late of the 5th Dragoon Guards.'

'A former soldier, I could tell,' said the young policeman in perfect, unaccented English.

'My word, you speak the Queen's English!' exclaimed the colonel.

'I was raised in England, sir,' said Emile. 'My parents are… or, rather, were… French.'

'And Mr Sickert is teaching you to paint?' interjected Henry.

'You know of me, then, sir?' said Walter, staring at Henry from a face that the vicar thought somewhat vulpine. Or that of a ruined saint.

'Why, Mr Sickert, you are famous throughout Dieppe.'

'And further afield too, I trust,' said Walter, struggling not to smile at the vicar's discomfort.

'Why in Paris and London too, I'll warrant,' said Henry, suspecting that Sickert was enjoying some sport with him, but not entirely certain. After all, these artists were jealous of their reputations.

'Now, my ball,' said the colonel, who had grown bored. He was looking around his feet as if the ball might have somehow returned like a dog that, repeatedly beckoned, had eventually slunk back to heel.

'I'm afraid we were too busy debating the exact colour of the sea to notice,' said the young policeman.

'The sea looks damnedly blue to me,' said the colonel, irritated by this presumed impertinence and resuming to flatten the grass. He had little time for the young, bearded or not. 'What now?'

His question was aimed over their heads and towards the road from Dieppe, where a young woman was pushing a bicycle up the hill and waving in their direction.

'Why, Emile. It's your admirer,' Walter muttered in French.

Emile could feel himself blushing. His landlady's daughter, Marie-Hélène, her hat askew and face puce with exertion, looked ridiculous as she now pedalled furiously across the grass towards them on her bicycle. It had pneumatic wheels and a chain-drive and she had won the contraption in a raffle. It would otherwise have been well beyond her mother's means to purchase. The bicycle was her biggest passion after her mother's lodger, for she was indeed enamoured of Emile. He was sorry now that he had ever shared this confidence with Walter.

'Emile… Emile!' cried Marie-Hélène, pulling off her hat and revealing that her flaxen Norman hair had become unpinned (Walter was thinking that he would like to sketch her in this exact moment) 'The commissaire wants to see you urgently. He sent me to find you.'

'But Marie-Hélène? I'm not on duty until tomorrow morning.'

'I have no idea why, Emile,' she gasped. 'He says that he's been looking for you all over town and when I told him that you were painting up here on the cliffs, the information seemed to make him even crosser and he sent me to fetch you at once. Take my bicycle, I can walk back.'

Even though it was his free day to spend as he liked, Emile could imagine his boss being exasperated by the idea of him painting pictures. The commissaire had little time for Emile as it was, and no doubt considered any form of artistry to be an unsuitable pastime for a guardian of the peace.

'We have a carriage arriving at four o'clock to take us back into town, mademoiselle,' said the colonel in English, bowing in a manner he considered courtly. 'If Agent Blanchet takes your bicycle, we would most gladly convey you home. Perhaps you would care to watch us playing golf.'

The girl stood gawping alternately at Emile and the colonel, before Emile translated the colonel's words.

'Take my bicycle, Emile. Hurry!' she urged. 'The commissaire told me it was vital that you be found.'

Emile thanked her and mounted the contraption – a Hirondelle of the type ridden by policemen in Paris. And once again he found himself cursing Commissaire Frossard for his refusal to introduce bicycles for the Dieppe police. The old dinosaur thought it would make officers look ridiculous to be pedalling after criminals, and now here he was reduced to borrowing his landlady's daughter's contraption so that he could rush to attend on Frossard.

* * *

Henry was feeling increasingly impatient as he watched Sickert pack away his painting utensils. It was getting late and he had to prepare for evensong. With the summer season fast approaching, visitors were trickling back to Dieppe to swell the English colony.

'The day Thou gavest, Lord, is ended, the darkness falls at your behest…'. John Ellerton's hymn induced a familiar melancholy as it came to mind. As a young man, Henry had met Ellerton at that great debate about Darwinism in Oxford between the Bishop of Oxford and Thomas Henry Huxley. He could however recall very little about the hymn writer now, 35 years or so later.

Sickert nodded at him in a rather knowing manner, thought Henry, before handing his painting paraphernalia to the coachman. Henry resented, or rather envied (which amounted to the same thing, he believed) the artist's freedom, although such a wild, abandoned approach to life also frightened him. Did Sickert have money of his own, or did he rely on the generosity of his wealthy friends?

There was a rumour that he lived off the earnings of a fishwife in Le Pollet. Henry shuddered at the idea of such degradation before worthier thoughts allayed his distaste. Didn't our Lord consort with fishermen and presumably some of them had wives? Did His disciples have wives? And didn't Jesus forgive the prostitute who washed his feet in perfume and wiped them with her hair?

He tried to imagine Lucy wiping his feet with her hair, and the thought made him laugh out loud (the colonel gave him a quizzical look before flicking away the end of his cigarette). Henry hadn't seen his wife with her hair down since the birth of their youngest, Edward, 25 years ago. Nor had he seen her undressed in all that time.

He sometimes tried and failed to remember her plump little body, these days concealed beneath petticoats, bustles and long dresses of black bombazine – worn, he always assumed, in honour of Queen Victoria and Her Majesty's seemingly endless mourning for Prince Albert. Henry resisted reading anything more into his wife's choice of attire. In any case, she seemed happy enough when with Alice, her female companion.

Lost in their thoughts, the three men silently followed Marie-Hélène aboard the cab, the driver giving a light flick of his whip before the horse clip-clopped resignedly forward towards Dieppe.

CHAPTER TWO

'Ah, there you are Blanchet!' snarled Commissaire Frossard. Those parts of his cheeks that were still visible above his beard and wide pointed moustache were claret-coloured with barely suppressed fury. Emile stood to attention a respectful distance from his boss's desk, biding his time as one might wait out a passing thunderstorm. Not wishing to infuriate his superior further than necessary, he had left Marie-Hélène's bicycle in the yard behind his lodgings and changed into his uniform. Struggling to button the stand-up collar on the blue tunic, he was perspiring heavily by the time he arrived at the station.

'I came as quickly as I could, sir,' he replied, immediately regretting any kind of riposte. Emile often felt that it didn't matter what he said to Frossard, it would always sound impertinent to the older man's ears.

Emile had encountered superiors like Frossard while serving with the army in Africa. It was usually one of the junior officers who had worked his way up through the ranks, the old sweats, who would take an almost instinctive dislike. Emile had often tried to work out what it was about him that caused such a strong and seemingly instant antagonism. He knew that he spoke French with a 'funny' accent that some described as 'English'. But growing up in London, he had only ever spoken French with his mother, Nathalie, and she had had an accent that was an unusual cross that reflected her own mixed upbringing in the Norman countryside and the sweatshops of Paris.

And no doubt Emile would have been thought of as 'putting on airs'. He was unusually well educated for a mere infantryman and his 'fancy' way of speaking would no doubt have been seen as somehow insubordinate. There was no doubt that Frossard thought so.

But beneath this more rational reasoning lurked a secret fear that Emile really was unworthy – an anxiety that stemmed from his physical likeness to his feckless father. Had he also inherited his father's character? Could others discern the same weakness – a defective personality bequeathed alongside his father's stature, curly chestnut hair and brown eyes?

He didn't remember this man who had died when Emile was four, but he was familiar with the photograph that used to adorn his mother's chest of drawers until one day it no longer did. And he was even more familiar with the disparaging remarks that his mother would make about her husband, who had long since drunk himself into an early grave. Was there something in Emile's aura that hinted at such an outcome in himself? Had he inherited bad blood?

'Painting pretty pictures in public, I hear,' the commissaire was saying in a cloddish accent that Emile had been told came from the Vendée region in the west of France. 'Most unbecoming for an agent of the police,'

'Yes, sir,' said Emile, deciding it would be futile to try and defend his new pastime. He had long since learned to swallow the commissaire's unrelenting hostility, just as he had learned to ignore those army officers in Africa. It was just a pity that his first police posting should have landed him with such a hostile chief.

'You'll be disporting yourself on the stage of the municipal theatre before long, I suppose,' continued Frossard, looking rather pleased with himself for this remark. Emile pursed his lips but made no reply as he could sense that the commissaire was finally coming round to the reason for his urgent recall.

'Now, then, I have a special job for you Blanchet. It will require your knowledge of English.'

Frossard grimaced as he said this, as if acquaintance with the English language was regrettable but necessary, like being a police spy - one of those wretches always hoping to earn a franc or two by relaying overheard snippets of criminal conversation.

'More importantly,' he continued. 'It will require your powers of observation, such as they are. You are to be at the quayside tomorrow morning at four o'clock when the packet boat arrives from England…'

'Four o'clock in the morning?' blurted Emile, forgetting to bite his tongue.

Grimacing again but otherwise ignoring the outburst, Frossard slid a small sheet of paper across his desk top. It was a photograph, evidently cut out from a newspaper or a magazine, of a well-dressed gentleman seated in a gilt chair. The man was of a large build, with fleshy lips and, thought Emile, a kindly demeanour. He would certainly stand out from the other passengers.

'Who is he, sir?'

'That is of no importance to you,' replied Frossard rather primly, and Emile sensed that the commissaire didn't himself know. A name perhaps, but nothing more. 'I have received a wire that this man is booked on the night crossing from England and my orders are that we keep a discreet eye on him.'

'A suspected spy perhaps? Or an anarchist?'

Anarchists were one of Frossard's pet subjects, and Emile knew that, given half a chance, he would happily expound on his hatred of these individuals' spreading terror with their bombs. It had long grown boring to listen to, but introducing the topic was a useful way of deflecting his unrelenting hostility. But the commissaire remained tight-lipped, which impressed Emile even further as to the importance of this mysterious arrival.

'He is English, though?' he ventured. 'Why else would you need my knowledge of the language?'

'Alright Blanchet, no more questions. That's enough.'

Frossard scraped back his chair and stood up. He was a short man, even when proudly erect and rocking back and forth on the balls of his feet, as was his habit.

'You are simply to observe who is at the quayside to greet this individual, and who else seems to be taking an interest in his arrival. Not counting the usual gawping locals. Not that there should be too many of those at that hour. Follow him to whatever lodgings he has taken, and note down anyone else who might similarly be interested in his whereabouts. Go and get some rest now, and report back tomorrow at midday.'

* * *

The Reverend Henry Gibson handed his golf bag to the servant girl, Clotilde, who eyed it with bemusement. He then pulled off his overcoat and passed that to the girl before creeping upstairs. Reaching the closed door of his wife's bedroom he stopped to listen, but none of the usual murmuring or laughter that accompanied Lucy's conversations with Alice disturbed the stale late afternoon air.

In their shared dressing room, he chose a shirt and jacket for evensong, and took them back downstairs to the little back room that served as a library, study and general retreat from a household that seemed to barely tolerate his presence. The feast of Ascension was less than a week away and, approaching his bookshelves, he retrieved a notebook containing past sermons about our Lord's departure to Heaven.

Henry could never truly reconcile himself to the idea of angels appearing in columns of smoke. In fact, he was becoming reluctantly ever more sceptical about all the supernatural elements in the New Testament, including the miracles. On which subject, the thought of plentiful loaves and fishes turned his mind to tea.

'Clotilde…', he exclaimed weakly, hearing the maid climbing the steps from the basement. 'Oh dear…' he said when no reply was forthcoming. More strongly now: 'Clotilde!'.

The girl's face appeared at the top of the stairs and Henry asked whether there were any cakes or pastries to be had, and what plans his wife had made for supper. No plans, it seemed, and she and 'Mademoiselle Alice' ('mademoiselle, my eye!', thought Henry) had chosen to dine at the casino.

* * *

For some months now Walter Sickert had been sharing a bed and dining table (at cost price) with a fishwife, the statuesque, fair-skinned and russet-haired Augustine Villain, otherwise known as "Titine". She not only cooked and washed clothes for him, but taught Walter the idiom of Le Pollet – a language said to have its roots in Venice. Walter liked to imagine that Titine had Venetian blood.

After his artistic cliff-top excursion with Emile, he had been hoping for a substantial fish such as turbot for his evening meal, perhaps served in one of Titine's rich cream sauces. But the market was closed on Sundays and Titine had nothing to bring home, so was cooking yesterday's herrings instead. As she clattered about in the kitchen, Walter played cards with her eldest daughter, Louise, who, though only six, had inherited her mother's guile.

But if the girl was beating him, it was also because he was preoccupied with the rumour about an unwelcome new visitor. Oscar Wilde, newly released from prison in England, was planning to make Dieppe his home. Walter, who felt a huge sense of ownership for this Normandy fishing port which he had been visiting since his childhood, could already hear Wilde's voice ringing across Dieppe's cafes and restaurants.

If true, he would dominate everywhere he went for the duration of his stay. Every conversation would be about the great mistreated poet (as the French would no doubt hail him) and how he had been abused by the barbarian English. How the barbarian English in Dieppe would greet him was quite a different matter. If only Wilde had refrained from suing Queensberry. Walter and others had warned him countless times that this foolish action was bound to expose his predilections.

And then in due course he would become bored and depart again, it being in his nature. A silver lining for sure, but in the meantime, there was going to be the embarrassment of meeting Oscar in the street or at social gatherings. He had nothing against the man, but wished he would depart Dieppe as quickly as possible and not disturb the equanimity of what had promised to be a most enjoyable summer. So thought Walter, as little Louise triumphantly scooped up the cards and began to deal again.

* * *

Emile looked once again at the cuckoo clock that, along with a wooden crucifix and a framed image of the Sacred Heart of Jesus, was the only adornment on the mustard-coloured dining room walls of his landlady's lodgings.

It was just after a quarter past seven and he thought he should retire to bed by eight-thirty. Not that there was much chance of falling asleep at such an hour. He wasn't in the slightest bit tired and it wouldn't yet be dark, while the rough red wine he was sipping with the cabbage soup had only served to liven him further.

Madame Remy was next door reheating last night's mutton stew, Marie-Hélène finding excuses to come into the dining room any time that Emile sat down to eat. She was now crouching in front of the dresser on the pretext of looking for bowls, while Emile knew full well that her mother had already retrieved these.

'Thank you for coming all that way to find me, Marie Hélène,' he said in an effort to break what was becoming an embarrassing silence. 'It was very kind. And that's a most excellent bicycle.'

She jumped to her feet with such a radiant smile that Emile instantly regretted instigating a conversation. The poor girl needed so little encouragement that he feared that this simple expression of gratitude would be enough to fuel her ardour for at least another month.

He understood that Marie Hélène's widowed mother was supporting what she saw as a favourable match for her only child, and Emile couldn't entirely blame her. The choice of potential husbands in her circle – small shopkeepers and laundresses in the main - wasn't extensive. There was a middle-aged grocer who, having recently lost his wife, had expressed an interest (Madame Remy had supplied this information in the hope of encouraging Emile to make his own suit). Marie-Hélène had said that the man looked like an old donkey and she'd rather die a spinster.

She was a robust, good-looking girl, with the flaxen hair and blue eyes of the Norman race, but Emile felt no affinity with her. Three years younger than him, Marie Hélène's experience of life was comparatively meagre, ranging little further than her mother's apron strings. Her conversation was limited to the comings and goings of the pension's other guests (there was only one other at that moment, a travelling salesman called Lambert, and their paths rarely crossed). Her sole other entertainment consisted of the needlework over which she would throw covert glances at Emile as he sat nearby reading a book or a newspaper. Even at this casual level of acquaintance, he felt stifled by her.

Her mother called Marie-Hélène into the kitchen, only for her to return with a bowl of the fatty reheated mutton stew, which she lay before Emile with the flourish of a top Parisian chef showing off his latest proud creation.

'Don't just stand there, girl, fetch Emile some bread,' her mother called, bustling into the room. 'Will you be retiring to bed soon? Jean, the night watchman on the swing bridge, has agreed to wake you at three o'clock. He'll tap on your window with his long stick.'

'That's very good of you to organise that, madame.'

'Think nothing of it,' she said, seating herself in a manner that suggested that she wanted to hear all about Emile's mission.

'I'm simply to observe the new arrivals from the cross-channel packet boat,' obliged Emile, keeping his mission as vague as possible. This wasn't difficult given the paucity of information that he had been afforded. 'I'm to make a report if I notice anyone suspicious.'

'Sounds like they are expecting someone important,' she said, before adding with lascivious relish: 'A fugitive criminal perhaps?'

'I really don't know any more than that,' said Emile truthfully, ladling a spoonful of the fatty stew into his mouth. 'Delicious,' he managed to add between supping down the watery gravy and beginning to chew on the grey, overcooked meat.

CHAPTER THREE

I proceeded to the quayside at four o'clock on the morning of Monday 20th May last to await the arrival of the crossing from England, the packet boat Sussex. Among its passengers I recognised the gentleman whose photograph I had been shown, a large fellow carrying a bulky parcel. His luggage followed, wheeled on a trolley by a porter…

Frossard had made Agent Blanchet transcribe the report because he had no confidence in his own handwriting. The commissaire had left his village school in the Vendée at the age of eleven and only learned to write once he'd joined the army. Even then, his was a childish scrawl with uncertain spelling and grammar. Blanchet had much a clearer script and an altogether surer grasp of words, another reason to resent the boy. Taking a tentative sip out of the steaming mug of coffee that had been placed before him by the station's maidservant, he continued to read:

The gentleman in question was met by two men of smaller stature and who - I quickly ascertained - by listening in to what conversation that I was able – were both English. I later learned by questioning the ship's purser, that the passenger's name was Sebastian Melmoth, which is how I will henceforth refer to the gentleman in question…

'Henceforth… ascertained…'. The words seemed to mock Frossard as he spat them out from under his breath. He recalled now the indignity of being taught how to spell by a junior officer when over-wintering near Tours during the Prussian war. The officer had been one of those educated types like Agent Blanchet, and he had wrongly believed that this teacher (who had in fact been giving these reading and writing lessons simply to pass the time) had been secretly sneering at him. But back to Blanchet's report. So, this mysterious passenger from England was travelling under a false name. Now that was interesting...

Monsieur Melmoth immediately handed the package to one of the two gentlemen, following which exchange they had a hushed and earnest conversation. The package seemed to be subject of this dialogue. The handover completed, Monsieur Melmoth appeared in much brighter spirits, laughing loudly and making his companions laugh in turn. It was difficult to ascertain the exact nature of their conversation, but it would in part seem to reference his recent experiences as a guest at some or another establishment.

Frossard found himself wondering about the contents of this package. His superiors had told him that this character, whose real name was Oscar Wilde, had been imprisoned in England for gross indecency. He now imagined the parcel to contain erotic literature, perhaps photographs of naked men and women. He had confiscated such images before – indeed kept some of them for closer inspection back at his lodgings.

Before following Monsieur Melmoth and his companions, I made a note (as requested) of anybody else taking a serious interest in the gentleman's arrival. Apart from casual onlookers, of which there were very few because of the early hour, there was one man taking a studied interest in Monsieur Melmoth's arrival. Indeed, he appeared to be taking notes, and when Melmoth and his companions headed off towards the seafront hotel of their choice – the Hotel Sandwich – this man followed them.

Falling in step with the fellow, I asked casually whether he was acquainted with the new arrival, but he seemed loath to answer. I spoke in both English and French, but the man ignored my questioning, and eventually brushed me off by walking ahead at a rapid pace. He was a slim, not particularly well-dressed man with a moustache and wearing a bowler hat. If I was to hazard a guess, I would say that he was English and perhaps a journalist or even a private detective.

'Don't hazard any guesses, you young fool,' thought Frossard, scratching out this last line with his pen. In the meantime, he was awaiting a report of his own. And if his suspicions proved founded in fact, then Agent Emile Blanchet's fledgling career in the police would soon be reaching an abrupt end.

* * *

Edgar Degas sat at the dining table in his rented home on rue Victor Massé in the 9th arrondissement of Paris. The three-floor apartment was costing him 656 francs a month but had the advantage of a studio on the top floor, so that he had only two flights of stairs to navigate on his way to work. Even so, he was going to have to write to his dealer, Durand-Ruel, for another advance.

As was her morning custom, Edgar's housekeeper Zoë Closier was reading aloud from the newspaper *La Libre Parole* ("La France aux Francais!" ran its masthead slogan). The editor, Edouard Drumont, was writing about his favourite subject (some said his only subject) the nefarious influence of Jews on French society.

'A military doctor stationed in Amiens has written in with the suggestion that vivisection be practised on Jews rather than on harmless rabbits,' read Zoë in a flat tone, squinting at the newspaper through a pair of thick-rimmed spectacles. Edgar himself, now aged 63 and his eyesight steadily worsening, could no longer bear to read much, complaining to anyone who would listen that he lived in a perpetual twilight.

'Vivisection, I ask you,' he guffawed, reaching for the Dundee marmalade. And as so often when he spread the orange jam on his toast, his thoughts turned fleetingly to his young friend Walter Sickert, for they both shared a love of marmalade. Walter had written just last week to say that he was now living permanently in Dieppe on the coast of Normandy and suggesting that Edgar pay a visit, just like in the good old days. Walter had further suggested he could perhaps stay with their mutual friend Jacques-Emile Blanche and that they could paint together as in former times.

'As long as he doesn't want me to go on any long walks,' thought Edgar, chomping on a piece of toast and recalling their painting expeditions on the cliffs around Dieppe. 'Nice but more Monet than I can bear,' he had once quipped to his young friend, so proud of the remark that he would go on to repeat it to anyone who suggested a trip to the Normandy coast. He had been younger then, and eager to shift Walter from the habits of his former mentor, the American bore Whistler. All those pallid washes! The self-obsession! Where was the life?

Unlike so many of his wealthier acquaintances, it seemed, Edgar had no desire to install a telephone. 'So, you're called and you come running,' he would say to friends who bragged about their devices. But he was seized now by a desire to telephone Blanche and arrange a visit to his comfortable beach-side home near the Dieppe casino, the Bas Fort Blanc. The summer season would have begun and the black-beamed Norman mansion would be filling with agreeable company. Painters and sculptors and poets whom Edgar could affront with his idiosyncratic views about art and life.

'See all the yids, yidesses and their brats burned,' Zoë recited from the newspaper, for all the world as if reading a stock market report. 'For God, the Nation and the extermination of the Jews.' She came to halt, suddenly aware that Edgar wasn't listening.

'I think... I think,' he said after a long silence during which he spread some marmalade on another slice of toast. 'I think I should like to go on a journey. What is for lunch?'

'Leg of lamb with Soissons beans... your favourite', replied Zoë.

'Very good,' said Edgar, his mouth instantly salivating. 'After lunch then I would like to dictate some letters. A little sojourn in Normandy might be just the thing.'

Zoë nodded and Edgar felt once again reassured that the 50 francs that he paid her each month was money well spent.

* * *

'Sebastian Melmoth, so that's what he's calling himself now,' thought Walter, working up a small quayside scene he had sketched the week before. The thought distracted him from a lecture he had been giving to Emile, about the advantages of small canvases such as the one he had just started to dab with cadmium yellow.

'Collectors will always prefer a small Corot to a large one,' he had been saying, Emile waiting for him to expand on this line of argument. He had no idea who this Corot is or was, and at first thought that his friend was talking, for some reason, about carrots. Either way, he always allowed Walter the free flow of his thoughts without constantly interrupting him over details. The important thing to grasp was that this Corot was presumably an important painter.

And in turn Walter enjoyed expounding his theories on art to the young policeman. It helped clarify ideas that he hoped later to enlarge upon in one of his frequent letters to *The Speaker* – a London periodical that kept him in front of his artistic peers in England while he strived away here in France.

But Oscar Wilde – confound him! The knowledge of his proximity was as aggravating as his actual physical presence. Even disguised as this Sebastian Melmoth, Wilde would cut an unmistakable figure, and Dieppe was so small that encounters would be inevitable and often.

And just when Walter felt that he had the little Normandy fishing port organised to his liking. The cheap studio overlooking the bustle of the port, the mistress who cooked and cared for him, and the jolly social interactions with other artists and writers. All this would be upended by Oscar's domineering presence. Oscar roaming and charming London or Paris was one thing, here in Dieppe quite another.

Also, there was Walter's own reputation in the town to consider. It was bad enough that the scandal surrounding Oscar's court case and subsequent imprisonment had tarnished artists of any originality, so that even Impressionism was lumped together in people's minds with the 'Oscar Wilde tendency'. But Walter, despite a long acquaintance with the disgraced writer, as well as the recipient of several acts of his kindness, simply didn't want to be associated locally with Wilde.

Of course, if Nellie had still been living with him as his wife, things would have been very different. She would have called him a prig for shunning not only an old acquaintance, but a dear friend to Walter's parents. Nellie however was back in England, having decided on divorce proceedings. Another cloud upon the horizon.

Emile mistook Walter's long silence for a sudden absorption in his painting. Perhaps a tricky piece of shading was puzzling him. But when Walter put down his brush and palette and began to stare out of the window of his little studio, he thought the time was right to resume the conversation.

'Smaller canvases?' he ventured.

'What? Yes, yes, quite so. And remember that Rembrandt began by painting heads on a small scale,' said Walter without conviction, his thoughts clearly elsewhere.

'By the way,' Walter resumed, this time speaking brightly and directly at Emile. 'I have this morning received a letter from my dear friend and mentor Edgar Degas. The great man is coming to grace us with his company in Dieppe. Now that will be an important art lesson for you.'

'The great Impressionist,' said Emile.

'Only don't use that term in his presence. He prefers not to be lumped together with the likes of Monet. And he would have groaned to have seen us painting up on the cliffs on Sunday.'

'I see,' said Emile, although he hadn't. 'In any case, I've taken up too much of your time this morning. I only dropped by to ask about this mysterious Englishman. A disgraced poet, you say, newly released from prison. Oscar…?'

'Strictly speaking, more Irish than English,' said Walter, dunking his brush into the turpentine with such force that some of the liquid splashed across the table top.

CHAPTER FOUR

From Walter's studio on the Tour aux Crabs, one of the last remnants of Dieppe's ancient fortifications against marauding English pirates, the police station was a short walk down the time-polished steps of the old rampart and along the quayside. It was another brilliant late spring day – still fresh in the bright sunshine. The fish market was in the process of packing up as Emile strode by. The last of the morning's catch was being haggled over, while gulls policed the freshly scrubbed cobbles.

He noticed the unmistakable figure of Walter's landlady, Augustine Villain, standing with balled fists on her hips, as she addressed one such latecomer. Madame Villain's produce was said to be among the best in the market, and Emile wished his landlady would buy her seafood there. Instead she frequented the cheap stall that was rumoured to purchase the catch that the other fishwives had rejected.

Walter had once introduced him to this Villain woman – a tall, pale-skinned, flame-haired Amazon, with two small children entwined around her feet. Emile found her impressive but not intimidating after his dealings with the female warriors in Africa, although he didn't care to think too much about those terrible encounters. The women of Dahomey were fiercer fighters than the men, and it took a period of adjustment for the French soldiers to meet them in battle and treat them like a male adversary.

Augustine Villain would have made a fearsome warrior if there was any truth in Walter's favourite anecdote. This involved a heated confrontation between Walter and Madame Villain's former husband, which was apparently terminated when she bit the latter upon his ankle.

Dieppe's buildings enclosed the harbour like a long sock, its opening to the sea invisible from the fish market. On the far bank lay Le Pollet, the fisherman's quarter and something of a law unto itself. The inhabitants had their own patois, some of which Emile now understood thanks to his acquaintance with Walter and his occasional police dealings with the locals. On the whole, however, the residents of Le Pollet weren't eager to become entangled with officialdom.

And here on the near side of the harbour were many of the administrative buildings that they elected to avoid – handsome 17th-century edifices that included the town hall and the police station. And joining the two sides of the harbour in a sweeping arc was a long arcade, with a number of cafes and restaurants, and the wrought-iron swing bridge that had been built ten years earlier, joining Le Pollet to the rest of the town.

Nearing the police station, he spotted the Reverend Henry Gibson from the previous day's encounter on the golf course. Dressed more smartly today, with a striped blazer topped by a jaunty boater, Gibson was striding in the direction of Le Pollet. Emile was about to call out , but the man was wearing a look of intense introspection – indeed he appeared to be muttering to himself. In any case, their acquaintance had been too brief for such a public greeting.

* * *

Shortly before Emile spied him, Henry had been strolling along the promenade listening to the high tide clattering on the pebbles and thinking of Matthew Arnold's poem inspired by Dover Beach.

The Sea of Faith
Was once, too, at the full, and round earth's shore
Lay like the folds of a bright girdle furled.
But now I only hear
Its melancholy, long withdrawing roar,
Retreating to the breath
Of the night-wind, down the vast edges drear
And naked shingles of the world.

'It's melancholy, long withdrawing roar', said Henry, repeating the line aloud. He had found Arnold's criticism of the miraculous elements of Christianity – including the Resurrection itself – deeply distressing at the time. Now he wasn't so sure that he didn't agree.

His congregation, seemingly content to woodenly perform the weekly rituals that he administered, had no inkling of Henry's doubts. Even Lucy – no, most of all Lucy – was ignorant of the turmoil in his soul. Could he even call it a soul, this secret inner life of his?

Absorbed thus, he found himself turning towards the quayside. It was Monday, which Henry treated as his day of rest. Men were slumped over fishing rods along the harbour wall. The fishing boats themselves – uniformly russet-sailed and blue-hulled - lay idle, their catch unloaded and awaiting the evening tide. Soon enough he found himself heading trance-like towards the iron swing bridge that led into Le Pollet.

He had hoped to see her again, but he also feared doing so. Henry didn't know her name for their paths had only crossed once before, exactly three weeks earlier on May Day.

He remembered the date because earlier that day an old woman had given him a sprig of lily-of-the-valley, a French good-luck charm that is traditionally distributed on the first of May. Wondering what to do with the flower, he had spotted the girl sitting on a doorstep, eyes closed and her pretty young face turned toward the sun.

'Here mademoiselle, for you,' he had said without thinking, stooping to hand her the sprig. She had opened her pale blue eyes and lifted a hand to shield them from the sun, and Henry felt instantly transported back into the presence of Florence, his one true love.

She had Florence's wide-forehead, freckled nose and pleasantly warm, rumbling laugh, as she thanked him for the flower. He had asked in his imperfect French about the significance of lily-of-the-valley and the girl shrugged and smiled and said she thought it was to celebrate the arrival of spring.

Feeling suddenly self-conscious, he had bowed and turned to leave but she had seemed as reluctant as Henry to terminate their encounter. She asked him whether he was English and how he found Dieppe. Henry scanned her face and, although coarser on closer inspection than Florence, the likeness was still remarkable. More than that, the girl seemed somehow to emit the same aura as Florence. Perhaps he could believe in miracles after all.

The courtship in Cambridge all those years ago had been short but intense. They had seemed destined for each other but Florence, who was among the first cohort of women allowed to study at the university, had chosen to break it off. She had stated that she could not follow Henry into his chosen vocation of the church.

Despite studying divinity at Girton College, she was not a believer, she had revealed. She couldn't therefore make a proper wife for a man destined to be ordained by the Church of England. And Henry, who had harboured fewer doubts in his youth, had reluctantly agreed that they should part.

It took him years to get over Florence – that is, if he ever did. Even now he occasionally dreamed of her; wistful, unhappy dreams that always ended with a sense of hopelessness and rejection. And here was this girl miraculously reawakening the feelings that had been dormant for so long. Sensations that had seemingly atrophied over the decades had now miraculously sprung back to life like a desert after rain. How could it be? It was surely a mirage, possibly even the work of Satan, but one that Henry felt irresistibly drawn towards.

In the three weeks since this encounter, he had prayed to be rid of his foolishness. Florence reincarnated on a doorstep in Dieppe – perhaps not in body but in spirit. The real Florence would now be same age as Henry, and he tried and failed to imagine how she might look now in her sixth decade. In any case, here he was now, striding towards the iron swing bridge that might just as well have been the gates of hell itself. Marching like the damned towards this sinful temptation, he also felt like a nervous young lover. His 19-year-old self. He was almost faint as he approached the doorstep on which he had encountered the girl, fearful lest she be nothing like he remembered. Or fearful lest she be exactly as he recalled.

But the doorstep was unoccupied. 'Stupid old fool,' Henry reprimanded himself, nevertheless hoping to encounter her as he continued up the steep winding lane beyond. What would he say if they did meet again? He must discover her name, for a name would give him a handle on reality. It would give this phantom some solidity and thus exorcise it. Inwardly though, he hoped for the very opposite. Let the phantom become flesh. Let Florence be resurrected.

* * *

Her name was Jeanne and at the precise moment that Henry was passing her doorstep, she was perched on the edge of her unmade bed – the same bed on which she entertained her customers. She was fully dressed, however, and leaning back on hands that were starting to feel numb from the lack of movement.

She maintained the pose nevertheless as Walter Sickert studied her, Jeanne's eyes resting on the top of her wardrobe where the funny red hat was starting to collect dust. The round, flat-topped hat that the Arab soldier had forgotten, along with the papers that also remained uncollected. Jeanne had thought about handing these to the madame, but there had been something so imploring about the Arab man, something so insistent that she should show them to nobody, that she had wrapped them in an old petticoat and stuffed them behind the wardrobe.

She thought about mentioning the papers to Walter now, but the Arab had said something about them being dangerous and to show them to nobody – for their sake. He would return after breakfast the following day, but that had been nearly a week ago now.

Jeanne turned her attention to Walter. From time to time, he would look up with an appraising glance as if Jeanne were a vase or a bowl of fruit. An object. Well, she was used to that. He would then make swift movements with his hand, Jeanne listening to his pencil rasp on his sketching pad.

Walter often paid her these visits and Jeanne wondered how long before he asked her to remove her clothes and pose naked. Indeed, how long before he paid her for a different service altogether.

But Walter had no intention of asking her to remove her clothes. In fact, that very morning he had begun writing a letter to *The Speaker* magazine disdaining the lazy depiction of the nude form. The way in which the models in art school were posed decorously on platforms in the unnaturally diffused light of the studio.

He looked now at the way in which the midday sun illuminated the tattered rug and the peeling wallpaper directly beneath the window while casting one half of Jeanne's face and body in shadow. The bed itself, with its rumpled blankets and stark iron bedstead told a far more interesting story than the meaningless velvet sheets that accompanied those reclining art-school nudes.

"A picture generally represents *someone, somewhere*," he had written that morning. "The error of art-school teaching is that students are made to begin with the study of *someone*, and generally *nowhere*."

Walter also had another concern. What would Madame Villain think if he started making naked portraits of her neighbours, however much she otherwise ignored, or professed not to care about, their means of making a living? Quickly sketching the folds in Jeanne's dress, he was amused by the thought that in a brothel he would at least be spared the presence of the great Oscar Wilde.

CHAPTER FIVE

Venetia Hall, more widely known as the popular novelist Edgar Stanton Lister, was taking tea with her toy poodle Tippet on the first floor-balcony of Maison Grisch, the most famous patisserie on the Grand Rue. Tippet had already wolfed down his brioche while Venetia was still applying apricot jam to hers.

'You are a greedy little boy,' she said, smiling at the way that Tippet, head cocked to one side, was watching her every movement.

Dieppe's main shopping street led in a wide, straight line from the harbour into the interior of the town and was invariably full of passers-by for her to spy upon. The daughter, granddaughter and great-granddaughter of soldiers, Venetia, under her masculine nom de plume, had earned considerable success with her tales of military life. Her latest stories however concerned the coming and going of the English colony in Dieppe.

There was so much happening in this little seaside town, with such a varied cast of characters, from the minor nobility and major painters to retired and mildly distressed gentlefolk and the sorts of ex-servicemen who lapped up her novels.

From beneath the rim of her various colourful hats (today she wore a purple straw hat with green shot ribbons), she liked to observe the pedestrians along the Grand Rue from her balcony perch. These days, the proprietor, Monsieur Grisch himself, gratifyingly greeted Venetia in English with 'Your usual table, madame?'.

Her copy of the London weekly periodical *The Citizen* had arrived on the morning boat and she impatiently turned its pages until at last she came to the society columns. And there, under the headline "Dieppe's summer visitors", was a jaunty account of the town's latest arrivals.

Dieppe is marvellously recuperative and healthy; no continental seaside resort can show a cleaner bill of health, three years without a single case of typhoid fever.

If the words seemed familiar to Venetia it was because she had written them herself, her regular anonymous missives about the Normandy port helping to supplement her income as a novelist. And now for the punchline: *Many people come to die but regain perfect health.*

She congratulated herself on this bon mot – albeit not an original witticism for she had overheard the remark being uttered at the casino. But then, glancing down upon the street, she realised that she had (to use that horrible new American expression) a 'scoop' on her hands – albeit one unlikely to appeal to the readers of *The Citizen*. For there, lumbering along the Grand Rue, was the unmistakable figure of Oscar Wilde.

Venetia noted how, as he raised his hat to passing parties, some would swerve like frightened horses and take a wide arc away from Wilde or, in one case, actually turn their backs on him. Leaving her brioche uneaten, and eventually followed by a reluctant Tippet (who gave one last longing look at his mistress's plate), she raced downstairs and out onto the street. It didn't take long to catch Wilde.

Laying a hand on his arm, and addressing him for the whole street to hear, she commanded: 'Oscar, take me to tea.'

* * *

Colonel Marsden sat in the sun-drenched morning room at Maison Lefèvre, nursing a second glass of Calvados while buried beneath a week-old edition of *The Times* of London. He was pretending not to listen to the gossip of two English ladies. Although their voices had begun as an infuriatingly low murmur, they had evidently forgotten the colonel's proximity (obscured as it was by a vase of orchids) and were now chattering at an unselfconscious volume.

'He came into the restaurant and I didn't know where to look or what to do,' said one. 'We were all very much vexed.'

'Mrs Peterson said she cut him when he greeted her in the street,' said the other. 'Greeted her in the street, if you will. She said she doesn't know the man from Adam.'

'His reputation precedes him.'

'Absolutely beastly.'

There was a gentle knock at the door and Madame Lefèvre herself appeared to announce that luncheon was served and to apologise for the lateness of the sitting. Apparently, some fish had to be returned to the market for not being perfectly fresh. The colonel sprung to his feet and the two ladies, suddenly remembering that he had been sitting nearby, looked flustered.

'That man of whom you speak, dear ladies, is an unmitigated blackguard,' he said, his face flushed with Calvados although its high colour could be mistaken for indignation. 'No beard or moustache... always a sure sign of moral corruption.'

* * *

After an unsatisfactory lunch of paté, Neufchatel cheese, bread and a stale custard tart, all washed down with rough country cider, Frossard returned to his desk in an ill humour. He had never married and his reliance on a succession of cooks and maids - none of whom stayed for long - meant that his diet was both poor and monotonous.

A letter that had been deposited on his desk during his lunch break however cheered him when he saw that it was from the police departmental archive records in Rouen. Skimming through the pleasantries and introductions, Frossard's eyes fastened on the particulars he had requested.

From information supplied by Emile Blanchet at his induction to the Rouen police in June 1894. Date of Birth:

12th October 1874 in London, Great Britain. Father: Gustave Blanchet, deceased. Origins unknown. Mother: Nathalie Blanchet (née Levallois) deceased, formerly of Bolbec in the department of Seine Inférieure.

Emile Blanchet returned to France from Great Britain in 1885 with his mother. He served loyally in the army of the French Third Republic for 18 months, stationed for six of those months in the African colony of Dahomey, helping to quell the uprising in that region. He is of sound health and good character and has sworn allegiance to the Republic.

'Sworn allegiance to the Republic,' muttered Frossard with distaste before noticing that attached to this letter was another. This was written in a different, more cramped hand.

For the confidential attention of Commissaire Frossard.
Dear Commissaire,

Further to the police departmental records, we have, at your suggestion, conducted a more thorough search of Agent Emile Blanchet's record and of his antecedents. These are indeed most worrying.

The reason for Blanchet's residency in Great Britain was that his mother, Nathalie Levallois, took a leading part in the Paris uprising of 1871. Such was her prominence that this woman was known to her fellow so-called 'Communards" as the Red Maid of Montmartre. She would undoubtedly have faced the death penalty if captured, but managed to make her escape to England. She lived in London until her return to France in 1885 under the terms of the general amnesty of 1881.

Furthermore, French police spies in London reported that Blanchet's father, one Gustave Blanchet, was active in anarchist circles in the British capital. The Special Branch of Scotland Yard also named this man as a dangerous agitator, who fraternised with Russian, French, Italian, Belgian and Spanish anarchists. His death was reported to have been caused by alcohol poisoning, although unconfirmed rumours suggest that he might have accidentally blown himself up with one of his bombs.

Given the spate of anarchist outrages in Paris in recent years, I suggest that Agent Blanchet should remain under strict surveillance. A discreet search of his lodgings might also be in order.

Cordially yours, but in strictest confidence, Colonel Wisehart

'Ha!' Frossard exclaimed, a smile of satisfaction blooming on his face as he began pacing up and down his small office. 'I knew there was something off about that boy. Sworn allegiance to the Republic, has he? Blood will out. Blood will always out.'

CHAPTER SIX

Emile had experienced another awkward lunch, smiling politely as Marie Hélène fussed around, administering course after course with a flourish that was entirely at odds with her mother's lack of the culinary arts. Today a leg of guinea fowl had been presented sitting in an indeterminant watery sauce, accompanied by hard chunks of undercooked turnip. Dessert had been the landlady's almost daily standby – 'pain perdu', stale bread infused with egg custard. At least this was relatively harmless.

He felt replete if gastronomically dissatisfied as, straightening his tunic and donning his kepi, he now stepped out into the bright May sunshine.

It might be pleasant to find a wife, he thought, although the only girl he had ever loved was far away in England and from too elevated a social stratum to consider such an attachment. Emile had been eight when they met and Mary Rogerson twelve, the eldest daughter of his mother's employers. The three years his mother, Nathalie, worked in the Rogersons' spacious house beside the park in Blackheath had been among the happiest of his childhood, made more precious by his adoration of that unobtainable goddess.

After her desperate flight to England and the death of her husband, Emile's wastrel father, Ludovic, his mother had eventually found work as a governess to the three Rogerson girls. She taught them French and embroidery and took them for long walks in the park.

Emile himself was sent to a local school, where he was a polite, shy pupil and therefore avoided the frequent canings that were meted out to the other more boisterous boys. But on weekends and during school holidays, he was included in the girls' outings, chatting in French to the two younger ones but generally ignored by their sister. On those rare occasions when Mary did deign to speak to him, Emile became light-headed and felt he might actually swoon.

And he was heart-broken when, shortly after his eleventh birthday, his mother announced that they were to go and live in France, a country he had never before visited. There had been a general amnesty for those who took up arms in the Paris Commune of 1871 and his grandparents had pleaded with his mother to return to their little farm in Normandy. They had grown too old to work their smallholding and needed looking after, and his mother had reluctantly agreed to do her duty as their only daughter.

And so, they exchanged the grand house on the outskirts of London for a low, beamed cottage in a small village near Bolbec, amidst the flat, featureless countryside of the Caux plateau. His grandparents spoke with a Norman accent as thick as the local cream and seemed to resent Emile's presence as an extra mouth to feed.

His mother had left home at 15 to work as a seamstress in Paris and, now that she had returned to her childhood home, they still treated her as a little girl. Not as the woman whose heroism during the Paris Commune had earned her the sobriquet 'the Red Maid of Montmartre'.

He remembered observing these so-called grandparents as they sat illuminated by the light of the fire. They never felt like blood relations, but indifferent strangers who had somehow imprisoned him in their own small, cramped world.

Emile himself was allowed the only candle, by whose light he would do the schoolwork on the kitchen table. One day he too could be a schoolteacher, everybody said. Everybody that is, except his mother.

He would watch Grandfather Levallois sitting uncomfortably on a three-legged stool, sucking on a long clay pipe and staring into the fire while Grandmother Levallois did her embroidery or mended clothes. She was almost blind so Emile wondered whether she did her stitching from memory and touch alone. And Emile would think: these are not my people. I am not of their seed.

His father's people were from the Occitania – a region in southern France that retained a mystical quality for Emile. His mother talked about it as a foreign country and said that Emile had inherited his swarthy looks from that side of the family. He hoped that these were all that he had inherited from his father, such was the shadow that this man had cast over Emile's childhood. He was like a character from a book, Emile would think when trying to dispel the fear of any hereditary traits – the drunken loudmouth. He recalled the Rogersons in London taking him to see plays by William Shakespeare – plays he couldn't really follow because of the complexity of the language. But there had been this one character, a carousing showoff, that he imagined was like his father.

Thrust suddenly into the cultural wasteland of rural Normandy, Emile was an oddity at the local school. Most of the children were of farming stock and could barely read or write. Indeed, he was eventually co-opted as a sort of unofficial substitute teacher, taking classes in mathematics and history. He made no friends.

The decision was eventually made to send him to college in Le Havre, about 20 miles away. He would have to board, although there was no money to pay for his fees and upkeep. In desperation, his mother wrote to the Rogersons in England and those kindly souls agreed to cover Emile's education for one year. What might happen after that year had ended, he was never to discover because his mother died suddenly of pneumonia.

Aged 16, Emile was now an orphan living with two increasingly deaf and frail old people whose patois he could barely understand. He realised that he was now utterly alone and would have to make his own way in the world. And the simplest means of escape would be to join the army.

Musing thus and approaching the police station, Emile realised that he was being hailed by a pair of unkempt-looking individuals. The men, both of unusually small stature, and whose raggedy trousers appeared to be soaked to above the knee, were waving frantically at him.

'Monsieur, monsieur… come quickly,' beseeched one in an accent that Emile now recognised as belonging to Le Pollet. The man hobbled across the street, while his friend, who had two wicker baskets balanced across his shoulders, hung back.

'A fellow has drowned,' he said. 'We were picking mussels and found him amongst the rocks.'

Emile agreed to follow the men, who, it transpired, lived in the caves that had been burrowed into the chalk cliffs flanking the far side of the port. These *hommes de caverne* were from the very poorest strata of society and had dug rudimentary homes in the cliff face that ran along Dieppe's eastern headland.

'My brother and I live there,' said the man who had first addressed him, indicating one of these cave dwellings.

The man said his name was Pierre Martin, and his brother was Paul Martin. He explained that they had been picking mussels at low tide when they noticed the body lying on its side, wedged amidst the rocks. Emile consulted his fob watch and realised that the tide would be in the process of turning and that they must proceed quickly to retrieve the body before it was reclaimed by the sea.

'We pulled him some way inland,' said Pierre Martin, and the policeman had the uncharitable thought that perhaps the brothers had rifled through his corpse in search of valuables.

'Is the man fully clothed?' he asked, as they jumped down onto the pebbles and started to crunch their way towards the flat sand and the jagged rocks exposed by the low tide.

'He is that, sir,' said Pierre Martin. 'Wearing the strangest clothing. A uniform maybe.'

'Possibly a foreign sailor fallen overboard,' thought Emile as they picked their way through the sharp rocks and towards the body. The dead man had been propped up against one such rock and, with his back to Emile, appeared to be gazing out to sea.

Emile saw what Pierre Martin had meant by his unusual attire. He was wearing russet-coloured trousers and a short blue Zouave-style jacket with gold braiding. It was his face that struck Emile most forcibly, however, the man being of unmistakable Arabic appearance. Streaked with sand, it might have been, but the features were familiar. He had known soldiers like this when he was stationed in Africa. Fighters from the Arab regiments of Tunisia and Algeria.

More men were now approaching, for which Emile was thankful as they must carry the body up above the high-water mark.

'Careful now,' commanded Emile, as the five of them lifted the bloated corpse and picked their way back through the maze of jagged, algae-capped rocks and up across the steep bank of pebbles. A crowd had by now gathered upon the promenade, Walter amongst them. As they lay the man down, and rested their own weary arms and legs, Emile noticed a gash in the back of the dead man's blue and gold jacket. It looked more like a cut with a knife or other sharp implement rather than a rip made by the rocks. Emile had also seen such wounds in Africa, often inflicted by spears.

Stepping forward with arms outstretched in order to try to force back the onlookers back, Emile noticed Walter had his sketch pad to hand and what could best be described as a look of hunger on his vulpine features. Walter slipped his sketch pad back into his shoulder bag. He had caught what he understood to be a look of disdain on Emile's face and had felt uncharacteristically ashamed of his impulsive desire to record the scene. He nevertheless pushed his way towards the front of what had grown into a sizable crowd and inspected the details of the corpse so as to be able to recall them in his studio.

Though the skin on his face had become wrinkled in the water, Walter noted that the dead man had the complexion of a North African. He was fascinated by the way the wet hair had become intertwined by pieces of seaweed so that he looked like some mythical creature from the deep. Neptune himself perhaps.

The clothes were colourful, especially the bright blue jacket with its yellow braiding, through which the dead man's bloated stomach was now protruding. Walter could certainly reproduce that from memory. The outfit as a whole seemed to belong more to the stage than the real military. It could be one of Gilbert and Sullivan's comic operas, of which Walter had seen many in the London of his youth.

'All he needs now is a bright red fez', he thought, the idea triggering a memory of seeing such an article of headwear recently. But where was it? In a shop perhaps? In someone's house? Yes, of course, he had meant to ask her about it. The fez had been sitting on top of the wardrobe in the boudoir of his model Jeanne.

* * *

Henry walked deeper into Le Pollet, the fisherman's quarter seeming to belong to a different city altogether. Naples, he imagined, with its dark narrow streets and the balconies that almost seemed to touch each other across the way.

It was past noon and the smell of cooking followed him from doorway to doorway and made him think of his own stomach. Monday was his day of rest and he usually dined in a restaurant - alone, of course, because Lucy only ever accompanied him to church. And even there she would sit with Alice like two spinster sisters, huddled together on the front pew.

He was drawn on, fascinated but also perturbed by the otherness of the quarter. Children with grubby faces, barefoot and some dressed in barely more than rags, stared at him as he passed. A woman leaned over a balcony and made a kissing noise before laughing and returning inside.

Henry increased his pace, unwilling to retrace his steps. And then, out of breath, he found himself emerging amidst the more generous, wider-spaced houses of Neuville. This road would eventually lead to the village of Puys, where the prime minister Lord Salisbury had his holiday villa.

When in France, his lord and ladyship were by far his most important parishioners, the family's stately procession to Sunday morning service one of the familiar sights of a Dieppe summer. Henry harboured a hope that one day preferment would be bestowed upon the Reverend Henry Gibson by his association with such an esteemed congregant. Perhaps a comfortable living near London was in the gift of the marquess?

Not that he had ever once been invited to the Salisbury residence, the Chalet Cecil, built (he had heard) in the fashionable style supposed to evoke the Swiss Alps. All turrets, balconies and carved wood. The Prime Minister kept somewhat aloof from the rest of the congregation, perhaps rightly suspecting that their attendance at church was merely to rub shoulders with such an eminent figure.

Henry also suspected that Salisbury disapproved of Lucy, the way she seemed to pay such little heed to her husband. A deeply conservative man in all matters – from opposing Home Rule for Ireland to resisting German and African incursions on the British Empire – he held firm views on the husband as head of the household, while a wife's duty was to keep him well-fed, well-lodged and well-pleased.

Henry finally emerged near the top of the cliff, where the imposing new church dedicated to sailors, the Chapelle Notre Dame de Bonsecours, stood like a lighthouse. Having never before visited, he now stepped inside, his nose assaulted by the smell of recently burnt incense. He could never quite reconcile himself to the fact that both Protestants and Catholics worshipped the same god. This chapel felt as alien as a Hindu temple as he gazed up at the stained-glass windows and the plaques covering the walls, all of them dedicated to sailors lost at sea in various shipping disasters.

Stepping gratefully back into the late May sunshine, he wandered over to the giant cross with its crucified Christ in

His agony staring out to sea. A packet boat from England bobbed about on the swell as it steadied to navigate the harbour entrance. People would daily gather to observe the arrival of the boat, it was one of the town's great amusements. But today, he noticed with interest, a crowd had congregated on the opposite side of the harbour, where normally only a few ragged cave-dwellers could be seen fishing for their dinner.

Extracting his pince-nez from his breast pocket, he tried to see what had happened to attract a melee to such a lonely spot. The throng now parted as two policemen wheeled a cart to the edge of the promenade, where a body lay spreadeagled. Henry noted that the young art student he'd recently met at the golf club, now dressed in his police uniform, seemed to be in charge.

Spurred on by the sudden thought that the deceased might be one of his own flock, Henry turned to retrace his steps back down into Dieppe. 'More likely one of those poor cave-dwellers,' he reassured himself. 'No doubt a Catholic soul.'

CHAPTER SEVEN

By the time the man's body, made weightier by its saturated clothing, had been lifted onto the promenade, two gendarmes had arrived with a hand cart. They would take the corpse to the mortuary situated on the street behind the police station.

Unlike the famous Paris morgue with its viewing platform, this one was not open to the public to come and gawp. Originally to help with the identification of the deceased, the exhibition of fresh cadavers had become a modishly macabre type of theatre.

Happily, to Emile's mind, the prefecture in Rouen rarely allowed such a display, although anyone who came forward claiming to know the dead person would be allowed an audience. Practice told him that there would a window of around three days for this to happen before decomposition began in earnest.

As they lifted the corpse onto the cart, Commissaire Frossard arrived, pushing himself through the crowd with a look of alarm.

'Is this the man?' he asked unnecessarily as he stood over the body. 'Have you checked his clothing for any form of identity?'

'Not yet, sir,' said Emile, a reply that, instead of annoying Frossard, seemed to satisfy him. 'And the men who found him. Which are they?'

Emile scanned the crowd but couldn't see the two wretches who had originally approached him. He did however notice that Walter had now made his way to the front and was staring intently at the dead body as it lay sprawled upon the cart.

'I can no longer see them here, sir, but I know where they live.'

'Very good, Agent Blanchet. We'll take the body to the morgue, and after we've undressed him, we will search the men's houses.'

'Yes, sir,' replied Emile, taken aback. Did he suspect the men of theft? Admittedly the thought had crossed his own mind, but the urgency behind Frossard's order struck him as nonetheless odd.

'Do we have anything to cover the body with?' Emile called out to the gendarmes. Walter, seeming to take this as a rebuke, stepped back from the cart and gave his friend an ironic salute.

'You can use my jacket if you like,' he said in English.

Emile was about to reply when his attention was suddenly snared by an intricate design – some sort of badge or regimental insignia – that was embroidered on the dead man's jacket.

'Do you have your sketch book to hand?' he asked the artist.

'Naturally,' said Walter, pulling his pad from his shoulder bag.

'What do you make of this?' asked Emile, pointing to the badge. 'Arabic perhaps?'

'Almost certainly,' replied Walter, who had already begun sketching.

'Quickly, before my boss notices,' urged Emile, keeping an eye on Frossard. The commissaire had his back turned as he consulted with the examining magistrate, Maitre Toussaint, who had now appeared on the scene. The crowd had swelled back towards the town, and Emile noticed with amusement that the arrival of the cross-Channel boat – usually the major draw on any afternoon in Dieppe – was this afternoon all but ignored.

* * *

Venetia Hall sat stroking Tippet's head while the poodle gazed longingly at the crumbs on the plates so recently stacked with dainty little cakes and pastries. The author of

The Regimental Mount and Other Stories of Military Endeavour was deep in thought.

Oscar had outwardly seemed his old self and had entertained Venetia with fantastical tales in which he recounted his recent incarceration in terms that made Reading Gaol sound like a holiday resort.

'The dear Governor, such a delightful man, and his wife is charming,' he had said. 'I spent happy hours with them, and they asked me to spend the summer with them.'

Impressed as always by his resilience and his effortless ability to turn everything into a beautiful joke, Venetia also detected a new vein of melancholy in her old acquaintance. It matched the noticeable coarsening of his face and hands that were the result of the years of hard labour.

This certainly wasn't the same carefree – careless, you might say - man she had known in London, and she worried for him in Dieppe. There may be some artists and bohemian types who would welcome him under their roofs, but it was a small town and the English colony here would be unforgiving. As Venetia herself had recently witnessed.

And, after all, the Dieppe English were exactly the type of audience she addressed in her books and her periodical articles. She knew them well, their likes and dislikes, their prejudices and preconceptions. They would be horrified but pleasurably scandalised by Oscar's so-called crimes, the precise nature of which they would of course feel unable to vocalise in polite society.

Paris or Naples would make a more suitable refuge, she thought, although those cities might return him into the orbit of the awful Bosie and therefore of his unspeakably vindictive father. And although Oscar had made plain that he was finished with Lord Alfred Douglas, Venetia was alive to his weaknesses as well as his strengths.

'You are aware you're being followed,' she had told him.

Oscar had taken a few moments to catch her meaning and then looked shaken.

'If you look under the awning of the fruit shop across the street you will see him now. He's been waiting there since we arrived.'

They simultaneously turned to look at the man, who was wearing a bowler hat and smoking a cigarette. Without returning their gaze but nevertheless seeming to sense it, he dropped his cigarette and ground it underfoot, before strolling nonchalantly away in the direction of the port.

'Oh yes,' Oscar had said. 'I do believe he was in the café last night. He was only person who didn't stand up and leave as soon as I entered. I had assumed he must be French.'

* * *

The body had been removed by the time Henry reached the quayside. The crowd had yet to disperse however, and had now separated into small groups, each conversing in an animated fashion.

He didn't recognise his little angel at first because she had her back to him as she spoke to a man in a wide-brimmed hat. It was only when she turned her profile towards the man that Henry saw that it was the very girl he had come looking for that morning – the girl who reminded him so strongly of his lost beloved Florence.

Henry was overcome with a sudden awful spasm of jealousy when he noticed that the man was none other than the artist Sickert. Already envious of the artist's lifestyle, he was also aware of rumours about the man's louche ways. Was he now planning to take the girl as his next mistress?

Turning swiftly on his heel lest either of them should turn and notice him (or worse still, he should note any gesture of endearment pass between them), Henry strode away. He was aware of a sudden hatred for Sickert that must surely be the work of the Devil. Was this punishment for his weakness in succumbing to temptation? He should have left the girl well alone.

And yet this illogical passion would surely not have arisen without the awful emptiness inside his marriage.

Henry had pondered this several times during the preceding weeks. Could he be punished if the wife to whom, before God, he had sworn lifelong fidelity, now carried on as if he didn't exist? Who, to all intents and purposes, had long ago abandoned her marriage vows?

Perhaps Sickert and the girl had only been exchanging pleasantries, although there was an ease between the two that suggested prior acquaintance. And unbeknownst to Henry, Jeanne did now fully turn, watching his retreating back through one swollen, bruised and bloodshot eye.

CHAPTER EIGHT

The casino dominated the western end of Dieppe's long pebble beach. With its domes of green copper and twin minarets, the Moorish-style edifice, built ten years earlier at a cost of one million francs, looked provocatively frivolous beneath the sombre, ancient castle brooding on the cliffs above.

Colonel Marsden stood nursing a calvados by the entrance to the roulette hall, observing the players as they sat hypnotised by the spinning wheel. It was mid-afternoon and he felt drowsy after a particularly fine lunch at Maison Lefèvre (poached guinea fowl with leeks and cream) and rather too many glasses of claret. He rarely had a flutter himself – his meagre army pension, supplemented by an unexpected legacy from his late wife's sister, was channelled towards gluttony rather than gambling. He couldn't afford to indulge both.

Occasionally the colonel joined the wives and children playing *petits-chevaux*, the little mechanically-operated jockeys on horseback that went round and round on a specially perforated board. These 'little horses' supposedly provided a more innocent form of wagering. It was certainly more fun than the often-mournful atmosphere of the grown-up gaming tables and, more importantly in the colonel's books, the bets tended to be on the lower side.

This afternoon, however, he was having a wager with himself. Clustered around the roulette table were five English gentlemen and one lady. It was harder to discern the more magnetic centre of attraction, the spinning wheel or the exotic, dark-haired woman sitting upright in their midst. For the Duchesse Caracciolo not only came with a colourful aristocratic lineage but also a delicious whiff of scandal. Delicious to the men that is, because as soon as any of their wives made an entrance, they would break off conversation with the duchess and look thoroughly abashed.

Married young to a Neapolitan duke, the half Portuguese and half-Jewish American duchess had abandoned her husband on the church steps and fled to her lover, a Polish prince and an equerry to Napoleon III. To add to her scandalous reputation, the duchess's daughter, Olga Alberta, was the goddaughter of Albert Edward, Prince of Wales. 'You can take God out of that equation,' the local joke ran, for Olga was thought to be the prince's own progeny.

The heir to the throne frequently visited his 'goddaughter' at the spacious new home named in her honour, the Villa Olga. His yacht would moor away from the others, the royal visitor brought ashore in a launch, while plain-clothes policemen paraded around the quayside. Despite such illustrious patronage, the ladies of the English colony shunned the duchess and her daughter, while the Prime Minister, Lord Salisbury, would stay out of Dieppe during the prince's visits.

The colonel's secret wager with himself was over how long it would take for the roulette table to empty once any of the English wives arrived. He thought ten minutes might be a decent interval, although any conversation between the husbands and the duchess would cease at once. The lady, long used to such social ostracism, did not appear to mind.

A rustle of a dress alerted him to the arrival of what he hoped would to be one of the wives. He found himself instead looking down on the small stout figure of Venetia Hall, who returned his surprised expression with a mock curtsy.

'Good afternoon, Colonel,' she said. 'Not playing the little horses?'

'Good afternoon, madam,' he replied muzzily. 'Just watching the roulette. Less onerous on the wallet that way, I find.'

'Quite so. And the duchess with some attentive male company, I spy. Not for long I should imagine, for a gaggle of wives are making their way here at this very moment.'

The colonel made a non-committal noise, not wishing to share his private wager with the author of several of his favourite books. Despite his enjoyment of the military tales of Edgar Stanton Lister, he didn't altogether trust the writer herself, suspecting her of using him as a model for one of her characters. His speculation was partially correct, for although the colonel thought that he was the basis for Major Pilson, a dashing cavalry officer in *The Regimental Mount and Other Stories of Military Endeavour,* he was in fact the template for Major Pilson's conceited and bibulous superior.

The duchess wasn't only unpopular with the English wives, but also with the French shopkeepers. They were annoyed by her habit of solely frequenting the town's two English grocers. A thorough-going Anglophile, she was often to be seen entering Litten's on the Quai Duquesne, which advertised 'Jams de Crosse and Blackwell, Stout de Guinness et soda water de Schweppes.'

But if a dark rumour that Venetia had heard, but kept strictly to herself, was true, then all of the French townspeople would be openly hostile to the duchess. For it was said that she had sent money and letters of support to the family of the traitor Alfred Dreyfus, the Jewish soldier whose trial and conviction for espionage had so shaken the nation.

It was now being claimed that this Dreyfus had been mistakenly identified as the author of notes communicating French military secrets to the German embassy in Paris. His supporters maintained that he had been wrongfully convicted and sentenced to life imprisonment on Devil's Island, but that the government and the army could not admit their error and risk their own disgrace.

Nobody of her acquaintance believed that Dreyfus was innocent. Indeed, they thought that the claims were all part of a Jewish conspiracy to protect their own. Venetia, who preferred facts to opinions, withheld her own judgement on the matter.

* * *

The clothes having been removed from the dead man, the still saturated garments were folded and placed on a table along one wall of the morgue. Emile looked at the man's marbled flesh and the way his veins now stood out so that his limbs and torso seemed enmeshed in dark purple netting. The skin on his hands and feet was sloughed and white, as if he were wearing dirty satin gloves.

Frossard appeared to be more interested in scrutinising the dead man's clothing, and, with a nod of approval from the examining magistrate, his hands delved into the pockets and ran up and down the lining to check whether anything had been concealed therein.

Dr. Paul Bernard, a small man in his fifties with a trim beard that suited his clipped manner, meanwhile began a thorough inspection of the naked corpse, an assistant jotting down the medical examiner's observations.

'In cases of drowning there is an added urgency,' he said, as if lecturing a class of medical students. 'Water, especially cold water, slows down the state of decomposition in the body, but once exposed to air, the decomposition will dramatically accelerate.'

He seemed to pay special attention to the side of the face where Emile himself had noticed an abrasion, and the man's back. Between the shoulder blades, there was a gash about four inches in length, about the same size and shape as a pair of parted lips. Emile recognised it as a knife or spear wound; he'd seen plenty enough of the latter in Africa. He was about to say as much when Dr Bernard crouched to get a better look at the gash, gave a little cough and addressed his assistant.

'In cases of drowning it can be difficult to differentiate antemortem injuries from postmortem changes caused by abrasions. The body being dragged against rocks and so forth.'

Frossard abruptly dropped the dead man's clothing and approached the body. Emile was about to say something about the wound when Frossard announced: 'Probably the rocks where we discovered him. They're damnedly sharp. Like razors.'

Dr. Bernard frowned, and then nodded. His assistant made a note and helped turn the corpse so that it now lay on its back. The pathologist began examining his hands and fingernails and then, forcing open the mouth, his teeth.

Seemingly satisfied with his external examination, the doctor was handed a saw. Emile's eyes dropped to the floor as he realised that he was about to slice the rim of the cadaver's head – removing it like the top of a boiled egg. Frossard, he noticed when he felt able to look up again, had his back to the operation and was staring at the dead man's clothing with an air of profound frustration.

Dr. Bernard was now inspecting the exposed brain, which he would occasionally prod with a spatula. The room, which had little ventilation, was beginning to reek of the blood that had been allowed to drain into enamel bowls placed around the dissecting table. Emile felt nauseous, but was determined not to show it or to succumb to any urge to vomit. He told himself that he had seen mutilated bodies before in Africa and not to be squeamish.

The examining magistrate was obviously experiencing a similar delicacy, for he whispered something in Frossard's ear before abruptly leaving the room. Frossard himself had now turned his attention to the operating table and was evidently unperturbed when the doctor was handed a chisel and, with the delicacy of a sculptor, began to tap away at the man's chest.

'It's very important not to destroy the sternum while opening the chest cavity,' Emile heard him say to his assistant, who duly jotted down his superior's observations. A sharp knife was applied to the bloated stomach, intestines and vile-smelling liquid starting to spill on to the table.

'Scoop them up quickly,' the doctor commanded his assistant. 'Bowl!'

Another wave of nausea rose up in Emile as the assistant grabbed an empty enamel bowl and placed them next to the exposed guts, which the doctor began to pull from the body like an impatient child opening a Christmas present.

'We can examine the intestines separately but first I must reach the pelvis to ascertain the man's age. The junction between the sacrum and hip bones should give some indication, as will the junctions in the lower vertebrae.'

Frossard peeled himself away from the table covered in the dead man's clothes and approached Emile.

'As soon as we are finished here, we must go and search the houses of the men who discovered the body,' he said in a loud whisper. 'There won't be a moment to lose.'

'Yes, sir,' replied Emile, once again surprised at the urgency of the commissaire's wishes to search the men's homes. What did he suspect them of stealing?

'On second thoughts,' said Frossard, before covering his mouth with a handkerchief. 'Let's go now. We can await the medical examiner's report.'

CHAPTER NINE

Walter strolled back to his studio, throwing open the window to expel the stale afternoon air. He loved this oasis on top of the old rampart, 32 time-worn stone steps up from the quayside. It commanded a good view of where the latest crop of passengers from England had now disembarked and were queuing to be interviewed by the customs officers.

After a long and often rough crossing, the Douane were a tiresome obligation. Walter had lost count of the number of his fellow countrymen affronted for being fined for carrying, of all things, safety matches.

Whenever he disembarked and noticed someone smoking in the queue, it was his habit to approach them and ask for a light. If they then produced a box of matches, he would advise them to surreptitiously throw the offending articles into the water.

'Matches are a government industry in France,' he would warn these bewildered travellers, who were unsure whether or not this raffish-looking stranger was playing a joke on them. 'The fine for attempting to take any matches through the Custom House is a franc apiece!'

Indeed, some would laugh in his face, suspecting that their leg was being pulled. They would later stare ruefully back at Walter when divested of a fiver by the Douane. Sugar and tobacco were also considered contraband, but it was the fine for a box of matches that began so many holidays on a sour note. The ensuing arguments further delayed the disembarkation, especially when the English passengers spluttered in bad French (when not insisting on speaking English *very loudly*) and the implacable customs officers replied in their thick Norman patois.

Not that Walter would be crossing and re-crossing the Channel at any time soon, having decided to stay in Dieppe for the winter. 'I cannot stand another winter in London,' as he told anyone expressing surprise at his decision to remain in the town beyond the summer season. 'London is too dark and life is too short.'

Besides, his wife Nellie was intent on suing for divorce and, having reluctantly agreed to end their marriage, they had to satisfy the legal requirement and show that he had deserted the marital home for two years. That should be easier with Nellie living in London and he in France, while Dieppe was considerably cheaper than the metropolis. His debts had kindly been covered by his brother-in-law, a Manchester businessman, while he was making modest sales with his Dieppe scenes. But money was always tight and he only too happy to spend it.

Walter turned to face his easel. Having squared up his sketches of Jeanne reclining on her bed and transferred them to the canvas, he now considered his colour palette. Her face was partly in shadow, as indeed Jeanne's face was now partly in shadow, that pig of a husband having since given her a black eye.

A drunken and mostly unemployed fisherman (few of the crews would hire him for he would prove a risk at sea), Pascal lived off Jeanne's earnings as a prostitute. Apparently, he had returned home after drinking all day and accused her of withholding money from him. Did he not realise that he was hurting his own livelihood by damaging his much younger wife's face with his fist? She hadn't been able to go into work today, she had told Walter, who had forwarded her ten francs from his pocket.

There was something else bothering him about Jeanne however. The body had been carted away to the morgue by the time she appeared, but Walter had shown her a quick sketch he'd made of the dead man's head, and of the insignia that Emile had asked him to copy. Jeanne recoiled when she saw his sketches, her bruised face taking on a frightened look. She seemed to shiver as she pulled away from Walter and, without bidding him farewell, strode off in the direction of Le Pollet.

Stepping away from the easel, he retrieved the sketch pad from his coat pocket. The hastily scribbled drawing of the motif on the drowned man's jacket revealed a hexagram of two equilateral triangles intersecting with a crescent moon. In the middle of the hexagram was some sort of script. Arabic probably. Taking a larger piece of paper, he attempted to copy the pattern, but the exercise didn't bring any fresh inspiration.

'It's no use,' he thought. 'I can't do any work today'. And he wondered whether he could be bothered to walk to the casino and hire a bathing suit. He hadn't yet been in the water this year and wondered whether the sea would be unbearably cold. 'Bracing,' he encouraged himself. 'It will be bracing'.

* * *

There was no one at home when the Reverend Henry Gibson arrived at the house on the Faubourg de la Barre, a short walk from the porch of All Saints Church. The Gibsons had lived in this handsome building for five years, ever since Henry had been appointed following a dispute concerning his predecessor.

This clergyman, the Reverend Dr. Merk, had apparently scandalised Dieppe's English colony by announcing his intention of marrying a woman of the Roman Catholic persuasion. A meeting ended with a call for him to resign and a letter was sent to the Bishop of London stating that Dr. Merk did not have the confidence of the congregation. Parents were concerned, it was stressed, as the vicar had decided that his own children would be brought up under the edict of Rome.

It was eventually decided to hold a ballot, Dr. Merk's opponent being a convivial type who liked to smoke and drink. The rival chaplains thereafter became known as "the drunkard" and "the atheist", the latter so dubbed because it was thought that no true man of God would consider having his children brought up as Papists. Those qualified to vote had to place a ball in a box that stood beside the church porch, choosing between either candidate

After a certain amount of suspected skulduggery (Mrs Venetia Hall was reckoned to have secreted several balls about her person), the 'atheist' Dr. Merk was elected, but departed Dieppe soon afterwards with his Roman Catholic bride. The 'drunkard' had meanwhile also mysteriously vanished, it being later reported (erroneously or not) that he had fallen into the dock at Le Havre and drowned. Henry received the calling soon afterwards, lifted from his comfortable parish in Surrey to sort out the mess and calm divisions.

He had been chosen because (in the bishop's words) he was "a clergyman of ordinary and extremely moderate High Church type" who could be relied upon not to try and "evangelize" Dieppe. Henry was however increasingly unsure whether he fitted this description. He certainly felt himself chafing against the limited expectations of his regular congregation.

The more he read the New Testament, the more he felt the need to replicate Christ's actions, however unpopular that might make him. He wanted to consort more with the poor, the needy and, yes, even with fallen women. He must try to overcome his violent feelings about the young woman he had seen with Sickert earlier today, and reach out to her with the chance of salvation.

Letting himself into the house, he decided however to start with the housemaid, Clotilde. How much did Lucy pay her? The girl was diligent and hard-working and Henry knew she had a widowed mother to support. Lucy ran the household accounts, paying shopkeepers and servants out of his stipend. She had capital and income of her own, an inheritance as well a monthly allowance from a family trust, and Henry hoped that it was this money that she frittered away at the casino.

'Clotilde!' he called, but the empty house seemed to swallow his voice. And no scurrying footsteps answered him as he again bellowed the maid's name: 'Clotilde!'

Henry went to his study desk and retrieved a batch of keys, selecting the one he knew unlocked his wife's bedroom. Returning to the hallway, he shouted the maid's name again, and receiving no reply, he climbed the staircase.

'Lucy!' he called after knocking on her bedroom door. 'Lucy dearest', he felt mischievously emboldened to say, confident now that she wasn't at home. And yet still he felt as nervous as a thief as he turned the lock and pushed open the door. 'A trespasser in my own house,' he thought. 'And this supposedly the marital bedroom.'

The room smelt strongly of perfume, a floral scent he recognised as the one habitually worn by Alice, while clothes lay thrown on the unmade bed and on the backs of chairs. Clotilde was only allowed in to clean twice a week - on Tuesdays and Fridays - and today was a Monday.

Henry himself occupied the larger of the two bedrooms that had originally been allocated to their children, Edward and Maggie. Neither had visited in five years, however. Edward, now 25, worked for a shipping company in Bristol, while Maggie, two years his senior, lived an increasingly lonely, spinster-like existence in London. Henry long ago realised that Maggie was odd, but also that his daughter resented her mother's close and seemingly exclusive relationship with Alice.

He walked over to Lucy's writing desk and sat down, wondering where he might find the book in which she recorded the household expenses. His eyes ran along the bookshelf above the desk, noting in amusement that amidst the Milton, Shakespeare and a copy of Henry Gibbon's *The Decline and Fall of the Roman Empire*, were a number of novels by Edgar Stanton Lister, otherwise known as their congregation member Mrs. Venetia Hall. His eye was however drawn to *Christ and Antichrist* by Henry Edward Manning, the Archbishop of Westminster.

'*There is a day to come which will reverse the confident judgement of men,*' he read, opening the leather-bound book at its first page. '*In that day the first shall be last and the first last. The wise of this world will be fools, and the fools in this world wise.'*

Henry recalled the archbishop's funeral. It had coincided with his last week in England before leaving for Dieppe. The funeral itself had been held at Brompton Oratory in London and, being a Catholic service, Henry had joined the enormous crowds standing outside the church in the murk of a winter's afternoon.

What had struck him most forcibly about the memorial to this great champion of the poor had been the procession that followed the archbishop's funeral car as it passed on its way to Kensal Green - great banners held aloft by working men from the docks and trades union and other socialist groups.

'This is what I must do... I must champion the downtrodden,' thought Henry as he turned to the inside cover to see whether the book belonged to Lucy or Alice. The bookplate, 'ex libris Alice Tait', confirmed that it belonged to his wife's companion. Held in place by the bookplate was a sheet of writing paper, which Henry unfolded and read. It was in his wife's handwriting and dated four years earlier, 12 August 1893.

Dearest beloved,

I want to know more about you, what makes you. Since last week so much has happened between us. I want you to talk to me. In short, I want you.

Henry folded the letter, which was singed 'L', and replaced it beneath the bookplate, and returned the book to the shelf. Looking around him to see whether he had disturbed any furniture, he retreated across the soft carpet and locked the door behind him.

CHAPTER TEN

Outside the cave entrance, washing hung over a makeshift fence made from driftwood and an old fishing net. This seemed to mark the boundary of a sort of front yard. Blocks of chalk had also been fashioned into a wall that separated each cave from its neighbour. Frossard shuddered to think what it must be like to live in such prehistoric conditions, deep within the cold and clammy chalk.

Stooping through the doorway that had been cut into the cliff face and entering the cave that had been widened into a living room, he had expected to be repelled by the miserable dwelling at the base of the cliffs. As his men fanned out and started upturning lobster pots and wooden boxes, opening desk drawers, and looking under rugs and blankets, he was instead overtaken by a profound sense of familiarity.

With the stove, makeshift furniture and low ceiling, it reminded him of his childhood home in the Vendée. The walls here were made of chalk instead of mud and horsehair, but the meagre size of the room and its layout were strikingly similar. That might even have been his old mother, her hands crossed across her lap and her unstockinged feet in wooden sabots, sitting in a low chair beside the fire.

And while the room may have been low ceilinged and cramped, it was tidy (or at least it had, before his men set to work), just as his mother had kept their long, one-floor cottage. He'd recently been thinking more and more about this dwelling; perhaps a sign of his increasing age. At the age of 44, he had begun the gradual process of turning time on its head, of starting to look backwards instead of forwards.

He had only once returned to his childhood village. It was shortly after the victory in Paris in May '71. Dressed in his smart uniform, with its scarlet trousers and brocaded blue jacket, and his first ever beard now neatly trimmed, Frossard had imagined himself the returning hero. He had decided to surprise everybody, a decision made easier by inability to write more than a few simple words and his unwillingness to dictate a letter to a more literate comrade.

People that he'd known all his life failed to recognise him as he strode into the hamlet, villagers warily regarding this sharp little soldier as he marched down the street with a look of enormous self-regard. Entering the family home, he'd discovered his mother sitting very much like the old woman here in the cave, recognition slowly creeping across her whiskered face.

"Pierre!" she had cried, the villagers who had previously failed to acknowledge him now gathering around the open door, their mouths agape. The brothers were out in the fields helping with the hay harvest, but they returned that evening. And over a hastily arranged feast of oysters, stewed eels and prune tart, Frossard had recounted his exploits, omitting the countless executions that already started to infiltrate his dreams.

It was the man with soot-covered face, his eyes shining out of the blackness like one of the minstrels Frossard had once seen in the musical hall. He was his first kill in that Parisian alleyway and his most persistent ghost. Frossard was haunted by the manner in which this filthy grinning creature had seemed to collude in his own demise. In these dreams the man's grin as his fate was sealed became ever more pronounced. Frossard wanted to shake him and shout, "Why are you allowing me to do this to you? You know you're going to die now, don't you?" And Frossard would wake in a cold sweat, cursing the phantom whose grotesquely grinning visage would stay with him for the rest of the day.

The prune tart consumed, dinner with his family was sealed by the appearance of the bottle of eau de vie - the colourless spirit usually only reserved for special occasions like Christmas, Easter and the Festival of Assumption. But it was while the bottle was passed around the table that the deflation had begun.

Having listened in awe to his stories about army life and liberating Paris from the revolutionaries, his family returned to discussing their own immediate concerns. The hay that needed cutting, the piglet that required fattening, and the white beans that they must buy from Luçon market.

Realising that these affairs were more important to them than the great events unfolding in the outside world, he sought someone less insular to talk to. He thought of the priest. Here was a man who would surely appreciate Frossard's exploits in defeating the anti-clerical mob that had threatened the very soul of France.

He would never before have dared to knock on the front door of the presbytery, or indeed have any reason to do so. The family had dutifully attended mass on most Sundays, but theirs was a passive, unquestioning faith and the priest was a familiar but remote presence in their lives. The long-faced, middle-aged man who opened the presbytery door regarded Frossard through stern grey eyes that clearly didn't recognise his caller.

Frossard had begun to babble away about the reason for his visit, but the more he tried to explain, the less coherent he became. Why had he come? Most probably to receive thanks, gratitude that was surely due from this representative of the church that he had helped save from the godless rabble.

'I have heard terrible stories,' the priest said instead. 'Would you like to receive confession?'

'That's not… that's not why I came,' Frossard had burbled.

'War… any sort of war… is a fearful thing,' the man had continued in a disconcertingly calm voice. Frossard hadn't come for a sermon. 'Thou shalt not kill, the Lord has commanded,' the priest continued. 'But there are times when killing another becomes necessary. But such an act can weigh heavily on the heart nonetheless. Would you like to confess, my son?'.

Frossard couldn't exactly remember what happened next, but he did recall shouting at this ungrateful priest. He yelled incoherently, losing all sense of dignity or decorum. Hadn't the man heard about the hostages, including the Archbishop of Paris, who been murdered by the revolutionaries, and of the churches burned to the ground? And then he was back out on the street, furious at himself for having approached this ungrateful village priest in the first place.

* * *

'Nothing here,' a gendarme said, nevertheless looking around in case he might have missed a clever hiding place. But for what? All Frossard had told his men was that he was looking for papers that might identify the corpse.

'What is it that you are looking for?' the old woman asked, the first words she had uttered since informing Frossard that her two sons were out foraging for seaweed. 'My boys would never steal anything from a dead body, sir,' the woman added, crossing herself.

'I'm sure not, dear lady,' said Frossard, looking up in annoyance as he had just noticed Agent Blanchet standing in the doorway. He had earlier dispatched him to the barracks to see whether they could shed any light on the insignia on the dead man's uniform. The task had a double objective in that it kept Blanchet out of the way while the search was being conducted.

'Any luck?' he almost snarled at the younger man.

'Nothing definitive, sir, but the barracks commander thought it belonged to one of the regiments based in Tunisia. The 'tirailleurs' based in Sousse was his best guess. In any case, he asked to hold on to the jacket unless we need it in evidence. He reckons he could get a definitive identification by the end of the week.'

'Very good,' said Frossard, giving the cave dwelling one final sweep of his gaze. 'Let him keep it as long as he likes. But send for the body for burial in the pauper's cemetery.'

* * *

The morning's writing had gone well. Over a thousand words had flowed from her pen as Venetia Hall continued her summer romance set in Dieppe. *The Tide Is Full* was being written not under the pen name Edgar Stanton Lister, the pseudonym she used for her novels about the military life, but under her own. Except she further embroidered it with a wholly fictitious middle name, Margaret, to give it a bit more drama. Venetia Margaret Hall.

Lunching on an omelette as she read through the morning's first draft - she rarely went to more than two - Venetia felt in sudden need of fresh inspiration. The book's heroine, Henrietta Douglas, was failing to come to life. Poor Henrietta felt too much like all the other heroines of Venetia's Dieppe novels: innocent, fresh-faced and on the verge of marrying the wrong man.

That didn't worry Venetia so much, after all the archetype was popular with her readers. It's just that Henrietta's speech felt dry and antiquated, somewhat like her own, she suspected. After all, she had been Henrietta's age around the time of the Crimean War, she thought somewhat disconsolately.

Venetia therefore decided that an afternoon visit to the casino might provide a spark for her imagination. She could listen to the frivolous chatter of the young English ladies who so delighted in playing the 'little horses'.

She was disappointed however to discover that, instead of frivolous young ladies, it was the vicar's wife and her companion who alone were bent over the gaming table, while the colonel watched from his usual perch at the entrance to the salon. Lucy Gibson was a short, dumpy woman with something of Queen Victoria about her. The resemblance was accentuated by her habit of wearing black, as if she too were a widow in deep mourning.

The poor Reverend Gibson, thought Venetia. It was he who should be in mourning for a marriage that outwardly appeared to be nothing of the sort. His wife spent all her time with her female companion, a gaunt, much taller woman called Alice Seagram, who exhibited a rather unfriendly manner to everyone but her beloved Lucy. Venetia watched them now as they concentrated on the *petits chevaux*, their bodies so close together that you would not have been able to run a sheet of writing paper between them.

'Good afternoon, Colonel. Has Madame Lefèvre been treating you well?' she asked, coming to halt next to the old army officer.

'Most excellently, dear lady,' replied the colonel muzzily. 'A most inspired cook, as you know.'

He'd heard that Mrs. Hall had been consorting with that Wilde fellow and wanted to ask her about the bugger's plans, whether or not he intended staying in Dieppe. But the colonel didn't know how to broach the subject. As if uncannily sensing his desire for this news, Venetia introduced the topic herself.

'I presume you've heard about our illustrious visitor from England?'

'Gad, which one? Dieppe seems full of illustrious visitors at the moment,' said the colonel, playing for time.

'Well, the great Oscar Wilde of course.'

'The "great", you say. The infamous more like.'

'Now, now, Colonel,' said Venetia, realising that the man was, if not drunk, then more than usually tipsy. 'He's served his time and deserves our Christian forgiveness.'

Christian forgiveness not being one of the colonel's more noticeable traits, he merely harumphed instead.

'Will he be staying long?' he managed to ask.

'I shouldn't think so. Café owners have been complaining to the Prefecture about how they are losing custom because so many customers up and leave as soon as

Oscar enters their establishments. I dare say he might try somewhere further up the coast. Somewhere more remote and less full of society.'

This last piece of information had been relayed by Oscar's friend's Reggie Turner, whom Venetia had met in the street the previous afternoon.

'Very wise,' said the colonel, followed by another harumph. 'Now these two ladies have a very fine friendship,' he added nodding in the direction of the gaming table, where Lucy was currently whispering in Alice's ear.

'Yes, but I worry for our dear vicar,' said Venetia. 'I never see him out and about with his wife.'

'That much is true,' said the colonel. 'On the other hand, any man would be happy to see his wife having such a close lady companion. Takes the strain off the marriage, if you know what I mean.'

Your poor dead wife, Venetia found herself thinking.

CHAPTER ELEVEN

Frossard having been called away to an urgent meeting with his superiors in Rouen and leaving by the early train, Emile had been ordered to visit the customs house and comb the passenger logs. He was to look out for any North African-sounding names, or anyone holding a military rank, it having now been confirmed that the drowned man's insignia was that of the 4th Tunisian Tirailleurs Regiment.

This was an infantry regiment of the French Army of Africa, stationed in Sousse. What on earth was the dead man doing on the Normandy coast? Had he fallen from a passing ship, or was he in Dieppe for a specific reason? Unless he had come on a restorative bathing holiday, which seemed to Emile to be highly unlikely, an intention of taking the boat to England seemed the most rational probability. But even that begged more questions than it answered.

By eleven o'clock, Emile had searched the passenger lists for the previous fortnight, the coroner having ascertained that the man had been dead for no more than one week, and found no name that seemed to fit the dead Arab. Unless of course he had booked under a false identity. But that would also require forged papers and Emile thought such subterfuge would be too complicated for a simple soldier.

Nevertheless, he made a note of any passengers with a military rank, or a surname that wasn't obviously English. And the vast majority of passengers were from Great Britain – the French seemingly finding no need to return the compliment by visiting England. Not for the first time, he found himself wondering about this English fascination with France and the corresponding lack of curiosity by the French about England. The country of his birth seemed only a useful bolthole when fleeing arrest or persecution, his own parents being a prime example.

His mother, Nathalie, didn't like to talk about her escape from Paris in May 1871, but once he had managed to persuade her to tell him about it. The story had seemed immensely thrilling to Emile, who must have been 11 or 12 at the time. How she had hidden in the homes of successive friends and comrades until she managed to get out of Paris and into Belgium.

But when the French government began pressurising Belgium to return wanted Communards (much to the disgust of Victor Hugo, who was then resident in Brussels), Nathalie and seven other comrades had sailed to England on a Flemish fishing boat. They apparently landed at dawn on the coast of Kent along with several baskets of herring. It was this mental picture that Emile most cherished.

His father Ludovic – the drunken armchair revolutionary – hadn't even participated in the Commune. He had exiled himself in London earlier to escape possible conscription during the war with Prussia, sustaining himself with occasional labouring jobs between writing pamphlets in support of socialism, anarchism and internationalism. Anything with an 'ism' as a suffix, thought Emile. Not that he had known the man, imbibing instead his mother's bitter assessment.

With over an hour to go until lunch, and with no further duties until Frossard returned from Rouen later that afternoon, Emile decided to drop in on his friend Walter Sickert at his studio on the nearby Tour aux Crabes.

Part of the town's ancient fortifications that had mostly been demolished in order to widen the quay, the Tour aux Crabes was approached up a timeworn stone staircase. It constituted a small elevated courtyard symmetrically planted with four cherry trees and surrounded on three sides with flint and brick cottages. Emile, like Walter, appreciated its air of discreet seclusion high above the bustle of the quays.

Walter's studio was a room in the smallest of these cottages, its protruding glass frontage apparently providing the north-facing light that was somehow considered important to painters. It was something to do with the constancy of the light, Walter had explained.

As Emile entered to the familiar smell of turpentine and paint, he was presented with a peculiar sight. Sitting placidly in one corner, and engrossed in playing with a woollen doll, was a girl of about two or three. Meanwhile, two women stood leaning against the far wall with their backs to Walter, their bonneted heads bowed forward. Walter himself was seated on an old armchair with a sketching pad on his lap.

'Ah, Emile, welcome,' he said. 'I'm just drawing the delightful Urquhart sisters.'

The child looked up from her dolly and stared at Emile, but the two ladies remained in their strange pose, almost like criminals who didn't want to be identified.

'They prefer to be drawn from behind. Polly thinks I make her face look like mouldy cheese. But good timing, my friend, as I believe I have finished this little sketch.'

Both women now slowly straightened up and turned. The older of the two, perhaps in her mid-twenties, smiled at Emile, but the other, younger woman, averted her eyes after a quick glance at the visitor. She had long fair hair and a pale complexion and Emile found himself transfixed. He couldn't say for sure – perhaps it was the shape of the face – but there was something of Mary Rogerson about her.

'May I introduce the Urquhart sisters,' said Walter, struggling up from the tatty old armchair. 'Mrs. Polly Middleton and her sister Lydia Urquhart. Agent Emile Blanchet of the Dieppe police.'

The younger woman, Lydia, looked at him now with open curiosity. The way that Walter had introduced Emile made it sound like he was here on police business.

'Just Emile, please,' he said, gratified to see that the corners of Lydia's mouth briefly turned up into a smile, before she again looked away. A squawk from the floor then reminded everyone of another presence in the cramped studio.

'Ah, yes, and this young lady is Lil, the daughter of Mrs. Middleton. Polly's child.' The child beamed at Emile, her lips smeared with red that the policeman surmised must have emanated from a bowl of strawberries by her side.

'We live across the courtyard,' said Polly Middleton proffering a gloved hand, which Emile pressed lightly while bowing. 'Mr Sickert minds Lil sometimes when we go out on errands. And spoils her something rotten. Enough strawberries now Lil!'

Polly was pretty, although the word didn't do her justice. 'Beautiful' wouldn't quite do it either, Emile would think later, and perhaps it was a certain nobility, or self-possession. Either way, it was tinged with sadness.

Lydia was altogether different. She seemed full of vitality, with a youthful bloom that had not been discernibly marked with any adversity. Emile bowed to her now, Lydia replying with an instinctive curtsy before bursting into unrestrained laughter. Walter followed suit and then Mrs. Middleton and finally Emile. Even little Lil began laughing, swept along by the hysteria that seemed to have enveloped the studio.

'I'm sorry,' said Lydia, struggling with her words. 'The formality…'

And suddenly Emile felt a wonderful familiarity. That he was once again in the bosom of the Rogerson family. He was back in that big house in Blackheath, laughing and joking with the daughters, while his beloved Mary Rogerson looked on. He had the delightful sensation that he had somehow come home.

Seeming as usual to read Emile's mind, Walter started looking for drinking vessels. 'I think we should mark the occasion with a toast. I am always happy when I'm able to bring my friends together.' But all he could find were two cracked and dirty china tea cups.

'Never mind, Walter,' said Polly Middleton, before turning to Emile. 'Perhaps you would like to come and dine with us soon.'

'I would like that very much,' said Emile, nearly adding that it would make a welcome change from his landlady's food. Despite feeling already delightfully relaxed in the women's company, he didn't feel he had made sufficient acquaintance for such a remark.

'A charming family,' said Walter after the ladies had departed. 'Polly's husband works in London, but she prefers to be in Dieppe with her mother and sister. Their father drank himself to death some 15 years ago and the family has lived in various towns across France ever since. Most recently in Dinan in Brittany, but now here in Dieppe I am glad to say. And you took a shine to Lydia, I surmise.'

'Oh please, how do you know that?' said Emile, his cheeks reddening.

'I can read you like a book, my dear Emile. A very entertaining book, whose latest chapters I am always excited to receive.'

'It's just that she reminded me of somebody.'

'Somebody special, no doubt? Lydia is a spirited young woman, quite untamed. By the way, how fares your investigation into the dead Arab?'

'Slowly,' replied Emile, picking up Walter's sketchbook and looking at his rear-view sketch of Polly and Lydia.

'Well, I'm not sure whether this is important or not', said Walter, yawning and stretching his arms out by his side as if recently awakened. 'But I was trying to remember where I had seen a fez of late. It was in the house of my model Jeanne, gathering dust atop her wardrobe.'

* * *

'I can't stress the importance, Commissaire Frossard, of finding those papers.'

Frossard had been surprised on arriving at the central police commissariat in Rouen, to be redirected to the army barracks on the other side of the Seine. Once there he was ushered to an upstairs room whose only furnishing consisted of a small table and two chairs. The windows were barred and the room smelt of stale cigar smoke. Left alone for some ten minutes, he paced up and down, listlessly staring out of the window bars at the great cathedral spire and adjacent twin towers that rose above the surrounding rooftops.

Sharp footsteps eventually heralded the arrival of two men, one a uniformed officer, the other in civilian clothes. Neither man introduced himself, but Frossard instinctively saluted the officer type. He was small and wiry, with deep-set eyes and a moustache that dwarfed his face. Frossard noted the number '74' on his collar – the 74th Infantry Regiment. The officer returned Frossard's salute and indicated one of the chairs, before seating himself behind the table.

The plain-clothed man, bulky and impassive with a large square bald head, remained standing with his back to the window, so that Frossard couldn't discern his face clearly. This man passed the officer a sheet of paper, which the officer then perused for a good minute.

'Frossard, I see from your army and police record that you are a true patriot,' he said at last.

Frossard felt himself straightening in his chair. He had longed to hear such words for far too long. Posted to the back of beyond, ignored and despised, he had forgotten the pride he once felt for the duties he had performed for France and for the army.

'Yes, sir, I am a true patriot.' He wanted to say more, but feared he might embarrass himself by starting to babble.

'And you were a keen supporter of our General Boulanger.'

Frossard had served under Boulanger - or 'General Revenge' as he had become known for his desire to avenge France's defeat in the Prussian war - in Tunisia. He had had high regard for his commander-in-chief's Catholic and monarchist views. And when Boulanger had returned to

Paris in '86, Frossard had followed him, resigning his army commission and taking up a post with the Paris police.

He had perhaps taken matters too far however when, as a serving police officer, he had attended rallies in support of Boulanger and openly campaigned for him when the general ran to become a deputy in '88

If only Boulanger had seized the moment, instead of deciding to fight in elections like any other run-of-the-mill politician. He could have marched on Paris in '89 and done away with those corrupt parliamentarians. France would have had a Catholic king again. The old order would have been restored and, just perhaps, Frossard might have found official favour.

Instead, by coincidence or not (Frossard felt not), the general's subsequent disgrace and suicide heralded a downturn in his own fortunes. Seemingly in line for promotion, his career stalled and superiors avoided his eye. He was posted from Paris to Rouen, and then to the backwater in Dieppe.

'Why, yes, sir, although...' Frossard now found himself struggling to answer. Was this a trap? Was he about to be disgraced further for his support of a long-dead hero.

'Yes. A damn shame about all that,' said the officer with a wave of his gloved hand, seemingly dismissing the subject, much to Frossard's relief. 'But the army needs men like you, Frossard. France needs men like you. Honourable men willing to go above and beyond duty to protect the *patrie*. And yet you seem to have been treated appallingly. A policeman of your talents and dedication should be stationed here in Rouen at least, or in Paris.'

Frossard didn't know where to begin, the gratitude he felt swelling up at hearing these words threatening to overcome him.

'Most mistreated, sir, and I can't understand why,' he managed to blurt.

'Oh, I can see why,' said the officer, tilting back in his chair and opening a drawer, from which he extracted a small cigar. 'We are ruled by men of little vision and no patriotism. If we are to remain a republic, alas, then let it be so, but nobody should seek to undermine the army. Nobody!'

Frossard shifted uneasily on his chair. As much as he was gratified to hear such sentiments, he wondered how they applied to his summons to Rouen. He didn't have to wait long.

'Now, this dead Arab soldier who washed up in Dieppe,' said the officer, leaning forward across the desk as pointing his unlit cigar at Frossard. 'You were directed that he might have been carrying some papers. Top secret papers, whose possession by the wrong people would be seriously detrimental to safety of the nation.'

'I was told in no uncertain terms to find them, yes, sir. But not of their contents.'

'Quite so. And no luck so far?'

'None, most unfortunately. I personally searched his clothes and the home of the men who discovered him. We still don't know how he died.'

Was it Frossard's imagination, or did the plain-clothed man standing by the window shift uneasily after he said this? Either way, he sensed an increased tension in the room. There was a long silence during which Frossard became aware of the officer studying him from his pale blue eyes above a droopy grey walrus moustache.

'Have you ever killed a man, Frossard?' he asked at length.

'Many times… in the course of duty,' Frossard replied, nevertheless taken aback by the question. An image of that grinning, rodent-like man in the Parisian back alley, a memory usually confined to his dream-life, sprung to mind.

'In the course of duty,' the officer echoed. 'Now how this Arab died, I know not, and frankly I don't care. That is not the question here.'

Frossard had the impression that the officer was struggling to find the right words.

'The thing is… I can't stress the importance, Frossard, of finding those papers. Spare no means in your attempts. The reputation of the army and of France is at stake.'

Frossard had to resist the desire to stand and salute. 'Yes, sir!' he half-shouted instead.

The man standing by the window now leaned across and passed the officer another sheet of paper. Frossard could see his face more clearly now. It was expressionless, as if set in stone.

'You may need some assistance,' said the officer. 'I see you have rightly expressed doubts about your deputy, this Agent Blanchet. While he has an unblemished army and police record so far – not difficult with someone so young – I agree that his background is a cause for concern. A mother who actively fought for the Paris uprising and a father who was an anarchist pamphleteer. I always believe that breeding will out, and this Blanchet smells like trouble.'

'My belief entirely, sir.'

'Well, we'll see what we can do, but in the meantime keep him on other duties, as far away from your investigation as is possible without raising any suspicion. Commissaire Frossard, I foresee only good things for you if we have a successful outcome to this business.

CHAPTER TWELVE

Henry Gibson breakfasted alone. It was Lucy and Alice's custom to keep to their room until he had vacated the dining room – the sound of his study door closing being their signal to emerge. He then attended to his toilet, doing so with uncharacteristic care and attention. He combed his sideburns and eyebrows and dabbed some eau de cologne on each wrist before donning a clean linen lounge coat and grabbing a boater from the hallway hatstand. Was it his imagination or did the maid Clotilde look up and give him a wry smile as he passed her scrubbing the floor tiles?

He stepped out of the front door and on to the Rue de la Barre, strode past the Café des Tribunaux with its look of a Munich beer hall, and down the Grand Rue. In his hand was a Bible. Nothing unusual in that for a man of the cloth except that he was gripping it with an intensity that wasn't matched by his somnolent gaze. He had the look of a very determined sleepwalker.

Henry failed to notice Venetia Hall taking morning coffee with her dog Tippet on the first-floor balcony of Maison Grisch, although she observed him and noted his unusually jaunty attire. He failed to notice Walter Sickert standing in the shade of a side street as he sketched a shop front.

Finally reaching the quayside where the boat train stood waiting for cross-channel passengers travelling on to Paris, Henry took a right turn by the Café Suisse and followed the arcades, deep in shadow in the late May morning sunshine. Café owners were putting out chairs and tables for the lunchtime trade as he passed by in this strange, trance-like manner. He then crossed the first of two bridges that led towards Le Pollet.

As he approached the modern wrought-iron swing bridge across the entrance to the inner harbour, separating Le Pollet from the town centre, Henry came to a halt. For the first time that morning he hesitated. Reflexively opening his Bible his eyes fell on a random passage from Paul:

"Casting all your care upon him; for he careth for you."

'He careth for me,' said Henry under his breath. He stood for a moment in silent prayer, passers-by casting curious looks at the gaily dressed gentleman who appeared to be contemplating the flagstones. He had come this far without a plan and now he must trust God to guide him.

The doorstep where he had first encountered the young woman, the vision who reminded him so strongly of his lost beloved Florence, once again rebuked him by being unoccupied. Without stopping to think and as if guided by the Holy Spirit, he knocked forcefully on the door above it. When no reply came, he knocked again, this time the door opening to reveal a stern-faced woman of about 60 years of age.

'*Bonjour monsieur*,' she said, her eyes running over Henry clothes and frowning slightly at the book in his hand. 'We are not open. Come back in two hours.'

'Apologies, madame, but I was looking for a certain young lady,' said Henry, unsure whether his meaning had come across in his faltering French.

'English?' the woman asked, before repeating, this time in English, 'We are not open. You come back.'

As she said this, the heads of two young women appeared from doorways further down the hallway. One of them was his "Florence". She said something in French to the old lady, who looked again at Henry, frowned, nodded and stood aside. Henry lifted his boater from his head and stepped inside the house.

She was barefoot and wrapped in a blanket, her hair unkempt and her face still full of sleep. Somehow the naturalness of her attire and drowsy disposition made her seem even more beautiful to Henry. She beckoned with her head, Henry following her naked heels as they climbed a steep narrow staircase.

On the first-floor landing she opened a door and smiled at Henry. It was then that he noticed the black eye.

'What happened?' he asked, pointing to his own eye.

She pulled the blanket more tightly around her and shrugged. The room was small and square and dominated by a large wardrobe and a double bed in considerable disarray. Her clothes were thrown over the bottom iron bedstead, while the tangled sheets lay half on the floor. She pointed to a wooden stool in front of a dressing table.

'What is your name?' he asked in French.

'Jeanne. And you?'

'Henry'.

'Nice to meet you Henry,' she said in heavily accented English.

'Ah, you speak English.'

'*Un peu.*'

Henry sat down and Jeanne perched on the edge of her bed, gently kicking her feet like a child. She looked at him through amused blue eyes, and Henry, returning her gaze, felt drawn in with an unabashed magnetism. He could stay like this forever, silently doing nothing. Just being with her. Was it possible that Florence could somehow have been replicated in this poor French tart? How strange is nature. How strange is God's purpose.

'What you like?' she asked, tugging the blanket from one shoulder so that her left breast was partly revealed beneath her petticoat.

'No, no, no!' exclaimed Henry, leaping from his stool with an outstretched hand. Jeanne pulled the blanket back over her shoulder and frowned.

'Not that,' he said, sitting back down. '*Je voudrais vous connaitre,*' he continued, unsure of his French.

'We can speak English if you like. Many of my clients is English.'

'Monsieur Sickert?' Henry blurted without thinking.

'*Oui*. Monsieur Sickert. But he only like to paint me.' And then she said: 'You want to marry me?'

'Heavens, no,' said Henry with a laugh. Then what did he want?

'I'm… I am already married.'

'I see,' said Jeanne. 'Me too… worse luck.'

In the silence that followed, Henry became aware of the bible sitting on his lap. 'Will you pray with me,' he asked.

'Pray?'

'*Prier*', he said, and she burst out laughing. And then seeing that he was serious, she nodded and put her hands together like a child in prayer.

'Dear Lord,' he began. 'Please look after your servant Jeanne and save her from mortal sin.'

He couldn't continue. For his selfish desires seemed to counter his wish for Jeanne's salvation. How could he reconcile holiness with his instinct to take Jeanne in his arms, to fall upon her.

'Kiss me… *embrasse-moi*,' she said, as if reading his thoughts.

Henry realised he had reached crisis point. The Devil was in the room, leering from the corner by the wardrobe.

'Jeanne… I…'

'Henry, I don't know what you want.'

A silence. And then she said: 'Will you do something for me?'

Feeling that the crisis had passed, that he had remained resolute and strong, Henry nodded gratefully.

'Anything, dear Jeanne.'

'Can I trust you? *Puis-je te croire*?'

'Absolutely'.

She nodded solemnly and stood up, padding over to the wardrobe. Henry watched as she crouched, her unbrushed auburn hair falling across her shoulders. Standing up again, it appeared that she had some sort of package in her hands.

'Please… keep this,' she said, handing him what felt like a bundle of papers enclosed within a large cardboard folder. This was tied to together with a silk ribbon and stamped with a wax seal. He tried to read the seal, but the identification had been worn away.

'Hide it. Don't tell anyone. *Personne… tu comprends?*'

She took the bible from his lap and held it out in front of him. He put his right hand on the holy book and said: 'I swear.'

Bending forward so that he could smell her warm flesh, Jeanne kissed Henry on the forehead. He had an urge to pull her on to his lap, but she retreated back towards the bed.

'These papers,' she said. 'I don't know… they are somehow dangerous. *Prends soin de toi.* Take care, Henry.'

CHAPTER THIRTEEN

Mid-morning and Emile sat inside the dingy café nursing a bowl of rough country cider. He had grown fond of the fermented apple juice – or at least its pleasant effect on his adolescent head - while living with his grandparents. The tipsy feeling proved a welcome escape during those unhappy years living marooned amidst the flat remorseless Caux plateau. The old couple made their own cider and drank it morning, noon and night. The association should have been enough to make him repelled by the drink, but instead he had developed a taste for it.

The café's mud-splattered window still afforded a good view of the steps leading in and out of the Hotel Sandwich. Emile was surprised when Commissaire Frossard had reassigned him the task of keeping an eye on the English poet calling himself Sebastian Melmoth. Of course, Melmoth's real identity was by now known by most of the town – at least by those that might be expected to take an interest. Emile had never before heard of this Oscar Wilde.

Walter had informed him of the nature of the man's crime, the one for which he had been imprisoned. His friend seemed amused by Wilde's carnal desire for another man, but Emile found himself bemused when he thought about the idea. He tried and failed to imagine himself wanting to kiss or caress another man. Either way, the English courts appeared to have treated Wilde severely for his transgression.

But why the need to follow him in Dieppe? Did the authorities perhaps fear that Wilde would corrupt the youth of the town? His task seemed such a waste of time, especially as he had received reports of a spate of thefts from the shops along the Grand Rue. Several complaints had been made in the past week alone.

A man stopped outside the hotel entrance, but only to light a cigarette before strolling on. Emile was the only customer and the patron had vanished into a back room, leaving him on his own. All the better for contemplating the events of the previous evening.

The invitation to dine with the Urquhart sisters and their mother had arrived sooner than anticipated. Emile had changed into his best suit and carefully attended to his toilet, immediately arousing Marie-Hélène's suspicions. She had been flustered when he'd announced that he was dining with friends that evening. Was there a lady involved, she had ventured to ask, while obviously fearing his reply.

'Three ladies to be precise,' he had answered, hoping to throw her off the scent. 'An English family newly arrived in Dieppe.'

The idea that there was a family involved seemed to partly satisfy Marie-Hélène, although she had later inquired about the ladies' ages.

'Did I say three ladies,' said Emile. 'I meant four. The oldest I believe to be in her forties or fifties, and the youngest is not yet four.'

He could see Marie-Hélène mentally calculating to whom the child might belong. But soon the task had seemed to defeat her, and she had left him in peace. He must find new lodgings, Emile had thought, not for the first time.

Polly and Lydia's mother, Mrs Elinor Urquhart, turned out to be a handsome woman in her late forties. She gave Emile a wryly amused look as he arrived like a suitor, complete with a bunch of pink cornflowers that he had bought that afternoon and hidden from Marie-Hélène under his coat. They were now crushed and starting to wilt.

Mrs Urquhart thanked him and passed the forlorn looking bouquet to a maid, who gave them a less tactful glance before carrying them away. There was no sign of Little Lil, but Polly and Lydia rose from their armchairs as he gave a brief bow – careful not to overdo it lest he once again triggered another bout of Lydia's laughter.

Polly and her mother had done most of the talking before and during supper, quizzing Emile about his early life. He hadn't been sure about how to broach the subject of his parents, but had decided it would be for the best that he should come clean on the matter. If they disapproved, so be it. But happily, he soon realised that Walter had already given a full picture of his mother's role in the Paris uprising and subsequent exile, along with his father's feckless ways.

He was more reticent about his time with the army in Africa. The so-called Second Franco-Dahomean War against King Béhanzin had proved victorious for the French, but Emile could feel nothing but shame for the one-sided struggle as line upon line of native fighters – many of them women – fell before French guns and bayonets.

'What an exciting life you have led for one so young,' said Mrs Urquhart. 'Like your own papa, my late husband was also overly fond of the bottle and we too have been forced to move from place to place as a consequence.'

Such easy acceptance relaxed Emile and he was soon regaling the company with tales of his life in London and of the kind family in Blackheath where his mother had tutored French. He spoke of the Rogerson girls, naturally without mentioning his boyhood passion for the eldest sister. And he told of his abrupt removal to his grandparents' house in Normandy.

From time to time, he gave a sideways glance at Lydia to see whether she was equally as engaged in his stories. She appeared to be listening politely, albeit remaining largely silent, with no sign of the ready laughter of the previous encounter. Perhaps her mother's presence somehow inhibited her, although nothing he had experienced so far of Mrs Urquhart warranted such reticence.

On the two or three occasions when Emile and Lydia did catch one another's eye however, there had been a distinct frisson. The connection was of such strength that both of them seemed unable to hold it for long. But even without addressing her or looking in Lydia's direction, he felt intensely aware of her presence. And was it his imagination, or was she also intensely aware of him?

Finally, after a supper that reminded Emile of the sort of meal that the Rogersons used to serve (watercress soup, beef pie and boiled vegetables, followed by a pink blancmange), Mrs Urquhart had disappeared into the kitchen and Polly had gone to check up on Lil. That left Emile and Lydia sitting silently and self-consciously as they faced each other across the dining table.

While Lydia sat with her eyes lowered but a smile upon her lips, Emile asked: 'How are you liking Dieppe?' The simple enquiry appeared to open a floodgate.

'Oh, very much,' she replied. 'And we are lucky to have Mr Sickert... Walter... as our neighbour. He seems to know so many disreputable people. Respectable people bore me. Do they bore you? Have you met his landlady, the fishwife? She's a holy terror... they say she bites anyone who disputes with her...'

'Yes, but fortunately disputes are rare as she is reputed to have the best fish in the market,' said Emile, feeling he ought to contribute to what was threatening to become a one-sided conversation. 'Walter is a fine man, almost the father I never had. But then...'

There followed a silence during which Lydia looked at him thoughtfully. Was Walter really the father he never had? He felt more like an older brother, although he had no experience of that relationship either.

'Oh, no, don't worry. I too never knew my father,' said Lydia. 'I was three when he died. So perhaps we're both orphans... Walter's twin orphans! By the way, do you like his paintings?'

'Yes, I do, very much.'

'I think they're horrid. He seems to see everything through dirty eyes. But otherwise, he's a sweetheart.'

Emile was taken aback by Lydia's comment about Walter's art. He too had once found his paintings rather dreary, but the more he watched him at work, the more he appreciated the artistry and the style. The ability to conjure up the impression of an object or a building with a simple brushstroke. And his admiration increased tenfold after his own miserable attempts at painting.

'Do you know lots of disreputable people?' asked Lydia.

'In the course of my work I have the occasion to meet a few.'

'Please, you must be my chaperone around the less reputable quarters of Dieppe. I would feel safe with an agent of the police by my side.'

It was at this happy juncture in his reverie, that the café door opened and a short, wiry man in a cheap suit and bowler hat entered. It was the man whom Emile had noted waiting for Oscar Wilde's arrival the other morning.

Noticing Emile, he seemed to hesitate, but then nodded and entered. The barman reappeared at the sound of the door opening, the man ordering a glass of wine in a bad French accent before seating himself at a table on the opposite side of the small room. After removing his bowler hat and lighting a cigarette, the man regarded Emile through watery pale eyes.

'He's rarely to be seen before noon,' he said in English – in an accent that Emile recognised as cockney. 'Not one to bother the larks, especially on a day like this.'

The morning was indeed dank and overcast, with a greyness that had banished the recent fine early June weather.

'Agent Emile Blanchet of the Dieppe police department,' said Emile, introducing himself.

'I know who you are,' the main replied curtly. He downed his glass of wine in one noisy gulp, rapped his knuckles on the table to get the barman's attention, and pointed to his empty glass.

'*Monsieur*,' murmured the barman, coming over with the bottle and refilling his glass.

'And you are some sort of a private detective, if I'm not mistaken,' said Emile, trying not to betray his irritation at the man's ill manners.

'Correct,' the man replied, not looking at Emile but turning his watery eyes in the direction of the Hotel Sandwich. 'And you speak very good English for a frog-eater.'

'I have never once eaten a frog,' said Emile. 'Tell me. Are you the sort of man who finds himself fighting a lot of duels.'

The man emitted an abrupt laugh and sighed. 'Duels are for nobs,' he said. 'I'm too poor and common to fight one. Common as muck, me. And unlike my current employer, I don't take anything seriously enough to risk dying for it. Have you heard of the Marquess of Queensberry?'

'Yes, I have,' said Emile, recalling Walter's recounting of the sorry tale of Oscar Wilde. 'He is the reason for this man's exile,' said Emile, nodding towards the hotel. 'And why we are both seated here today in this dingy establishment.'

'Sodomy, if you'll excuse my French, is the reason for that man's exile. He's a backgammon player, if you catch my drift, a molly who goes by the windward passage. I'm here to make sure that his predilections no longer involve the marquess's son and heir.'

'He is the innocent party then, this son and heir?' said Emile, riled by the man's rough tongue. 'Well, whatever this Oscar Wilde has done, I'm sure it doesn't require the attention of both of us,' said Emile, aware that he was disobeying a direct order as he scraped his little table across the tile floor and stood up.

He would be more usefully employed talking to the shopkeepers who had been reporting thefts than waiting for this English poet to rise and shine. 'If you would be so good as to report your latest findings to the police station this evening and I am sure we will be only too happy to continue facilitating your stay in France.'

'What the devil?' said the man, his watery eyes hardening as they focused on Emile. 'Are you threatening me?'

'Is six o'clock convenient?'

'Or what?'

Emile didn't reply, holding up a one-franc coin for the barman to see. Picking up his kepi, he placed it on his head, bowed, and made for the door. Wondering whether the man would take his threat seriously, he stepped out into the street and made his way to the Grand Rue. Perhaps he ought to drop in at the police station and report his findings. That there was no sign of Monsieur Melmoth and that anyway he had just recruited an unwilling police spy.

Frossard could always send him back with a flea in his ear, if so minded, but Emile was damned if he was going to spend another minute sharing a thankless vigil in the company of the rude little private detective.

As he approached the station, he noticed an old woman standing outside. It was the mother of the two cave-dwellers who had discovered the dead man's body. Leaning forward on a walking stick, she was staring up at the station's imposing portals like a dog waiting for its master.

'Madame,' said Emile, raising his kepi.

'Oh monsieur,' she wailed. 'They have arrested my sons and destroyed my home. Everything thrown about and broken. What have we done to deserve this? What have we done?'

* * *

Henry sat at his study desk attempting to turn his mind to that Sunday's sermon. The congregation would be swollen not only by summer visitors but the usual increase in numbers each time the Prime Minister attended All Saints.

Lord Salisbury and his family had arrived in Dieppe earlier that week and his secretary had let it be known that the usual retinue would be in church that Sunday. Henry understood this to mean that two pews should be reserved for his lordship and ladyship and whatever family, servants and private detectives would accompany them.

For the past few Sundays Henry had been working his way through the Book of Ezra, struggling to find parallels between the English colony in Dieppe and the return of the tribes of Israel following their exile in Babylon. Venetia Hall, accosting him after the previous Sunday's sermon, had asked him whether he might be referring to the schism between All Saints and Christ Church.

All Saints was considered 'high church' – all candles, rituals, incense and vestments – and attracted the higher social echelons of the English colony. The upstart 'low' establishment, Christ Church, was on a mission to "evangelize" Dieppe and tended to attract the English tradesmen and their families, along with teachers and visiting sailors.

Henry had assured the lady novelist that this was far from his mind, but afterwards he wondered whether subconsciously he had been referring to this unfortunate rivalry between the town's two English churches.

But now Henry's thoughts strayed from 5th-century BC Jerusalem to that bedroom in Le Pollet. Jeanne tugging at her petticoat to expose the top of her breast. Her hands clasped in prayer. The smell of her as she kissed him on the forehead. 'Kiss me… *embrasse-moi*'.

Much stirred, he stood up and went over to the bookcase. From among the pamphlets and collected sermons that took up one shelf, he pulled the folder that Jeanne had entrusted to him. Putting his nose to the cardboard cover he could smell her perfume.

On closer examination, the wax seal had been marked with what looked like an official stamp. Military perhaps. He tugged at the edge of the cover to see whether he could read any of the papers held so tightly within. What looked like a piece of personal writing paper was partially dislodged, Henry reading the words '29 Avril, Sousse' and then, in English, 'Dear Madame'.

He thought about pulling the whole letter from the folder, but remembered Jeanne's serious countenance, her look of fear, as she told him to hide the folder and inform no one else of its existence. Hadn't she made him swear with his hand on the Holy Bible?

He pushed the letter as best he could back into the folder, and clambered up the little wooden step ladder he used for reaching the top shelves of his bookcase. Putting the folder to his nose and inhaling Jeanne's perfume one last time, he removed two large and dusty books and placed the folder so that, after replacing the books, it was hidden behind them. The dust along the shelf was so thick that it had collected into grey tufts, and Henry felt reassured that Clotilde would not be disturbing his new hiding place. In fact, she rarely ventured into his study unless invited to do so.

Just as he had dismounted the steps, he heard voices coming from the hallway as Lucy and Alice returned from wherever they had been. They were discussing something with Clotilde. Putting his ear to the study door, he heard Lucy making arrangements for their supper, which they planned – as so often – to take in their room.

He still hadn't discovered how much they were paying Clotilde, and Henry thought the best way might be to ask the maid directly. He listened now as footsteps made their way up to the staircase.

'And did you see our dear lady novelist Mrs Venetia Hall,' came Lucy's voice. 'With that awful Oscar Wilde. What was she thinking? Perhaps she's decided to become a decadent playwright.'

Alice's manly laugh was followed by the key turning in their bedroom door. For once, Henry felt no resentment towards his wife and her lady companion. He must return and see Jeanne again soon, although with what intention he did not know. Let God once again be his guide.

CHAPTER FOURTEEN

As Emile entered the police station, his colleague Renard tried to block his path.

'What's the matter, Renard?' asked Emile, struck once again by how well the man's name suited him. He looked as cunning as a fox and as wantonly vicious.

'I'm sorry, but I have strict orders. Nobody is to enter.' He didn't look very sorry.

'But I'm not a nobody,' said Emile, pushing past Renard and entering the station proper. The main room, where Emile and two others had their desks, was empty, but the door to Frossard's office was closed. He could hear muffled voices from the other side.

Without stopping to think, he knocked and entered. Frossard, who was leaning across his desk and resting on his knuckles, turned to glare at Emile. Seated in front of him and looking dismally at the floor was the cave-dweller who had first brought his attention to the drowned Arab. Pierre Martin was his name, remembered Emile.

Blood had collected around the side of Pierre's mouth, which looked swollen, and, as he turned to stare at Emile, it was clear that one eye was also inflamed to the point where it appeared closed. He looked like a boxer who had had been beaten in a fight.

Standing behind the cave dweller was the man called Bastin, the biggest and oldest of Emile's colleagues and who had a high regard for Frossard. He was also a notorious thug, who enjoyed the more violent side of the job rather too keenly. His enormous hands, like two slabs of meat, rested on the back of the man's chair.

'What the hell are you doing here, Blanchet?' spat Frossard. 'I gave strict orders…'

'I told him, sir,' said Renard, who had now appeared in the doorway.

'What's going on, sir?' asked Emile. 'Why have you arrested this man? Did he steal from the dead man?'

'Get out!' screamed Frossard. 'Get out now!'

'Very good, sir,' said Emile, turning to look at Bastin, whose hands remained on the back of the unfortunate cave-dwellers chair. The brute smirked at him.

The door slammed shut behind Emile, leaving Renard in Frossard's office. Emile walked over to his desk and sat down, immediately leaping again to his feet as a thought struck him. If both the brothers had been arrested, where was the other man?

Before Renard could return to his post, he went to the cupboard where the keys to the station's three cells were kept. Scooping all three from their hooks, he rushed to the stairway that led to the basement where the cells were located. Only one of the cell doors was closed, and Emile found the key that fitted its lock – first looking through the spy-hole. The other cave-dweller, who was sitting on the edge of bench that was fixed to the far wall, looked up as the key rattled in the lock.

'Blanchet?', he could hear Renard shouting. Ignoring the summons, he let himself into the cell and approached the cave-dweller. He bore similar marks to his brother, a swollen mouth and eye, along with a red abrasion across one cheek.

'Why have you been arrested?' he asked.

The man raised his mottled face towards Emile and shrugged. 'I don't know. Please, sir, look after our mother,' he said.

'Why have they been beating you?'

'They keep saying we have stolen some letters, sir, but it's not the truth. I swear to God.'

Emile nodded. He could hear the sound of feet hurrying down the stone steps that led to the basement.

'Don't worry, I'll sort this out,' he said, just as Renard's eye appeared at spy-hole. The gendarme pushed open the door and stood there breathless, just staring at Emile. It seemed he didn't know quite what to say.

'Frossard wants you,' he muttered after eventually collecting himself. Renard seemed confused. Emile handed him the keys without a word and left the cell. He found Frossard standing next to his, Emile's desk. He looked quite mad, thought Emile as Frossard inhaled and exhaled like an enraged bull.

'What the hell are you playing at, Blanchet?' he spluttered.

'Nothing, sir. I simply returned to the station only to discover that the two cave-dwellers had been arrested. Is it too much to ask what developments there are in the case?'

Emile knew as soon as he spoke those words that they were going to infuriate Frossard further. He could hear his own insubordination.

'Too much to ask? *Too much to ask?* Who the hell do you think you are, Blanchet? And why aren't you following orders and keeping a watch on that English poet?'

'He left his hotel early this morning and isn't expected back until tonight,' answered Emile, repeating a lie he had prepared earlier. Frossard stared at him, his face rigid with rage.

'How do you know that to be true? He could come back at any time.'

'Sir, I thought it expedient to come back. I have discovered some new evidence that I believe has a strong bearing on our case. It concerns a hat – a fez – that the dead Arab might have been wearing.'

* * *

The tennis courts outside the casino were deserted that gloomy Wednesday afternoon as Venetia Hall made her way inside to the gaming rooms. The early summer weather had turned unseasonably cold, while the grey sky had made a lurid, sickly green of the sea. The tide was high and the jetty that carried bathers modestly out to the deeper water was closed. The few people strolling on the promenade were outnumbered by the wheeling, screeching gulls.

Oscar Wilde had finally left Dieppe, she had learnt, exchanging the busy port for a village a few miles down the coast. What the inhabitants of little Berneval would make of this extravagant figure in their midst, she couldn't even begin to imagine. Either way, she was certain that his sojourn (Venetia didn't think Wilde would stay beyond the summer) would remain the most notable event ever to happen in that quiet little coastal community.

She was still feeling angry with the artists and the so-called friends who had failed to offer him hospitality or, in some cases, even acknowledgement. At dinner at Venetia's home, the Pavillon de Berri, Oscar had complained in his usual wittily back-handed manner. 'To be spoken of, and not to be spoken to, is delightful,' he had said wearily, like an actor forced to recite a line that had grown stale with repetition. Venetia nevertheless jotted it down in her journal of 'bon mots' after Oscar had departed.

He had however failed to hide his bitterness at his treatment from Walter Sickert. The man was a hypocrite and only disapproved of Oscar's extra-marital relationships because Sickert had (as Oscar put it) "a preference for Messalina over Sporus". Only later was Venetia able to confirm his meaning by consulting her edition of Suetonius's *The Twelve Caesars*. Oscar had been referring to the Emperor Nero's two 'wives', Sporus being a castrated boy.

While cognisant of the many kindnesses that Oscar had shown to Sickert and his family, especially towards his mother Eleanor in the aftermath of the death of Sickert's father, Venetia rightly suspected the real reason for Sickert shunning his old friend. It wasn't that he was a prig. After all, Oscar's predilections were well known in London society. It was because he was afraid of being associated with what people were calling 'the Oscar Wilde tendency' and therefore being shunned in turn.

Sickert had feathered a comfortable nest for himself in Dieppe, and he had no wish to rock any boats that might interfere with his pleasant lifestyle. Thinking thus, Venetia entered the great hall of the casino. Standing near the doorway to the 'little horses' gaming room, she thought she spied Colonel Marsden at his usual observation post. She was about to address him when the man turned and glared at her.

'Apologies, monsieur, I mistook you for an acquaintance.'

It was the beard that had confused her. The stranger was in fact taller and stouter than the colonel, with melancholy brown eyes that surveyed Venetia in silence. He bowed and returned his gaze to the gaming table, where the Duchesse Caracciolo sat playing amongst the usual group of English husbands.

'Apologies, madame, but my eyesight is poor,' he said in English, not removing his gaze from the gaming table. 'The lady amongst those gentlemen. Is she Jewish?'

Venetia, taken aback by the question, did not reply. The man turned to her then and announced: 'Edgar Degas, madame. Visiting from Paris.'

The famous painter, thought Venetia, but having taken an immediate dislike, she didn't betray any recognition of his name.

'Venetia Hall, visiting from England,' she replied stiffly. 'The lady is of Portuguese and American descent, I believe.'

'Ah, American,' replied Degas, as if this proved his point. And then he said, squinting at the gaming table: 'My mother was also American. Of French descent.'

'Will you be staying in Dieppe for long?' she asked after another lengthy silence, her curiosity getting the better of her distaste.

'We'll see,' he said wearily. 'As long as I'm not taken on any more intolerably long walks along the cliffs.'

'And will you then perhaps be painting in Dieppe itself during your stay. Modern artists seem to find the town and its surroundings endlessly fascinating.'

Degas now looked at her with amusement, Venetia's admission that she had in fact heard of him but had chosen not to acknowledge this, had piqued his interest. He waved a slim ebony cane in the general direction of the gaming table.

'I would prefer to paint these gamblers,' he said. 'In any case, I shan't want to trespass on the town claimed by my artist friend Sickert as his own subject.'

'Indeed,' said Venetia, causing another look of wry amusement to cross Degas's heavily bearded face. Unlike Oscar Wilde, here was a famous person about whom she could write in her next missive to readers of *The Citizen*. She would have to observe him closely, and pen an amusing sketch of the celebrated artist.

Waving his cane once more in the direction of the gaming table, he asked in stilted English: 'Madame, could you inform me of the identity of the lady so exciting the attention of her gentleman companions?'

'The Duchesse Caracciolo, monsieur. She has a somewhat scandalous history and as soon as their wives appear, expect her admirers to scatter like pigeons on hearing a gunshot.'

Degas gave such a hearty laugh that all the gamblers, with the exception of the duchess, turned to look in his direction.

'Do tell me more,' he said to Venetia, replying to the men's stares with an ironic bow.

'The duchess's daughter, Olga Alberta, is the goddaughter of the Prince of Wales. You may note that her second name is in honour of His Royal Highness Albert Edward.'

'*Une filleule*. A goddaughter. But why?'

Venetia merely raised here eyebrows in response, before explaining: 'This daughter, or goddaughter, is a great beauty and much in demand from the young artists of the colony. They love to paint her. The Prince of Wales also greatly favours her with visits. The duchess herself is a great anglophile and her house is supposedly decorated with more chintz furniture than Queen Victoria's.'

At this point, the lady in question rose from the gaming table. She seemed to levitate without any effort and glide towards the doorway where Degas and Venetia were standing. Venetia had never been this close to the subject of such scandal in Dieppe, and noted the faded alabaster skin on her face, and deep almond eyes that half-closed as she passed by, as if in anticipation of an insult.

I surmised correctly,' said Degas after she had moved out of earshot. '*Une juive*. A jewess.'

CHAPTER FIFTEEN

Walter, who had been so excited by the imminent arrival of his old friend and mentor Edgar Degas, now found that he was unexpectedly nervous. It was twelve years since that formative summer in Dieppe during which Walter had been 'adopted' by Degas and drawn away from the influence of his first artistic 'parent', James McNeil Whistler.

Walter would never forget those hot summer days of '85, striding out each morning with Degas, armed with their *pocharde* boxes to paint some new vista or other. All the while, the master – twice Walter's age and with an established reputation - would impart his knowledge and experience to his eager young protégé.

He recalled the first time that the great man had viewed his paintings at the house Walter and Ellen had taken while honeymooning in Dieppe. Degas had run his fingertips along the smooth surface of his little panels and remarking with admiration how they had been "painted like a door". "Nature is smooth," he had added.

Walter had been young and hungry for knowledge and lapped up Degas's suggestion to move away from the low tones he had learnt from Whistler ('It all seems a bit like something taking place at night') and to paint people. To fully realise figures and not simply to make them suggestive daubs in a landscape.

Over the intervening years, Walter had regularly visited Degas at his studio in Paris, each time greeted with gratifying effusion and bombarded with yet more technical tips and artistic insights. The visits had become less frequent of late, a regular round of letter-writing taking their place – his maid Zoe's hand-writing now as familiar as her master's. With his growing blindness, Degas now dictated his correspondence.

But Walter was more self-assured now and felt less in need of a mentor. Having pleaded with Degas to visit Dieppe, he felt responsible for his well-being. The great man would be staying once again with Jacques-Émile Blanche at his black-beamed manor house situated underneath the cliffs, on the old Napoleonic coastal gun battery known as the Bas Fort Blanc. But while not responsible for Degas's comfort, he would be expected to sit and listen to his old mentor. And on this score, his recent letters weren't encouraging.

They revealed a growing obsession, not with developing his art but with the supposed Jewish subversion of the French state. This mania, as Walter saw it (not having feelings one way or another towards the Israelite race), was threatening to become boringly all-encompassing. What Walter did not know was that, having been dictated immediately after breakfast, a meal accompanied by Zoe reading aloud from the antisemitic newspaper *La Libre Parole*, such thoughts were usually uppermost in Degas's mind.

He finished cleaning his brushes and looked out of the studio window. The cherry blossom that had adorned the trees so gaily was long gone, replaced by small green fruits. Just at that moment, Polly and Lydia Urquhart emerged from their cottage across the courtyard. Carrying shopping baskets, they headed towards the steps leading down to the quayside.

Walter had been having second thoughts about the wisdom of throwing Emile and Lydia together. Delighted as always to unite his friends in what he saw as one great happy family, he now realised that Lydia might be too flighty for the serious young policeman. She was too much of a flibbertigibbet, he believed, to be a suitable companion for his young friend. And yet Emile seemed besotted, while Lydia was seemingly equally infatuated in return. Perhaps the passion would be fleeting and burn itself out. A novelty that would soon become wearisome.

'Let nature run its course', he told himself before turning his attention to lunch. La Villain would have finished at her fish stall and would now be cooking something suitably replenishing. He would return to their house in Le Pollet, with the added incentive that he had an appointment that afternoon to make further sketches of Jeanne.

It would probably be the last time he would need to visit the little back-street brothel. Jeanne's home was a few doors down the same road and Walter suddenly felt a desire to see where she lived with that brutish layabout of a husband. What squalor did they inhabit? He would like to sketch her at home, seated at her kitchen table or laying on her rumpled marital bed.

But if he called there and was met by the husband, it would no doubt lead to Jeanne receiving another jealous battering. The coward wouldn't lay a hand on Walter, of course. Could nothing be done to liberate her from this insupportable marriage?

There was one bright spot upon the horizon however and that was the rumoured departure of Oscar Wilde. Walter had earlier that morning bumped into the shockingly emaciated figure of his old friend and Yellow Book collaborator Aubrey Beardsley, who was staying in Dieppe on his doctor's orders.

Beardsley, it transpired, had been as eager as Walter to avoid any embarrassing encounters with Wilde. Looking now little more than skin stretched tautly across bones, he had flagged Walter down in the street to say that he had heard from Blanche, who had heard from his fellow artist Charles Condor, that Wilde had left town on a horse and cart. Walter now found himself laughing aloud, following by an unexpected wave of affection, at such an incongruous image; the dandyish figure of the famous writer perched atop a humble rustic cart.

Condor, one of the few old friends who would still associate with Wilde, said that Wilde planned to settle somewhere quieter up the coast. That was still too near to Dieppe for Walter's comfort, but at least it negated the need to scurry away or appear oblivious every time that great bulk loomed around a street corner.

A chilly gust of wind disturbed the branches of the cherry trees as he crossed the courtyard, his sketching pad under one arm. Tugging at his fisherman's casquette hat so that it sat firmly upon his head, he descended the ancient stone steps. A packet boat was preparing to leave for England, steam from its funnels driven horizontally towards the largely deserted pavement cafes of the Quai Henri IV. Walter paid no heed to the small, bowler-hatted man standing on deck and smoking a cigarette. The detective was one passenger among many peering down at the quayside as dockers prepared to cast off the ropes.

The sight of the boat was a melancholy reminder of England and Ellen - that he had agreed to exchange letters with his wife confirming his persistent adultery. He had repeatedly put off this unpleasant chore, partly because he still somehow hoped for a rapprochement. Or at least a stay of execution, for Walter's more realistic side realised that he could never change his ways.

Passing through the long, low covered fish market, he noticed that the Villain's stall had been dismantled for the day, while the remaining stalls had largely been emptied of their morning catch of conger eels, langoustines and rays. Gulls strutted along the cobbles, ever alert for scraps or discarded fish.

He would write to Ellen that night, he had decided by the time he arrived at the Villain's front door. This had been left open as usual. The large, tall figure of Augustine herself appeared in the hallway, wearing her usual black dress, sleeves rolled up and with a blue and white check apron round her shapely waist.

'You have a visitor,' she said, nodding with her head towards the bedroom. Through the open doorway he saw Lydia Urquhart, holding a broom and looking flushed, in the middle of the rush mat that partially covered the bare floorboards. The bed had been made, and Walter noticed with alarm that the skeleton of a herring, which he had been intending to paint, had been removed from the plate upon which it had been left.

'What have you done to my fish bones?' he demanded, dispensing any pleasantries

'I threw them away,' Lydia replied defiantly. 'Out of the window. There appears to be a rubbish heap below.'

'You little interfering wretch, I was just going to paint it.'

'Doesn't your landlady clean for you?'

'My landlady knows not to interfere.'

'Anyway, I came to see where you live,' she said, looking around her with distaste. 'And to give you this.'

Walter took a folded piece of paper from Lydia's outstretched hand. 'It's for Emile,' she said. 'Inviting him to guide me around the more disreputable corners of Dieppe.'

* * *

At that exact moment Emile was standing in the cave dwelling of the Martin brothers and their mother. Learning of their imminent release from custody, he had waited with the mother for their safe return, in the meantime helping her tidy the mess that Frossard and the gendarmes had left behind them. Some of the rickety furniture was beyond repair, seemingly broken for no reason other than sheer malice.

When the brothers returned, they each in turn fell into an embrace with the tearful old woman. Apart from their swollen eyes and bruised faces smeared with congealed blood, they didn't seem to have come to any great harm.

Pierre Martin shook Emile's hand and thanked him for his help. The police, he said, were adamant that they had stolen some important letters from the drowned Arab. What use would they have with any letters, he had answered, since neither of them could read. But still they insisted, the chief's anger intensifying the more that they professed their innocence.

Why wouldn't Frossard confide in him about the nature of these letters, wondered Emile? If they are so important as to warrant assaulting these innocent men, then surely he ought to share his information with his most senior agent. What exactly was it that they were looking for? And then the thought struck Emile that perhaps Frossard himself didn't know.

'And the chief didn't say anything about the contents of these letters?', he asked Pierre Martin. The brothers shook their heads in unison.

'Only to say that they were of national importance,' said Pierre.

Emile was about to apologise for their treatment before thinking better of it. If such an utterance were to make it back to Frossard, he would be sacked on the spot. As it was, he felt that he was skating on thin ice following his earlier behaviour back in the station. No doubt Frossard would already be applying to have him posted elsewhere, or perhaps dismissed altogether.

A week or two earlier, the idea of being posted to a different town would have appealed to Emile. Frossard's hostility had become oppressive - no doubt as the commissaire had intended. He didn't have an ally among the other agents, all of whom were scared of their boss. Only his friendship with Walter had seemed like a reason to stay in Dieppe.

But now. Lydia.

He had lain in bed the previous night saying her name out loud. It was curiously satisfying to speak the word softly under his breath, and then louder, but not so loud that Marie-Hélène might overhear it. His landlady's daughter sometimes stood outside his bedroom door, listening. He could see the shadow of her feet in the crack at the bottom of the door, and occasionally even hear her heavy breathing as if mustering up the courage to enter.

He remembered how, when living with the Rogersons in Blackheath, he had done the same thing – uttering Mary's name aloud as he lay in that attic bedroom next door to his mother's room and that of the maids. The thrill it gave him then was multiplied a hundred-fold now because there was a real chance that Lydia might reciprocate his interest.

He had had no real friends while growing up in England, his mother being his closest confidant. But he had never once revealed to her his ardour for Mary Rogerson, perhaps fearing it might jeopardise their position in the household. Or that she might laugh at his childish passion, albeit lovingly.

What would his mother think of him now - a policeman and therefore a representative of the French state against which she had risked her life fighting? At least there was no longer any possibility of the monarchy returning and the Republic was slowly but surely easing the Church out of the business of government and the ordering of society. No, she would be pleased with the direction of public affairs, and in turn he felt proud to be representing the Third Republic.

But then what would his mother have thought about the prospect of dying in bed, coughing and sweating and complaining of chest pain in a Normandy cottage, her parents looking on helplessly? They were unable to afford a doctor and were trusting in God to carry their daughter through the coming crisis, despite the fact that Nathalie Levallois denied the existence of their deity.

Feeling helpless himself and unable to bear his grandparents' prayerful utterances, Emile had taken a long walk in the February gloom, marching blindly down the seemingly endless straight roads that led to the vast, empty horizon of the Caux plateau. He even began to pray himself, although without any clear idea about who or what he was addressing; he promised this unknown deity to live a full and fruitful life if only his mother was saved. He could still recall his breath pluming into the chill winter twilight as he made his desperate pleas to the universe.

He had never forgiven his grandparents. He couldn't pardon them for summoning his brave, intelligent mama back from England simply to skivvy for them. Little more than a beast of burden. But why had she agreed to return?

What sense of duty had compelled her to give up that rewarding life in Blackheath for drudgery in a meagre Normandy smallholding.

When serving in Africa three years later and receiving news that his grandparents had died, one soon after the other, he felt no sadness. If anything, their deaths seemed to compound his bitterness. It was all such a tragic waste. In fact, in all those lonely years in that mean little cottage, he had often wished them dead, to have met the same fate that one day would befall his mother. Then they could both return to Blackheath and the Rogerson family.

Old Mrs Martin, the cave-dwellers' mother was looking at him as if reading his thoughts. But that wasn't possible because she put her hand on Emile's forearm, looked into his eyes and said: 'Thank you, sir. You are a good man.'

CHAPTER SIXTEEN

Gustave Geffroy, the former art critic of the Parisian newspaper *La Justice* and now recently appointed to that role on the new radical publication *L'Aurore*, stood pondering the painting he had just torn from its brown paper wrapping. It now stood propped up against an office cabinet.

Delivered that morning by the framer, it was a portrait of Geffroy, surrounded by books and seated (rather stiffly, he thought) in his study at home in Paris. The painter was Paul Cézanne. Geffroy, who had written several articles praising Cézanne's work, had been introduced to the artist by their mutual friend and fellow Impressionist Claude Monet.

It was Cézanne who had suggested painting Geffroy's portrait in gratitude for being a lone voice in championing his work. The sittings had spanned three months during which subject and painter discovered that – although their ideas on art were broadly aligned – a certain mutual antipathy existed between them.

Perhaps it was their different temperaments. Cezanne, the son of a Provencal banker and Geffroy with his flinty Breton heritage. More likely it was their differing religious outlooks, Cézanne being a staunch and traditional Catholic, while Geffroy believed that the church and all its works were a hinderance to republicanism. Their conversations on the subject had curtailed after the first two sittings.

Whatever the reason for their animus, Cézanne had left the painting unfinished and disappeared back to Provence. When it became clear that the artist considered the matter closed (Cézanne had written to Monet to say that he was disappointed with the portrait), Geffroy decided to have it framed in its current condition. He didn't particularly like the painting, but was flattered to have been captured by an artist whose work he at least admired.

The critic was suddenly aware that he had been joined in appraising the picture. Georges Clemenceau, the founder and director of *L'Aurore*, stared at the painting impassively before giving a gentle nod, a smile breaking out over his rather simian features.

'Do you intend to hang it in here?' asked Clemenceau.

'I don't think we have the space,' replied Geffroy, surveying the cramped office, whose desks had already accumulated great piles of paper despite having only been open for three weeks. His desk was stacked with books, including Geffroy's own *Histoire de l'Impressionnisme* – the first-ever book about the artistic movement.

'You should hang it up behind your desk. It might give the place a more homely atmosphere that these infernal contraptions', said Clemenceau, waving a hand towards a desk on which squatted an enormous typewriter, and near it, a telephone. 'And how was your visit to Normandy?' he enquired, taking a seat.

'Brief. Brief but interesting,' replied Geffroy, who had joined a weekend house party in Dieppe hosted by the portrait painter Jacques-Emile Blanche at his beachside home, the Bas Fort Blanc.

'Quite the gathering. Degas was there, spouting his eternal hatred of the Jews to anyone who cared to listen. Does the man have any other subject these days? Aubrey Beardsley, the bourgeoise-shocking English illustrator, was in attendance as well. Thin as the skeleton that alas he will very soon become, the poor man. And Walter Sickert, the English painter, appeared every mealtime without fail. Like a dog who has heard the rattling of saucepans in the kitchen.'

'I don't know this Sickert,' said Clemenceau, filling a pipe with tobacco.

'Has his own unique style… Impressionism but with a more sombre palette than Monet or Cézanne. He seems most influenced by Degas, even somewhat intimidated by the great man. Anyway, he told me something that might interest you in your former capacity as mayor of Montmartre.'

'Go on,' said Clemenceau, lighting his pipe, a great plume of smoke rising to the ceiling and dispersing across its yellowed surface.

'It seems that Sickert has befriended a young policeman by the name of Emile Blanchet.'

'Blanchet? Should I know the name? A policeman, you say?'

'You would know his mother,' said Geffroy, waving away a gust of pipe smoke. 'Her name was Nathalie Levallois.'

Clemenceau frowned as Geffroy's words sunk in. 'Good God,' he exclaimed. 'The Red Maid of Montmartre, herself. Extraordinary. But you say her name *was* Nathalie Levallois. The last I heard she was living in exile in London. She is no longer with us, I presume.'

'Died of influenza, but not before returning to France.'

'I am very sorry to hear that,' said Clemenceau, taking on a distant, dreamy look. 'During the Prussian siege she organised relief for refugees and as well as a cooperative making balloons for that wonderful madman Nadar. Perhaps you are too young to recall the Paris Commune...'

'I was 15, but living in Lyon at the time.'

'Ah well, yes. Nadar used to take photographs from his balloons – the first photographs of Paris from above. And then he began using the balloons for delivering letters during the Prussian siege and afterwards during the Commune. Nathalie organised a cooperative at the old dance hall, the Elysée-Montmartre, and later at the Gare du Nord. She organised seamstresses working at sixty sewing machines, stitching together balloons for these flights. Remarkable woman.

'The last time I saw her she was wearing the uniform of the National Guard – part of the Montmartre Women's Vigilance Committee. And valiant, by all accounts, during those bloody May weeks of the Commune. Died in her bed at least. She was lucky to leave Paris with her life in '71.'

There was a long moment of silence as Clemenceau sucked contemplatively on his pipe before asking: 'And the boy? Has the apple fallen far from the tree?'

'Well, I mean, surely being a policeman speaks for itself, I told Sickert. But he told me something even more interesting. Apparently, this young Blanchet is a good, honest sort and spirited too. But he's at odds with his boss. A commissaire by the name of Frossard. Pierre Frossard.'

'Ha!' exclaimed Clemenceau, snapping out of his reverie. 'Frossard? The knuckle-headed police officer who made speeches in support of General Boulanger. Bring back the monarchy and all that nonsense? That Frossard? I thought we'd heard the last of him.'

CHAPTER SEVENTEEN

'What in heaven's name made you join the police?'

Emile looked down at Lydia, who smiled back up at him, instantly dissipating any offence he might have taken at the tone of her question. They were making their way on foot towards the mound on which stood the ruined castle at Arques-la Bataille, so named after a supposedly famous 16th-century battle. So famous indeed that nobody he had asked – including Walter, his landlady and his colleagues in the police station - could supply him with any details.

He had managed to dissuade Lydia from taking a tour of Dieppe's more (as she put it) disreputable corners, arguing that it would be unseemly for an official of the town's police to conduct such an excursion with a female civilian. She had countered by saying that he was being pompous, but he had settled the argument by suggesting that if news of such an unusual expedition were to be broadcast, it might cost him his job.

It was an hour's pony and cart trip from Dieppe, for which Lydia's mother had insisted on paying. Their elderly driver let them off in the centre of Arques and immediately settled down for a sleep, Emile agreeing to return within two hours.

Somewhere along the steep grass path that led up to the ruins, Lydia had slipped an arm through the crook of his elbow.

'I mean, why the police?' she repeated, twirling her parasol with her free hand.

They strolled on in silence, their locked arms giving Emile the most delightful frisson and sense of relief. It was if they had effortlessly passed one hurdle in their courtship. The weather had turned fine again, and a hot June sun beat down from a cloudless sky. Somewhere in the forest above Arques, a cuckoo was calling.

'Well now, as I told your mother and sister and yourself at dinner the other week, I was in the army for a year and a half,' Emile said after a lengthy silence. 'Following the death of my mother and a miserable time living with the strangers that were my grandparents, the life of a soldier proved surprisingly agreeable.'

They continued walking as Emile tried to gather his thoughts, or try to discern where they might be leading. The image of his grandparents' miserable farm that remained with him most vividly was of his mother – his brave, cultured mother, who had stood upon the barricades of Paris and tutored the children of a well-to-do family in London – carrying milk churns. His intelligent, courageous mother yoked like an ox as she carried two pales of milk across her shoulders.

The grandparents had always regretted not having sons, and now that she had returned dutifully to help them in their old age, they worked his mother like a man. Or a beast. She would milk the cows, draw water from the well, and once – to his immense shame – he had watched her pulling a small plough across the vegetable patch. She must have been so worn out that it was little wonder that she had succumbed to pneumonia.

Emile was aware of Lydia looking at him.

'The discipline and the routine meant that I was always busy and had no time to think,' he continued in something of a gabble. 'This came as a considerable relief, I must say. I hadn't quite realised how unhappy I had become... how futile life had seemed. I made some friendships at the training barracks and was looking forward to being posted to exotic, faraway places. The sorts of places that you read about in books.'

'Unlike my sister, I'm not a great reader,' remarked Lydia with a coquettish twirl of her parasol.

They came to a halt at the top of a ridge which looked down on a grassy ditch that must have been the castle's moat. They were unable to pass a group of largely female sightseers, however, whose open parasols combined to create a giant shroud above their heads. A stout man in a boater and striped blazer, a guidebook in one hand, was addressing the tourists in English.

'The castle dates from the 11th century,' he said in a ringing voice better suited to the theatre stage than this bucolic setting. Lydia put a gloved hand to her mouth to suppress a giggle, and Emile feared she might set him off laughing too. As he had already discovered, there was something infectious about her ready amusement. Her ability to see the silliness in everything.

'It was built by the uncle of our old friend William the Conqueror,' the man continued, gurning like a theatrical at his captive audience. 'But William besieged it, fearing the castle might prove a menace to his own power.'

'Shall we turn?' suggested Emile, and Lydia nodded. The tourists, ignoring their guide, collectively swivelled their heads and regarded Emile and Lydia as they strolled away, arm in arm.

'And you were saying?'

Emile wasn't sure what he had been saying, letting the story flow so that perhaps a coherent reason for his joining the police could be discerned lurking within. He had never before been asked directly about his rationale for signing up to such a widely despised profession. Except, of course, at his initial police interview when his replies had been crafted to satisfy the examining board.

'After six months in barracks in Chinon, I was accepted to train as an officer at the prestigious academy of Saint-Cyr,' he continued. 'It was a huge honour since most of the officer cadets there came from prestigious aristocratic families.

'My training was meant to last for three years, but after just six months I was suddenly called away to Africa,' he resumed, judging that a chronological reiteration might uncover some vital nub of truth. 'I don't know why I wasn't allowed to finish my officer training but I have my suspicions. I believe they discovered the identity of my parents and this was held against me.

'Your parents were socialists, Walter told me,' said Lydia. 'My mother and my sister are socialists.'

'I did not know that,' said Emile, seeing Mrs Middleton and Mrs Urquhart in a new light.

'I think socialism is silly,' continued Lydia. 'Men and women are not equal and never can be. And some people need to be workers and others need to run businesses, otherwise the whole thing just doesn't work. Don't you agree?'

Emile's thoughts had turned to his parents. His mother's courageous and very active pursuit of her own beliefs, and his father's dissipated life talking about revolution as he drank himself to death. But Lydia's thoughts had moved on.

'Anyway, you were saying. Africa...'

'Yes, so, there I was in Africa, helping to suppress a native rebellion in Dahomey. I don't know if you ever read about it.'

'I don't read newspapers,' said Lydia with another twirl of her parasol. 'But pray continue.'

'But the people we were fighting against…,'. He spoke now as if in a trance. 'The extraordinary thing was that the best fighters in this rebel army were actually women.'

'Like your mother,' said Lydia, stopping and looking at him with a glint in her eye.

'Yes, I suppose. But these were proper Amazons. Fierce. But…'

'You don't think fighting women is a fair sport?'

How could he explain? Once they had been in close combat, it had come down to bayonets. But how do you describe ripping a woman's belly as you screamed at her like a savage? How do you explain to this innocent creature the terrifying cries of the fearless Amazons armed with swords and machetes? The simple yet horrific choice of either killing or being killed. Perhaps she would find these stories 'fascinating', like the 'disreputable' corners of Dieppe. But the reality was too horrifying to be made into a colourful anecdote. It was a reality that had melded with his worst nightmares, the ones that beset him on a regular basis.

'Anyway, once we shipped back to France I resigned my commission,' he said flatly.

'You poor man,' said Lydia, tugging at his elbow with her own. And then, smiling up at him: 'I should hate to be a soldier.'

They walked on in silence, Lydia eventually unlinking her arm. Emile had the sudden feeling that a fork in their relationship had been reached, and he felt helpless in not knowing which direction he should take, if any.

Looking over her shoulder Lydia giggled and said: 'Quick, the cattle are after us.'

A cloud of parasols was indeed heading in their direction, led by the stout tour leader, guidebook swinging in his hand.

The conversation on the journey back along the dusty road to Dieppe felt strained to Emile. Something had broken and he wasn't sure what. Although their upbringings shared similarities – the long-dead feckless father, the subsequent itinerant lifestyles - perhaps their personal experiences were too different. And now, despite the intimacies of the afternoon, Lydia seemed almost a stranger to him. Tiring of the impersonal observations about Dieppe that had begun to enter their conversation, Emile turned now to his companion.

'What plans, or dreams, do you have for your life, Lydia?'

The question seemed to please her, because she smiled at him for the first time since they had boarded the carriage.

'Oh, I shall probably become a spinster living with my mother and my sister in whatever new French town we've alighted upon because of its cheap lodgings. Or perhaps…'

She let her sentence hang in the air.

'Or perhaps?' asked Emile. Was he being ungallant? Was he supposed to suggest an engagement?

'Or perhaps we could try Italy. Rome is said to be very inexpensive. And so full of history.'

He must have looked disappointed, because Lydia gave an affectionate laugh and nudged him with her elbow.

'Emile, whatever happens, I am sure we will remain good friends,' she said.

'Yes,' said Emile, noting that they had entered the outskirts of Dieppe and were passing the great flint walls of the town prison. Was she telling him something, or challenging him? 'Yes. That would be most agreeable. I would wish to remain good friends always.'

'Always?' said Lydia, before jumping half out of her seat. 'Goodness!' she exclaimed. 'Who on earth is that calling to us?'

Emile looked up and saw Marie-Hélène furiously pedalling towards them on her bicycle, one hand outstretched and waving shakily as she struggled to maintain her balance. Pulling to a stop, she threw her bicycle on the ground and rushed towards their carriage, Emile noting her angry glance at Lydia.

'Quick, Emile, there has been a murder,' she shouted in French. 'There has been a murder.'

He felt Lydia stiffen by his side, unsure whether it was from horror or excitement.

'A murder did she say?'

'*La prostituée Jeanne de Le Pollet*', shouted Marie-Hélène. '*Le putain*.

Emile jumped down from the carriage, not wishing Lydia to overhear any further details.

'I was going to bicycle to Arques to find you,' said Marie-Hélène, doubling up to catch her breath.

'How did you know where to find me? Did the commissaire ask for me?'

'No, not the commissaire. But I spoke to your English friend, the artist. He told me. It was he who found the body.'

'Walter. Good God!'

Emile thanked the girl and climbed back into the carriage. Marie-Hélène bicycled beside them for a short while before haring off, her mission accomplished and humiliation complete. Emile would later feel sorry for her, but for now he was trying to assemble his thoughts.

Jeanne was a well-liked young prostitute who did some modelling for Walter and who was married to a former fisherman – a violent drunk by all accounts. Walter had spoken about him recently because he had given Jeanne a black eye. How had Walter discovered the body? How had she died?

'Did she say that the victim was a prostitute?' asked Lydia.

'A fallen woman, yes,' replied Emile archly, unsure of the extent of Lydia's knowledge of such matters.

'How terrible. And we have missed the excitement because you wouldn't show me around the disreputable corners of Dieppe.'

But Emile was no longer listening. His mind was racing. The husband… it must have been the brute of a husband. He'd taken it too far this time. It was probably inevitable.

Noticing that they were now nearing the junction by Le Pollet, he called to the driver to stop and told him to take the mademoiselle back into town. Jumping down and turning back as the carriage clattered off, he didn't see Lydia scowling at him beneath her parasol.

CHAPTER EIGHTEEN

The front door to Jeanne's house was closed but unlocked, Walter had discovered on turning the handle and giving it a slight shove. He had already knocked loudly several times and called out her name, the elderly brothel-keeper having informed him that Jeanne hadn't yet turned up for work and that she was probably still at home.

'You were supposed to be the first client of the day, monsieur, but two other gentlemen also called for her this morning. I told them she wasn't due at work until two o'clock and they went away. I hope nothing's happened. I did think it was odd to have two gentlemen callers so early in the day, and asking for her by name. Not the police, I hoped. They didn't say. Now that I think of it they did look like police. Oh dear, she is usually never late.'

Not unduly alarmed, Walter had thanked her and walked up the street towards what he knew to be Jeanne's home. His prior curiosity about the state of her domestic arrangements and his desire to sketch them was about to be met with a scene that he could not have anticipated in his wildest imaginings.

It was a tall, narrow red-brick house, the front door leading directly into a kitchen that also seemed to serve as a dining room and lounge. The place was in utter disarray, with drawers pulled open and discarded on the floor. A dresser had fallen, or been pulled, forward onto its front, so that it leant against the dining table, its contents strewn across the table-top and the floor. Smashed crockery, copper pots and pans and other cooking utensils lay among cushions that had been ripped apart, feathers coating everything like a dusting of snow.

'Jeanne?' shouted Walter from the bottom of a narrow staircase.

Hearing no reply, he climbed the creaking wooden staircase, noticing that clothes and bedding lay heaped on the landing. A door to a bedroom was ajar, a bare foot and ankle visible on the floor beside the bed. Gently pushing open the door, he realised that it was being blocked by the rest of Jeanne's naked body. She lying face down on the floor.

'Jeanne,' he said, stepping forward and crouching to touch the back of her shoulders. Her flesh was cold and unresponsive to his touch. Her hair was matted with blood and, on turning her, Walter was met by one open but sightless eye. Twisting her head her further, he was horrified to notice that the other eye was protruding half out of its socket.

'Jeanne,' he whispered this time, holding her head, blood smearing his canvas jacket. 'Jeanne. Christ almighty! Who did this to you?'

He had never seen Jeanne naked before, preferring to sketch her in her clothes, but he couldn't help but look now, noticing her freckled white skin blemished by a line of fresh bruises down the left side of her back and across one buttock. A pool of blood had started to grow beneath her head, and Walter let it drop gently on the bare floorboards. Pulling a blanket from the bed, he draped it over her.

The bedroom, he noticed, was in the same disarray as downstairs, with drawers pulled out from a chest and the contents of a wardrobe thrown around the place as if attacked by a wild animal. Standing, he felt suddenly nauseous, but fought the urge to vomit. There was clatter and the sound of a man shouting downstairs.

'Jeanne!'. The man's voice seemed to ricochet around the house. '*Merde!*'

There was then silence as if the owner of the voice was listening, before footsteps began stomping up the wooden staircase followed by a thump as the man – presumably Jeanne's husband Pascal – seemed to stumble, cursing as he resumed his ascent. Walter looked around for a weapon in case he needed to defend himself. After all the husband couldn't be blamed for drawing the wrong conclusion from the scene that awaited him.

Nothing obvious came to hand however and Walter now found himself face to face with Pascal. He was a short, stocky fellow dressed in a soiled white vest and whose furious expression now turned to slack-jawed incomprehension as he stood alternately staring at Walter and the body of his wife.

The man let out a bestial scream and launched himself at Walter, who became engulfed in the stench of stale sweat and alcohol. Shaking himself free, Walter stepped back, unbalancing Pascal, who tripped backwards over Jeanne's corpse and fell against the side of the bed. He slid down between the bed and his wife's body and lay there in a grotesque parody of conjugal togetherness.

Walter rushed from the room, down the staircase and out on to the street. To his surprise a small crowd of women and children had gathered while others looked on from balconies and open windows. He was glad to note the lack of menfolk otherwise he might have been seized and apprehended.

'Quick, we must fetch the police,' he shouted, addressing the nearest adult. 'Jeanne has been killed. Murdered,' he added for emphasis.

'It's Pascal who has done this, the drunken pig', a woman said, seemingly unsurprised at the news and turning to her neighbour.

'He's inside now,' said Walter, surprised at the woman's equanimity. 'Be careful. He is drunk.'

'The pig,' said another woman in the crowd. 'I always said he would end up murdering poor Jeanne.'

It seemed that the commotion had reached the ears of the woman who ran the brothel and who had now joined the gathering.

'Jeanne?' she asked. 'Did you find her?'

At that moment the door of the house was pulled open and Pascal stood there, his vest now smeared in blood like a butcher's apron. Pointing at Walter, he bellowed: 'He… he killed my wife!'

'I found her, 'protested Walter. 'She was already dead.'

The man launched himself at Walter, but was beaten back by several of the women, who began lashing at him with sticks, bags and anything they had to hand.

'Enough!' the brothel keeper shouted. The crowd immediately hushed. 'I can vouch for this gentleman,' she said, turning towards Walter. 'He came looking for Jeanne but ten minutes ago. She hadn't turned up for work and they had an appointment. He is an honourable man… an artist.'

Unsure whether the good citizens of Le Pollet would agree with the woman's equating his occupation with being of good character, Walter was relieved to see four uniformed policemen striding up the street. Ahead of them was short, wiry man who Walter recognised as Emile's boss.

'Commissaire… commissaire…,' Pascal implored, addressing Frossard. 'My wife has been murdered.' And pointing at Walter, he added: 'And this is the culprit. I found him standing over my wife's body.'

But Frossard didn't even glance at Walter. Instead, he ordered two of his men to enter the house and search the crime scene. To the other two gendarmes, big brutish types, he said: 'Arrest this man and take him to the cells.'

'Come along peacefully, Pascal,' said one of the gendarmes, pulling the man's arms behind the back of his blood-smeared vest while the other slipped on a pair of handcuffs.

* * *

It was a peculiar sensation (but one that the Reverend Henry Gibson had repeatedly experienced of late) that he never felt further away from God than when in church. Particularly his church, if he could apply such a possessive pronoun to the gloomy edifice set back behind the shops on the Rue de la Barre.

He sat perfectly still for a moment and listened. The building felt as cold and as eternal as the tomb and the unresponsive silence, rather than comforting him as it once did, now unsettled Henry.

The sun had returned to Dieppe and was illuminating the stained-glass windows that had been bought on subscription under the previous incumbent. The ascended Christ stood with open arms before the multitude of saints. But the multi-hued refraction failed to lift the oppressive gloom of the interior. Nor could the flowers that had been recently arranged beneath the altar by Mrs Venetia Hall.

This alarmingly eccentric melange of larkspur, peonies, roses and sweet peas had been plucked from the lady author's garden and reflected Venetia's unconventional mode of dress. At the previous Sunday's morning service, she had appeared in an extraordinary straw hat trimmed with yellow roses and aigrette made of tall grasses.

Henry appreciated Venetia however. She seemed more worldly and generous than most of the ladies of his congregation with their incestuous small-town tittle-tattle. And warmer to Henry himself. He sometimes contrasted her benevolent amusement with the absolute indifference of his wife and her companion. These abstractions were how he thought of Lucy and Alice now. He could hardly bear to give them names.

The sight of Venetia's floral display triggered the memory of that sprig of lily-of-the-valley that he had placed in the hand of his dear Jeanne that May Day morning. Her faced upturned towards the sun. Her eyes slowly opening. The freckles on the bridge of her nose. The resemblance to his darling Florence. 'Do you want to marry me?'.

But it was a Friday and he needed to begin thinking about this Sunday's sermon. He was still working his way through the Book of Ezra, and was reaching the troubling passages where Ezra had returned to Jerusalem and was attempting to prevent Jews from marrying non-Jews. How to approach such a topic without inflaming what Henry knew to be the already ingrained prejudices of some of his congregation? Many of them would agree whole-heartedly with Ezra, but from an inverted standpoint. They wouldn't want their Christian sons and daughters marrying a Jew.

His thoughts turned instead to the more agreeable task of choosing the hymns. *Eternal Father, Strong to Save*, with its seafaring associations, was always given a rousing rendition here in Dieppe, many of his flock being regular passengers on the cross-Channel boat. Henry had himself once started singing it during a particularly rough crossing. Other passengers had joined in as the ship pitched and rolled.

Love Divine, All Loves Excelling was also usually accompanied by hearty singing, and gone were the days when Church of England congregations baulked at hymns written by Charles Wesley. In any case, any Methodists in Dieppe were likely to worship at Christ Church. There would be no dissenters at All Saints to make a show of singing Wesley's words with meaningful fortissimo.

Picking up a copy of *Hymns Ancient and Modern* from a book holder on the front pew, he began leafing through the bewildering choice on offer. And then he remembered that Lord Salisbury would be attending that Sunday, the prime minister always appreciating hymns with a patriotic, pro-Empire sentiment. Nothing too controversial, at least.

These musings were superseded by a more corporeal sensation. Henry's stomach was rumbling. On Fridays, Lucy and Alice were in the habit of joining him for lunch, an odd sort of tradition that had grown up over the years as if this ritual compensated for their living virtually separate lives during the rest of the week.

He closed the hymn book and replaced it, walking back up the aisle and out of the church while noting that the laurel bushes that lined the path needed clipping. He'd talk to the gardener who cut them back last summer. The usual 27 steps returned him to the front door of the house on the Faubourg de la Barre, just ahead of Lucy and Alice. He heard them before he saw them.

'A prostitute… it's all so awful,' he heard Alice say.

Henry froze. Had they found out about his visit to Jeanne? In an instant, he envisaged his disgrace and downfall, regretting his impulsive trip over to Le Pollet. Or had they somehow discovered the booklet that he had hidden on his book shelf?

They had seen him now and instantly stopped talking. Alice nodded curtly while Lucy gave a perfunctory smile and wished Henry a good day. He was relieved that no accusations had yet been levelled at him. Perhaps it was too distressing to be addressed publicly.

'Have you heard?' asked Lucy. 'There's been a sordid murder on the other side of town. '

Henry replied that he'd been in church all morning and had received no news of anything.

'A fallen woman by all account. I believe I overheard that her name was Jeanne.'

He couldn't recall later precisely how he managed to disentangle himself from the bearers of this appalling news and make his way to his study. He thought he had blurted out something about needing to prepare a sermon.

CHAPTER NINETEEN

'I've been suspended from duty.'

'Whatever for?' asked Walter, cleaning some paintbrushes with a rag.

'Insubordination and for disobeying orders,' said Emile, slumping into a tatty old armchair in the corner of Walter's studio. 'Apparently there will be a hearing.'

Frossard had summoned him that morning, curtly dismissing Emile but not before ordering him to leave his kepi and the rest of his uniform in the station store cupboard. This seemed unduly terminal for what was supposed to be a suspension from duty.

Unable to face returning to his lodging, and the quizzical looks of his landlady and Marie-Hélène, he had made his way at once to Walter's studio. Emile now found himself staring at a sketch of a woman sitting, fully dressed, on the edge of a bed. Walter had drawn lines vertically and horizontally over the sketch, dividing it into equal-sized squares.

'Is that…?'

'Yes, that's her. That's Jeanne. *La pauvre Jeanne.*'

'Have we… have the police questioned you about it?'

'No, and they should, shouldn't they?' said Walter, placing the clean paintbrushes in a low wooden box. 'Perhaps they will later, but in the meantime, they just carted off that dumb brute of a husband as if they'd already decided that he was the culprit. I almost felt sorry for the confounded man.'

'Do you think he did it?'

'The whole affair is so queer. I mean, yes, he's a violent, drunken beast, of that there can be no doubt. But murder in such a frenzied manner? And to ransack his own house like a crazed wild animal…'

'Drink does terrible things to people,' said Emile rather sanctimoniously, thought Walter. But Emile had been thinking of his mother's stories of his father's endless carousing. He never raised a hand to her, by all accounts (he wouldn't dare, thought Emile), but the verbal violence had apparently been difficult to bear.

'I mean, surely I must be the prime suspect,' said Walter. 'I was discovered in the dead woman's bedroom by her husband, my clothes were covered in her blood, and the whole situation must have seemed so damnedly compromising.'

Walter began pacing the studio, his hand to his brow in an almost theatrical manner. Emile weighed up his friend's words and decided that his presence in the victim's home was indeed worthy of further questioning. He of course believed Walter's reason for being in Jeanne's house, but to a disinterested observer, it would surely warrant an investigation of a more searching nature.

It was now almost exactly 24 hours since the discovery of the corpse and the husband's arrest. Emile felt helpless that he could no longer follow the course of the investigation, while he had no allies within the station with whom he could make discreet inquiries.

'Perhaps you should go down to the police station and make yourself available for questioning,' he suggested.

'I did think so but La Villain was of the opinion that it would be a foolish course of action,' replied Walter. 'My landlady has a low regard for the police, I'm sorry to tell you. Her philosophy regarding *les mouches*... 'the flies' as she calls them, is that if they are not bothering you then it's for the best not to bother them. *Ne reveillez pas le chien qui dort.*'

In the case of Frossard and his former colleagues in the Dieppe police department, Emile could find no reason to challenge La Villain's assessment. They were not a group of individuals to inspire much respect. In fact, his qualms had been growing about his suspension from duty that morning. His dismissal was beginning to feel less an issue of discipline and more a matter of convenience. They had wanted him out of the way.

'I have a good mind to investigate the matter myself,' he said.

Walter gave him a wary look and shook his head. 'It seems to me,' he said at length. 'That it would be better if you kept your head down and spent your time preparing the defence you plan to give at your upcoming hearing. By the way, will my clothing be needed as evidence, do you think? Polly Middleton has kindly offered to take it to the laundry. And yet...'

Walter walked over to wardrobe and pulled out a linen jacket, its front smeared heavily with dried blood.

'La Villain didn't want it in the house, so I'm keeping it here,' he said, holding the jacket as if exhibiting a work of art. 'I think I might keep it this way.'

Noting Emile's frown, he smiled and added: 'My wife Nellie always said that I had a morbid streak.'

'The poor woman... Jeanne, I mean.'

'Yes, quite so. Hard to think that this same blood was still coursing through her young veins yesterday morning. A kindly soul, very sweet natured. And happy too, despite her position in life.'

'But don't you think that the whole case is accursedly curious,' said Emile, returning to his earlier thoughts. 'I'm sure something is not quite right with this investigation. That husband of hers will be convicted and beheaded before the week is out, if the alacrity of current proceedings is anything to go by. What evidence do they have of his guilt?'

The men's conversation was interrupted at that moment by a knocking at the door, which then swung open without their having had time to respond.

Lydia Urquhart strode into the room, followed by an alarmed-looking Polly Middleton with little Lil in her arms.

'Oh my God, Walter. Polly just told me that you found the body,' blurted Lydia.

'I'm so sorry Walter,' said Polly, entering the room and placing her free hand on her sister's shoulder. 'I tried to restrain her. The silly girl seems to think this tragic event is terribly exciting.'

'What happened?' she asked Walter, ignoring Polly and, it seemed to him, also making a point of ignoring Emile.

'Lydia, please'. Polly spoke firmly this time. 'This is not a fit subject for discussion. Kindly refrain from being a walking Inquisition.'

'But I'm interested,' pleaded Lydia. 'Perhaps Monsieur Policeman will tell me,' she added, giving Emile what seemed like a somewhat aggrieved glance. She obviously hadn't forgiven him for leaving her in the carriage while he went off to investigate the murder.

'Emile is no longer a policeman,' interjected Walter. 'He has been suspended from duty.'

'What the devil? Why so? That's so beastly of the police, dear Emile.'

The words "dear Emile" felt like balm and he smiled at Lydia.

'Not following orders,' he said. 'I'm sure I will be reinstated in time.' As soon as this terrible business with Jeanne is finished, he thought to himself. Why did they want him out of the way?

'Well, every cloud has a silver lining, as the novelists say' chirruped Lydia, fixing Emile with a glint in her eye.

'How so, you silly girl?' asked Polly.

'Well, now that Emile is no longer a serving police officer, he can show me those disreputable corners of Dieppe.'

A collective groan greeted her words. And then Walter began to laugh, joined by little Lil and finally Emile himself. Only Polly remained stern and unmoved.

'Silly girl,' she repeated. Emile caught her eye and she appeared to soften. Returning his look with a resigned smile, she turned to address the child in her arms.

'Come on then, Lil. Let's find you some lunch.'

As Polly and Lil left the room, Emile turned to find both Walter and Lydia scrutinising him.

'What?' he asked. 'What is it?'

Neither answered, but Walter gave him a sly, wolfish grin.

* * *

The maid being busy tidying the bedrooms, Madame Remy herself answered the front-door bell. Standing there was a short but upright man with a pointy moustache and wearing a dashing blue uniform. He reminded her of a cockerel, the very emblem of France. The man removed his kepi and bowed before speaking.

'Madame Remy, I don't think we've had the pleasure. I am Commissaire Frossard of the Dieppe police. May I come in?'

'Why, of course, monsieur', she said hesitantly. 'But may I ask about the nature of your visit?'

'Worry not, dear lady. I have merely come to discuss your lodger, Emile Blanchet.'

'Emile? Has something happened?'

'Not exactly. May I come in? I fear the matter is in strictest confidence and best not discussed on the street.'

'Of course, of course,' said Madame Remy, embarrassed by what she took to be her lack of manners. Stepping aside, she closed the door behind Frossard.

Marie-Hélène appeared in the hallway at that moment, inquisitive about the visitor. Frossard bowed deeply towards the girl, who blushed.

'Go and fetch some coffee for the commissaire,' barked her mother, and Marie-Hélène scuttled off.

'A fine-looking young woman,' said Frossard. 'May I inquire of her age?'

'Nineteen… nearly twenty. And high time she was married, monsieur' said Madame Remy, gesticulating towards the dining room. The words had become a mantra, issued without thought whenever anyone would ask politely after her daughter's age or wellbeing.

'Alas, I myself never found time to marry,' said Frossard. 'Too busy with my army and police career. It's the one big regret in my life however. Too late now, I suppose, to find a woman who can cook and sew and keep me company in the evening. To be my helpmate in this arduous life of ours.'

Several questions crowded in on Madame Remy at this point. How old was the commissaire? Her age? He seemed somehow older, like most proper gentlemen. He was fine-looking in his way, but his accent was odd. Where was he from? Paris? And would he make a suitable husband for Marie-Hélène? Or perhaps even for herself?

They sat down. Madame Remy noticed that the commissaire had placed some sort of pamphlet on the table.

'My dear lady,' he began. 'Have you heard of a group of people calling themselves anarchists?'

The word rang a faint bell with Madame Remy, but only that.

'These anarchists hope to overthrow the present good order of society and to do so they will kill innocent people,' Frossard continued. 'They use dynamite indiscriminately, bombing cafes, theatres and any place where crowds gather. They also target our leaders. Surely you remember our own President Caro, three years ago stabbed to death by an Italian anarchist in Lyon.'

'Oh, those ones.'

'Yes, madame, those anarchists. But in short, for what end?'

Madame Remy had been trying to follow Frossard's words, but she was mainly asking herself: why is he telling me about these terrible things?

'For what end?' she echoed feebly.

'Precisely. I have here one of their pamphlets,' said Frossard, pushing the booklet towards her.

She looked fearfully at the pamphlet as if it might actually be one of the sticks of dynamite that he had been talking about. Was she supposed to pick it up and read it? She wasn't very good at reading.

'What does this have to do with Emile?' she asked instead.

'Well, yes, indeed. A very pertinent question. I have been worrying that Agent Blanchet might have become infected.'

'Infected?'

'Infected. By his parents, you see. Emile's father was one of these anarchists. He blew himself up with one of his own bombs…'

'No! How terrible! I never knew.'

'For the best, some might say. And his mother. Perhaps you recall the terrible events of the Paris Commune.'

'Why yes. I was but a girl…'

'Emile's mother was in the thick of it. A Communard, as those miserable wretches called themselves. She would build barricades, take up rifles and fire on the French Army. A woman. I ask you. Even so, she would have been executed for treason had she not escaped to England. Do you see my point?'

'I had no idea,' said Madame Remy, raising her hand to her mouth

'No. And it seems that Emile has been deceiving a lot of people. Why did he join the police? That is my question.'

Did it require an answer. Madame Remy thought for a moment and ventured: 'Some sort of spy, do you think?'

'Or worse.'

'You mean…'

'Imagine planting a bomb inside a police station. Or stealing all the records of known criminals.'

Frossard pushed the pamphlet further towards Madame Remy.

'Take this,' he said. 'Acquaint yourself with its nature, madame. And should you find anything similar when perhaps tidying Emile's room, you could inform me. Directly. Discreetly.'

Frossard gave what he thought was a tender smile. Marie-Hélène returned at that moment with a small enamel tray bearing two coffee cups and a sugar bowl, which she placed on the table.

'Mademoiselle, your mother tells me that you are on the lookout for a suitable husband'.

Marie-Hélène looked at her mother and blushed.

'I'm afraid that she has rather her heart set on Emile.'

'Oh dear,' said Frossard, reaching for the sugar bowl.

'Why, what has happened?' asked Marie-Hélène.

'I am rather afraid to tell you both that I have had to suspend Agent Blanchet.'

'But why?'

'For disobeying orders. And also, while I make further inquiries about his activities.'

'You mean his painting?' asked Marie-Hélène.

'No, child, I'll explain later,' said Madame Remy.

Marie-Hélène backed out of the room with a look of confusion upon her face.

'Keep this pamphlet, madame,' said Frossard in a low, conspiratorial voice. 'If Emile shows any interest in it perhaps you could let me know. Perhaps you could even leave it in his bedroom for him to read. Don't say it was from me. Just say that someone pushed it under your door. See if he has any questions. Let me know. Charming girl your daughter.'

Finally, at last, Frossard saw a glint of cunning in his hostess's eyes.

'I will let you know, for sure, Monsieur. And we must find you a suitable wife.'

* * *

Slightly to her later annoyance, Venetia Hall heard nothing about the murder until after she returned to Dieppe. She had set out early that morning, Tippet splayed inelegantly across the tartan rug on her lap, for the village of Berneval, six miles up the coast. The carriage driver had estimated a journey of two hours and Venetia had packed a picnic basket with pastries for herself and Tippet and some macaroons and a jar of confit duck (his favourite) for her host for the day.

Oscar - or Sebastian Melmoth as he was still calling himself - had been living in this unlikely backwater for the past fortnight. He had sent her a postcard to say that he was staying at the Hotel de la Plage and that the food was quite passable once he had persuaded the chef to refrain from serving him snake for dinner. She later discovered that this was quite true and not just one of Oscar's fanciful stories.

Venetia found the 'wounded lion of Berneval' (as his friends had begun calling him) fresh and hearty from a morning swim in the sea and in much better spirits than he had ever displayed in Dieppe. The change of scene was evidently suiting him.

'And how is our foremost novelist of military valour?' he teased as they sat for coffee on the hotel's narrow and somewhat rickety veranda. The sun shone directly on to their table and Venetia considered requesting that they move inside. But Oscar, the tips of his long hair still damp from the swim, had seemed so delighted to bask in the sunlight that she demurred.

Displaying his usual disregard for economy, he had taken the best two rooms at the hotel and even hired a valet. Changes were afoot, however, and there was talk of building a chalet in the village, the hotel proprietor acting as his estate agent. While the required funds were raised, he planned to rent a nearby house – an ugly redbrick edifice known as the Chalet Bourgeat that Oscar later took great pride in showing her.

According to her host, Venetia was one in a long line of visitors to Berneval, the village having seen nothing like this colourful mix of society in its entire existence. Apart from his close friends and confidantes, More Adey and Robbie Ross, a constant stream of young poets, painters, publishers and hopeful Parisian theatre producers had beaten a path to this unprepossessing hotel.

Venetia herself had come armed with the latest gossip from Dieppe, but she now saw that Oscar would not be in the slightest bit interested. He had moved on and was already constructing his own gay little world here in this out-of-the-way spot; this *petit trou de campagne*, as he called it.

There was talk of a new Biblical play to follow the success of *Salome*, this one called *Pharoah* and which was to be staged in Paris. Oscar told Venetia of others attempting to persuade him to write a play, rather than a poem, about his time in Reading Gaol. The idea had been inspired by Dostoevsky, whose novel *From the House of the Dead* had been a fictionalised account of his incarceration in a Siberian prison camp.

But Venetia could tell that Oscar was having too good a time being feted by his visitors and spending the money raised by his supporters to give much serious consideration to writing. Furthermore, there was the Bosie question, and Venetia was shocked by the change in tone when Oscar spoke about Lord Alfred Douglas.

He now referred to Douglas as "a most delicate and refined poet" and how they loved each other deeply and how "their souls touch in myriad ways". A potentially catastrophic reunion, which had seemed a distant prospect just a few weeks earlier, now appeared inevitable. What alarmed her even more was the fact that she had noticed that the private detective – no doubt hired by Douglas's father – had returned to Dieppe in recent days. It surely couldn't be too long before the man was also lodged at the Hotel de la Plage.

Venetia also wondered how Oscar would endure the long grey Normandy winters, when the cold wind blew in off the sea, the green fields turned to bare earth and the visitors returned to London and Paris. She herself found Dieppe dull and withdrawn from late September onwards and she couldn't imagine Oscar in such high spirits in the shuttered depths of January and February.

But for now, June was reaching its zenith and Monsieur Melmoth, as he was universally greeted around Berneval, was organising a party for the village children. This was in order to celebrate the Diamond Jubilee of Queen Victoria – a portrait of whom, Oscar confided, stood watching over his hotel bed.

'I hope she averts her eyes,' Venetia said to Tippet as the pair of them set off to return to Dieppe. The dog had of course been horribly spoiled by Oscar, who had even shared a morsel of his beloved confit duck with the gluttonous beast. She hoped the scamp wouldn't become ill.

* * *

Henry closed the study door behind him and reached for the Bible that stood permanent sentry on his desk. It was a long-held habit of his, much disapproved of by Henry's various early mentors (one even went as far as to call it "sorcery"), to randomly open the Bible whenever a crisis arose. At such times he would try to discern God's message in whatever passage lay arbitrarily before him.

Closing the Holy Book, which, in preparation for that Sunday's sermon, lay open at the Book of Ezra, Henry then reopened it. His eyes fell on the following passage from Luke's gospel:

And Jesus being full of the Holy Ghost returned from Jordan, and was led by the Spirit into the wilderness, being forty days tempted by the devil. And in those days, he did eat nothing: and when they were ended, he afterward hungered.

Had Henry not been tempted by the Devil? Hadn't Satan lured him across town and into the very bedroom of a wanton young woman, fooling Henry with her likeness to his lost love Florence? Instead of the freckled face of Jeanne, her eyes closed as she innocently turned her face to the sun – how Henry had first encountered her – he now saw a trap laid by the Evil One. He had been lured by his sentimental weakness to the very edge of the pit.

These thoughts were interrupted by voices and laughter from without the study. Lucy and Alice were in the hallway, Clotilde with them to judge by the way in which Lucy had begun to speak in her badly accented French. Her understanding of the language was nevertheless much more fluent than Henry's faltering grasp.

'*Dites au maitre que nous ne déjeunerons pas avec lui aujourd'hui,*' he heard her say in a loud voice that was presumably intended to carry to Henry's ears.

Why weren't they going to lunch with him today? Presumably it was so that they could gossip more freely about Jeanne's murder while at the casino, thought Henry. And pick up the latest news about the hideous crime. A sudden feeling of revulsion had him striding across to the study door, his hand resting on the doorknob, before he stopped himself.

His anger was too great and there could be no telling what he might say if confronted by his wife at this moment. The sin of anger. Perhaps this was also part of the devil's plan for him, to unleash dismay and destruction upon the very bedrock of their marriage.

Some bedrock, he thought, retreating to the desk and closing the Bible. He would take no lunch today, first making sure that Clotilde relayed this information to Lucy. And neither would he dine that evening. Was it possible to fast for 40 days, in imitation of our Lord?

Lucy and Alice were still in the hallway, now talking in low voices between themselves. Henry felt trapped in his study, the bookcases the walls of his prison cell. Crouching down, he put his hands out upon the carpet to steady himself before lowering himself on to his knees and prostrating himself.

As usual when preparing to pray, he closed his eyes and attempted to empty his mind of thought – allowing instead free access to his spirit (Florence had once described his 'spirit' as Henry's 'feelings', but that didn't do justice to the sanctity of the space that remained after the abandonment of the conscious mind). God, he felt, could respond to whatever you called these sensations more readily than He could to the inconsistent ramblings of the intellect.

His primary sensation now, he discovered, was an intense anger towards Lucy and Alice. This rapidly dissolved, however, replaced by a sensation of pity towards the poor Jeanne. Why would his Lord fill his soul with pity if Jeanne were a trap laid by the devil? He recalled again Jesus and his association with prostitutes. "They that are whole have no need of the physician, but they that are sick: I came not to call the righteous, but sinners to repentance."

Levering himself uneasily to his feet just as he heard the street door slamming shut, Henry grabbed the library steps and positioned them within reach of the folder that Jeanne had entrusted to him. Reassuringly, the package had gathered dust since he last handled it. The smell of Jeanne's perfume no longer attached to it he was however disappointed to discover.

Gently manoeuvring the ribbon around the top corners of the package, so as not to break the seal, Henry was able to discern the first lines of a good quantity of letters and other notes – all, as far as he could see, written in French. The topmost letter was however addressed in English and inscribed using a typewriter. Managing to slip it out of the package, Henry carried the letter over to the window and began to read:

Sousse, Tunisia. 19th May 1897.

Dear Rachel Beer,
Please excuse this correspondence from a stranger but I feel that the matter I lay before you will be of great interest to you and your readers, and of even greater public importance.

For reasons of my current position in the French Army and the patriotic duties incumbent upon me, I am unable to share the enclosed information within my own homeland. I feel sure, however, that no such reservations apply in Great Britain and that publication of the enclosed proof concerning this long-standing and terrible miscarriage of justice against Alfred Dreyfus will not face the febrile opposition that might be expected here in France.

But please allow me to introduce myself. Two years ago, I was appointed director of the Deuxième Bureau, the army's intelligence section. Part of my brief was to investigate the theft of French military intelligence that was subsequently passed to the German embassy in Paris.

As you will know, the unfortunate Dreyfus was charged with and convicted of this act of espionage and imprisoned on the penal colony of Devil's Island in French Guiana.

In the course of my investigations, I was able to uncover the identity of the real culprit. However, I was hindered in these investigations and subsequently relieved of my post and sent on regimental duty to Tunisia in North Africa. It is from Tunisia that I now address you, dear madam. I hope you will excuse any errors in my use of English, but this letter has been translated for me by a fellow officer who is also privy to the information contained herein.

I have it on the good authority of a mutual acquaintance (and who must remain anonymous here, in case this letter should fall into the wrong hands) that you are sympathetic to the plight of Monsieur Dreyfus. I sincerely hope and trust that you would be willing to assist in unmasking the real traitor in this most unfortunate case.
Yours very sincerely,
Lieutenant-Colonel Georges Picquart.

CHAPTER TWENTY

Gustave Geffroy sat behind his desk at *L'Aurore*. On the wall behind him hung Paul Cézanne's portrait of the art critic. Both the man himself and his likeness in oil paint sat in an identical pose, their elbows splayed and hands resting on an open book. The tome in question was Geffroy's own *L'Histoire de l'Impressionisme*, published three years earlier and the very first printed record of the artistic movement. His editor at the newspaper, Georges Clemenceau, sat at a desk on the other side of the cramped office.

'And how was your lunch with Degas?' asked Clemenceau, filling his pipe.

'Oh, the usual. Leg of lamb with Soissons beans, all washed down with endless Jew-baiting.'

'Does he think of nothing else?' asked Clemenceau before applying a match to his pipe.

Edgar Degas had been on accommodating terms with Geffroy ever since the critic had written that it was Degas who had taken the initiative in organising the first Impressionist exhibition in 1874. He was given regular previews of the great man's work and this lunchtime Degas had offered to sell Geffroy one of his famous pastel works. And at a decent price too. But this wasn't what he was eager to discuss with Clemenceau.

'Degas has been visiting Dieppe and I have news about young Emile Blanchet.'

It took a few moments for the name to register with the other man, who stared blankly at Geffroy through a cloud of tobacco smoke.

'Ah, yes. Nathalie Levallois's boy. What about the lad?'

'Only that his boss, that old reactionary Frossard, has him suspended for no particular good reason.'

'And how does Degas know all this?'

'He's been staying with the English painter Walter Sickert and Sickert has befriended young Blanchet. It seems that Dieppe has been experiencing quite a few sensational events this summer. First, Oscar Wilde chose to make it his home after being released from prison. And then there have been two recent murders in the town – one of a young prostitute, the other of a Tunisian soldier.'

Clemenceau's expression now took on the peculiarly simian caste that it did when he was deep in thought.

'What do we know about the Tunisian soldier?' he asked eventually. 'Which regiment?'

'One of the ones stationed in Sousse. Under Georges Picquart.'

There followed a long silence while Clemenceau sucked on his pipe and stared Geffroy through a cloud of smoke. He then put down the pipe and said: 'That is most interesting. Most interesting indeed.' 'Murdered in Dieppe, you say?'

* * *

Colonel Aubrey Marsden stood at his usual observation post in the doorway between the gaming halls of Dieppe's casino. After another highly satisfactory lunch at Maison Lefèvre (the andouillette had been particularly succulent, the colonel having long ago overcome his distaste for this type of offal sausage) he had been hoping to gossip about yesterday's sensational happening. The murder of a young trollop in Le Pollet.

He had spent the previous afternoon milling with a large crowd of onlookers outside the police station. He was told that an arrest had been made and that the culprit was currently inside the station being questioned. The murderer was rumoured to be the woman's husband, a drunkard with a violent temper. But then what would you expect of a poor man wedded to a mutton?

The colonel had been hoping that he might catch sight of the young police agent he'd met on the golf course – the officer with the excellent spoken English and the deplorable lack of facial hair. By capitalising on his brief acquaintance with the young man, he would attempt to learn the latest news about the case and thereby make himself the centre of attention at the casino. He would be loath to admit it – and indeed was far too proud to even consider the matter – but the former army officer felt ignored by large sections of the English community in Dieppe. Gossip was the currency in this town and he intended to bank some now with gory details about the murder.

It had been different in Aldershot, which had been awash with old soldiers like himself. Many there had also served in the Crimea or in China during the Opium Wars and had stories to exchange and experiences to share. The colonel had spent the majority of his later career at the Royal Military College in Sandhurst, but not before helping put down the Indian rebellion of '57, fighting courageously during the defence of Delhi.

Dieppe by contrast seemed to be full of painters and poets, ruined European aristocrats and distressed spinsters – hardly the colonel's ideal companions. At least that wretched Oscar Wilde had left town, fleeing to some godforsaken village up the coast with his tail between his legs, according to the lady novelist Mrs Hall.

He had to admit however that Dieppe was considerably less expensive than back across the Channel, and the food incomparably better. And however proud the demeanour of his fellow countrymen in this little French port, one had to remember that it was their search for cheaper living that was often their primary reason for them being here.

Standing outside the police station he noticed the coming and goings of a short man with an upright military bearing, along with a full beard and a fine pointed moustache. This policeman had the unmistakable bearing of an old soldier, he thought, turning to a neighbour in the crowd to enquire about the policeman's identity. This character hadn't known, but another had leaned across and informed the colonel that the officer in question was a Commissaire Frossard – "*un véritable patriote.*"

The remark only confirmed the colonel's initial impression. He had met such proud and upright French soldiers in the Crimea, where Britain and her Gallic ally had shaken off centuries of enmity to face the threat of the Russian Empire. The colonel's father, with his vivid memories of the Napoleonic Wars, could never come to terms with the alliance.

Was it his imagination, or did this Commissaire Frossard single him out from the crowd, acknowledging the colonel as a fellow military man, before stepping smartly back inside the police station? He had certainly looked in the colonel's direction.

Regretfully, he hadn't in the event been able to locate the beardless young policeman. And now disappointed by the turn-out at the casino, the colonel was about to set out in search of an armchair in which to have a discreet snooze when he spied the vicar's wife and her lady companion. He watched them approach, arms entwined, with a feeling of envy. How he would like to have a confidante with whom to share the joys and sorrows of this life.

He had by now largely forgotten the way in which, following his retirement, he had expended considerable energy in attempting to avoid his late wife, Violet. Fishing, golf and cricket had all provided excellent excuses for not being at home, while Violet had been so averse to his old-soldier acquaintances that whenever he invited them over to play cards, she would make her excuses and sit in the other room embroidering or reading.

'Good afternoon, dear ladies,' he said, giving a courtly bow as Lucy and Alice approached.

'Good afternoon, colonel,' replied Lucy. Since the couple appeared to be about to pass him by without a further word, the colonel hastily interjected: 'A dreadful business about that poor woman, wouldn't you agree?'

'The poor woman, colonel?' said Lucy.

'Haven't you heard? A lady of the night.'

'Oh, yes, quite so,' said Lucy, the couple ceasing their progress towards the gaming tables as they recognised the possibility that gossip was about to be shared. 'Have you heard any more, colonel?'

'That her blackguard of a husband has been arrested.'

From the ladies' reaction it was clear to the colonel that this was old news.

'The detective in charge of the investigation is called Frossard,' he hastily added, hoping that he had remembered the name correctly.

'Oh, yes, the commissaire,' said Alice. 'They say he's a true patriot.'

'That's exactly what I heard,' replied the colonel, feeling somewhat deflated as the ladies walked off.

* * *

After Degas had departed for Paris, Walter was sorry to have been so apprehensive about the master's visit. Unlike his letters, which seemed entirely preoccupied by his hatred of the Jews, in person the great man wanted solely to discuss his art and to reminisce about the past. All those jaunts they'd made together to the clifftops bordering Dieppe, their pochards and sketch pads to hand.

Young Emile had been present in the studio one afternoon when Degas demonstrated some of the eccentricities of his pastel technique – how for example he might place a drawing on the ground, cover it with a board and then stomp on it to grind the pastel into paper.

The great man explained how pastel was a more versatile medium for the large-scale works Degas had been forced to create because of his deteriorating eyesight. He told Walter that his blind spot had been worsening so that he could only really see around the spot at which he was looking, and never the spot itself. He added that he attributed the affliction to the fact that, during the siege of Paris, he had slept in a studio with a high window from which the cold air poured down on his face at night.

This was the same studio – but a different window – in which he had painted *Femme à fenetre,* Degas relating a curious story about the woman depicted in the picture. He said that he brought her, as a present, a piece of horse-flesh, and that her hunger for meat was such that she seized it and tore it with her teeth, without waiting for it to be cooked.

Walter owned one of Degas's pastel portraits of nude women which so scandalised the last Impressionist group exhibition in Paris all those years ago. "It's as if you looked through a keyhole and saw them bathing, washing, drying, rubbing down, combing their hair or having it combed for them," Walter recalled his friend telling him excitedly at the time.

Walter also understood that the quick execution of pastel colouring negated the delays associated with oil painting, his friend and mentor concerned that his failing eyesight would only worsen. A pastel is always ready to get on with. Everything was a race against time; against the drying of the paint.

As he was leaving, Walter promised to visit Degas in Paris that winter, asking whether he could bring Emile with him. Degas had seemed well disposed towards the young policeman, especially after he informed the great man that Emile had never visited the city from which his mother had fled.

'She fought for the Commune, young man?' he asked. 'I salute her memory. I was in Paris while the barricades were being put up but I had left by the time that terrible slaughter began. I was here in Normandy, in fact, staying with friends and sketching their horses and children.'

That conversation had taken place two days earlier and now the studio felt empty in the absence of Degas. Walter walked over to the easel on which sat his ink and pencil sketch of Jeanne. He had squared it in red ink that morning, numbering each column in preparation for transferring her image to canvas.

The way in which he had shadowed her face so that the details were mostly obscured now felt distasteful to Walter, as if in veiling her features he had somehow been presaging her death. At least he had asked her to keep her clothes on, that beautiful young body now laid out on a mortuary slab.

Stepping forward he ripped the sketch from the board upon which it was pinned. Scrunching the paper, he threw it into a wastepaper basket before locating his sketch pad and ripping out all but one drawing he had made of Jeanne. This he pressed to his lips and slid into a drawer along with other long discarded sketches.

Walking over to the open studio door, he noted how the cherries on the courtyard trees were beginning to take on colour. He must pick them before the birds consumed the fruit. The breeze carried a pleasant warmth along with the salty tang from the harbour below. Suddenly he knew what he must do to shake off this feeling of deflation since Degas's departure. He must recreate their painting excursions, but with him as the master and Emile as the pupil. It would help take the young policeman's thoughts off his suspension – to prevent him kicking his heels and growing frustrated. And it would grant Walter the opportunity to dissuade Emile from making a match with Lydia.

The idea that this would be a disastrous liaison had been growing until now he felt he ought to step in and say something. Furthermore, he noted a growing friendship between Polly and Emile, although he doubted whether Emile had noticed such was his youthful obsession with Lydia.

* * *

Emile was at that very moment seated by a window in a small, darkened café on the Place Nationale – the large square that hosted a market on Thursdays, Fridays and Saturdays. Today was a Tuesday, however, and the square was deserted save for three seagulls who had been squabbling over a herring that must have fallen out of a fishwife's basket. A skinny ginger cat was in turn watching the seagulls.

The square's permanent resident was the great 17th-century naval commander Abraham Duquesne, whose swaggering likeness, a ship's anchor at his feet, stood on a plinth at one end. Duquesne was Dieppe's most famous son, born and raised here before his various exploits against the Spanish and the pirates of the Mediterranean. A year before Emile's arrival in the town, there had a great celebration because the admiral's heart, which had been placed in a silver box after his death and sent to Switzerland, had been repatriated to his birthplace.

Emile knew all of this because Walter, who had painted the statue on a number of occasions, was curiously proud of this dashing sailor. He almost seemed to identify with Duquesne, thought Emile, who had admired Walter's recent painting in which the statue had been entirely in shadow with sunlit houses behind it.

He turned in his seat to see whether he could recreate the picture's viewpoint, but the café was at the wrong angle. The bell in the church of St Jacques rang twice and Emile sighed at the thought of the long afternoon stretching out before him.

Unwilling to return to his lodgings and face being interrogated by Marie-Hélène and her mother, he had skulked around town like a fugitive or a vagrant before taking lunch at a restaurant far enough from the police station to not risk encountering any of his former colleagues. Returning aimlessly in the direction of the port he had remembered this little bar, with its dark interior and anonymous clientele.

He had drunk a bowl of cider and considered moving on to something stronger, but as always when it came to question of drink, thoughts of his father stayed his hand. He ordered a coffee instead, unable to still the always lurking fear that he was indeed destined to be a good-for-nothing wastrel like the man whose seed had begotten him.

Hadn't his aunts, who had followed his father to London and who had made fleeting appearances in Emile's young life, always marvelled at his physical likeness to that drunken sot? But just because he had inherited the tight chestnut curls and dark eyes, as well as the tall, lean stature of the man, did that necessarily mean Emile was fated to fall heir to his weak character and overpowering vices?

Damn it! Perhaps he ought to tell the barman to bring a bottle of brandy over to his table. Why not? "And bring two glasses and join me for drink, my good man," Emile could imagine his father saying in such a setting as this. And he would waste away the afternoon talking to the man, and to anybody else who would listen.

Perhaps Emile could do the same. Prattle on about his bastard boss, how Emile had been unfairly treated, and how something fishy was afoot with the murder of this poor *putain*.

And then what? He sipped his coffee and his thoughts turned to Lydia. What would she think if she saw him drunk and babbling to strangers about his troubles? Maybe she would think it funny and call for a glass for herself. The idea didn't seem implausible and the possibility disturbed him. What would Polly think? She would have been saddened, but perhaps more understanding. And he was suddenly struck by the realisation that he cared more about Polly's approval than that of her sister.

He drained his coffee, dropped some coins on the table and left the café with only a curt "*bon après-midi*" to the barman. The square felt dazzling in the sunlight, the air warm. Summer had properly arrived. He strolled over to the statue of the proud old sailor, his long cloak and feathered cap now streaked white with seagull droppings but his face looking defiantly outward to the far horizon. Perhaps Emile needed to broaden his own vista, leave this town and its police station with its obstructive and hostile boss.

But wasn't that what Frossard wanted? He certainly wished him out of the way. If for now he wasn't personally able to delve into the mystery of the drowned Tunisian and the murdered prostitute then there were other ways that he could make his mark on the case.

He must persuade Walter to visit the police station and repeat the story that he had told him yesterday. The one he told him after Emile had visited the studio and met the famous artist, Edgar Degas.

Walter had apprised them both of how, when he visited the brothel to sketch Jeanne, the proprietor had informed him that Jeanne hadn't arrived for work as usual. And how there had been two gentlemen callers asking for Jeanne by name earlier that day. If they had come as a pair, then it was surely unlikely they would have been seeking Jeanne's professional services. Surely these men would be of interest to the police and had questions to answer.

Emile could understand why Walter might be fearful of approaching the police. After all, having discovered Jeanne's body and having no legitimate reason for being inside her home – her bedroom at that – then surely, he must be a prime suspect. It was now four days since the murder and no attempt had been made to question Walter while, as far as Emile knew, Jeanne's husband was still in custody. Perhaps the husband had hired these men to kill Jeanne? In that case, Frossard should be made aware of their existence.

* * *

Henry, that same warm Tuesday afternoon, sat alone in his church. He was grateful for coolness of the darkened nave - a blessed relief from the oppressive sun that had caused a stream of parasol-wielding ladies and boater and blazer-clad gentlemen to make their cheerful, chattering way towards the seafront. The town centre felt deserted, save for those poor souls whose lives allowed no time for leisure.

Clutching the letter from the folder given to him for safe-keeping by Jeanne, he sat down on a pew and then slid forward on to his knees. The Lord would provide guidance, he knew, as he laid bare his thoughts – contemplation that required Henry to ask forgiveness as he again recalled Jeanne's petticoat sliding from her bare shoulder.

"Do you want to marry me?" the lamb had asked him. Henry's subsequent confusion at this naïve and objectively absurd question baffled him then and baffled him now. How it had stirred him! If Jeanne were somehow a reincarnation of his beloved Florence, then he was being offered a second chance at happiness. And yet how absurd…

Having asked for forgiveness, he allowed his thoughts to turn to the letter and its possible meaning. Should he show it to another? Not to Lucy, for that would be an admission that he had visited a prostitute and been taken so far into her confidence to be entrusted with her dangerous secret. And to reveal its existence to the police would be incriminating in a different way, now that the girl had been so cruelly murdered.

But what troubled him most were the contents of the letter. Although he paid little attention to the newspapers and took little interest in the politics of his own or any other nation, he was aware of what was widely known as "the Dreyfus affair". How an army officer called Alfred Dreyfus, a Jew from Alsace, had been arrested and imprisoned for spying for Germany.

There were those who claimed that Dreyfus was innocent and that this fact could not now be admitted because so many important people, especially in the army, had nailed their colours to the mast of his guilt. And although he had overheard many heated arguments about the affair (Colonel Marsden was particularly vehement in his belief that this Dreyfus should have been executed instead of being sent to a penal colony), Henry himself could muster little interest in the business.

On several occasions during the course of his lifetime, Henry had been described as unworldly. And Henry was proud to be aloof from the affairs of this world. "Set your affection on things above, not on things on the earth," as Paul wrote to the Corinthians. But now he felt that the world had come to him and landed in his lap.

'I am afraid, Lord,' he whispered.

'Oh, I'm sorry. I didn't see you kneeling there, Vicar.'

Henry scrambled to his feet. Venetia Hall stood staring at him from behind a spray of flowers. In fact, she seemed to be immersed in blooms, since she was wearing her familiar purple straw hat adorned with yellow roses.

'I couldn't help but notice while taking Communion on Sunday that the arrangements on the altar were wilting,' she continued, seemingly as flustered as Henry to have discovered the vicar so deep in prayer. 'And I have such a wonderful showing of roses at the moment that I thought I'd replenish the vases here...'

'Quite so, Mrs Hall. Quite so. I was just…'

'You were praying. Yes, my apologies again for arriving unannounced. Now that I am here however, I ought to put these roses in water or they too will wither and die.'

'No. Yes. Please proceed, dear lady,' said Henry, gathering himself as Venetia, after glancing at the letter still clasped in Henry's hand, strode towards the chancel. Watching her as she made her way down the nave, he wondered whether her visit was part of God's answer to his prayer. After all, Venetia was wise in the ways of the world, and was acquainted, he believed, with many eminent persons. Indeed, she was one of the few congregants whom the prime minister, Lord Salisbury, deigned to address after the Sunday service.

But would the lady's worldliness extend to the fact of Henry having visited a prostitute – however benign were his intentions – and a prostitute most foully murdered? He had only once dipped into one of Venetia's novels, purchased by Lucy. It had been a romance, he dimly recalled, whose hero became involved in a duel over his wife's honour. He hadn't felt the urge to further his acquaintance with the lady's oeuvre, although Colonel Marsden was an avid advocate of her tales of military gallantry.

Henry closed his eyes again, but felt no further communication from the Holy Spirit. His suddenly quietened mind seemed proof that He had spoken and said all He needed to say; that Venetia had been sent by Him who is most holy. And opening his eyes again, he noticed Venetia staring back at him before hurriedly looking away and busying herself with her flower arrangement.

Folding the letter and placing it in the inside pocket of his jacket, Henry strolled up the nave in what he thought was a nonchalant manner, his features displaying what he hoped was an expression of admiration.

'Such lovely pink roses,' he said. 'The warm weather we're experiencing must be encouraging them to bloom.'

'Tell me, Vicar,' said Venetia, ignoring his trite meteorological observation. 'What do you make of French girls?'

Noticing Henry blanch, Venetia hurriedly explained: 'I'm writing an article for my readers back home about the difference between English and French girls. I mean young girls… of an age before courtship and marriage.'

Relieved that Venetia hadn't been referring in any way to Jeanne, Henry attempted to ponder the matter.

'From my limited observation I would say that French girls in Dieppe tend to be better attired…'

'Quite so,' interrupted Venetia. 'Very chic. As faultless as a fashion plate and just as vapid.'

Henry's laughter at this witticism appeared spontaneous and genuine and Venetia made a note to include it in her finished article.

'But they have no roses in their cheeks, no spring in their step,' she continued, disappointed this time by her audience's lack of response. But Henry had been thinking of Jeanne and how he had first encountered her on that doorstep on that fateful May morning. She had roses in her cheeks. Or rather the bloom of a ripening apple.

'Tell me, dear lady,' he said now. 'You have a wide circle of friends in Dieppe, and I was wondering whether you have the acquaintance of a Mrs Rachel Beer.'

'Rachel Beer,' echoed Venetia. 'Rachel Beer.' It was indeed a name familiar to her and she tried to recall whether she was a regular at the casino.

'Wait a minute, if it is Rachel Sassoon Beer to whom you refer, then yes, I do know of her.'

'Sassoon Beer? The name is not familiar to me. Is she by chance a member of our congregation?'

'I very much doubt it,' said Venetia with a laugh. 'The Sassoons are a fabulously rich Jewish family. Made their money in China and India, although from Mesopotamia originally, I believe. Rachel Beer is a remarkable woman. She married into the Beer family, who are not Jewish. Following her marriage, Mrs Beer converted to Christianity, after which her family disowned her.'

'How regrettable for the poor woman,' said Henry, who often felt that his own family had disowned him.

'Poor? Not in any material sense. The Beer family are also fabulously rich. They own newspapers in London, which Mrs Beer now edits. The *Observer* and the *Sunday Times*. Like I said, a remarkable woman.'

CHAPTER TWENTY-ONE

'What is this?'

Emile realised that he was shouting but was too enraged to care. He was holding the pamphlet that he had been shocked to find on his bedroom table the night before. It was four roughly printed sheets of paper advocating violence against all forms of authority, including the police. He read:

Raise fires in the four corners of our cities, mow people down, wipe everything out, and when nothing whatever is left in this rotten world perhaps a better one will spring up!

He had seen nonsense like this before, on pamphlets confiscated by the police after being left on café tables. They were the work of violent anarchists. But how had one found its way into his bedroom? Madame Remy looked sheepish.

'Somebody must have slipped it under our door,' she said. 'I cannot read very well, so I left it for you to look at. Perhaps it was meant for you.'

Marie-Hélène was looking at her mother in a nervous fashion and then, when Emile looked at her, her eyes dropped to the floor. She had been out of sorts ever since Emile had first appeared at breakfast in Walter's old tweed jacket and breeches – a gift for use on their painting expeditions. His landlady had also looked at him in a manner in which a doctor might observe a very sick patient.

Marie Hélène had actually gasped when she had noted his attire, asking in a pained voice when he was likely to be reinstated. Emile felt that his value to the household - not to mention Marie Hélène's marriage prospects - was directly connected to their lodger wearing his smart blue uniform. They were proud to have a policeman beneath their roof, not this shabby bohemian, who was now slinging his satchel of paints around his neck.

'I have no word as yet of when my hearing might be conducted,' he said stiffly, draining his coffee and waving the pamphlet. 'This is dangerous nonsense. It doesn't belong to me and should be thrown away. If I was not suspended, I would take it straight way to the police station.'

'What is it that you have done to be suspended?' asked Madame Remy following him into the hallway.

'Fear not, madame. It's only a minor disciplinary matter that will be sorted in due course. And don't worry about my being able to afford your splendid food and lodgings for I have enough savings put away.'

Stepping with relief on to the street, Emile wondered whether his landlady had detected his intended note of sarcasm. He was still furious that she placed the anarchist pamphlets in his bedroom. In any case, he decided that he didn't care if she did discern his disrespectful tone, for the food was fast becoming unbearably awful and Marie-Hélène's constant attentions oppressive. He would look into living elsewhere, and maybe not even in Dieppe.

He had a fancy to visit Paris, the city where his mother had lived and fought so bravely for her beliefs. Her stories of heroism and despair made the city seem both magical and terrible. There had been talk of visiting Walter's friend Monsieur Degas in the autumn, which would be an opportunity for Emile to discover the reality behind what had, in his mind, become a city of myths and legends.

It was another hot, cloudless morning, as he passed the fish market. Walter's statuesque landlady, Madame Villain, was holding up a whole turbot for a customer to inspect. As usual nobody was examining the seafood displayed on a barrow by the fishwife patronised by his landlady. No doubt Madame Remy would appear as usual at a quarter to twelve to scrape up any of the poor specimens still unsold at closing time.

Trotting up the steps to Walter's studio, Emile nearly collided with Polly and Lydia coming in the opposite direction. Pressing himself against the wall to allow them to pass, he noted again the difference in their demeanours.

There was an air of sadness about Polly, albeit borne with a resigned good humour. Lydia could not be more different, with her ready, excited laughter and carefree manner.

'I hope you haven't left Lil in Walter's charge,' he said, doffing his hat. 'We are off hunting for pretty views to paint along the clifftops.'

'Don't worry, Emile, she is with our mother,' said Polly with her sad smile.

'Could I join you?' asked Lydia. 'It's too warm to going visiting.'

'We're calling on some friends visiting for the summer,' explained Polly. 'Come on Lydia, they are just as much your friends as mine.'

Lydia pulled a face at her sister and waved a gloved hand at Emile, before the pair disappeared beneath their parasols and continued their descent. Walter appeared at that moment at the top of the steps. His pochade box was strung around his neck and he was apparently ready to leave for the cliffs.

'I see you encountered the delightful sisters,' he said as they made their way along the Grande Rue and the Faubourg de la Barre, and so on to the Pourville road with its twisty uphill lanes bordered by Swiss-Norman style chalets. 'I had wanted to talk to you about them.'

Sensing that his friend had some bad news to impart about Lydia - perhaps this 'friend' from England was a rival suitor - Emile stopped and looked at Walter.

'What is it?' he asked.

'Ah, now…,' said Walter, suddenly abashed. 'You see, I've been thinking upon your courtship with mademoiselle Lydia… it is a courtship, isn't it?

'I suppose so, although a queer sort of courtship, I will warrant. Anyway, I like her very much.'

'No doubt. And she is a lively companion. Delightful in many ways, if a little frivolous at times.'

'She certainly has what we French call a *joie de vivre*.'

'That indeed she does,' said Walter, seemingly unsure how to progress. 'Delightful in many ways. But excuse me, Emile, for I believe I know you well and have your best interests at heart. And you are a serious young man, of that I have little doubt.'

'You have no doubt? And so, you are saying?'

Walter shook his head and put a hand on Emile's shoulder. They were emerging now out of the cooling shadows of the deep-sided banks and tall villas and near the open summit of the Pourville road. To the left was the new golf clubhouse and to the right, the glistening sea.

'What I am saying… and please don't take offence at this… is that you and Lydia are both delightful young people. But, I fear, you are not well matched.'

Emile drew away, Walter's hand falling back by his side.

'How are you to say we are not well matched when I love her so?'

'You love Lydia?'

And now that he had said the words aloud, they did seem to ring oddly hollow. False even.

'Well, true love is a fine thing, never to be despised', said Walter, dabbing his brow with his handkerchief. The morning was becoming intolerably hot for such an expedition. Emile pulled off his jacket and hung it over his arm.

'I am extremely fond of her,' said Emile.

'Ah, oh yes. And I am extremely fond of Lydia. And of her dear sister Polly.'

'Polly is most agreeable too,' agreed Emile.

'Most agreeable. And have you never considered that she would make a more suitable match?'

'Polly?' exclaimed Emile, looking at his friend to ascertain whether or not he might be joking. But Walter showed no outward sign that he was in jest.

'No, I have never considered such a thing. And she is married and with a child and, quite apart from that, has shown no sign of being interested in me.'

'Are you sure of that? I know for certain that she *is* fond of you. And as for being married, her husband long ago deserted her. He now lives a dissolute life in London, by all accounts, strongly of the Oscar Wilde persuasion.'

'You mean?'

'Frankly it's a miracle that little Lil was ever conceived.'

They walked on. A heat haze shimmered over road ahead of them.

'But would he consent to a divorce?' asked Emile.

'I'm glad to see that you haven't dismissed the idea out of hand,' said Walter smiling at Emile. 'Polly and he were married in France and French divorce laws are so much less onerous than in England, as I have been discovering to my cost. Did you know that during the French Revolution, a law was passed allowing husbands and wives to part if either one of them simply felt like doing so. Napoleon changed all that. Boney thought it detrimental to the stability of the family and all that. But the good old Third Republic has made it once again relatively simple to cast asunder one's marriage vows. I am very envious.'

'This is madness.'

'Not at all, merely an observation. I have noticed in recent weeks that you cast more looks towards Polly than to Lydia. Don't deny it.'

Emile was silent as the truth of Walter's statement sank in. He did find himself looking more at Polly these days than at her sister. But why was that? He thought that a silent alliance of sorts had grown up between them, a joint mockery of Lydia's foolishness. But he thought that this was friendship. And yet…

'*Au contraire*. In fact, the more I think about it, the more sense it makes,' said Walter, breaking into his thoughts. 'You have no parents or other family to disapprove of you marrying a divorcee, and Polly would make a wonderfully supportive companion as you progressed in your career…'

'Ah, my career,' said Emile, kicking a stone to the side of the road.

'I have no doubt that you will go far, my dear Emile.'

'But Polly… she is older than me and more settled.'

'She is exactly the same age as you. 23. It's Lydia who lags behind in maturity. You are five years her senior and so much more experienced in the ways of the world. I believe her youthful frivolity would eventually drive you mad. But here we are. Shall we set up our easels and speak no more on the matter for the time being?'

They had chosen the same spot above the cliffs from where, weeks earlier, they had been interrupted first by the golfers and then by Marie Hélène on her bicycle. Questions crowded in on Emile as Walter busied himself setting up his easel and sorting through the tubes of paint.

Had Walter already discussed this matter with Polly and Lydia? Indeed, had Lydia herself instigated it? And if not, then what would she think if Emile were transfer his affections to her sister?

And Emile had to admit that the idea of Polly as fiancée was not without its attractions. He simply couldn't deny how his eyes were drawn to her sad countenance rather than Lydia's invariably gay features. For wasn't there indeed something tiresome about such relentless high spirits? But there was more to it than that. For he felt strangely compelled to look at Polly rather than her sister.

Nevertheless, they may be the same age, but he was a mere child in matters of the heart. She had already been courted by a man - a man of 'Oscar Wilde tendences' admittedly (had the husband deceived her in this regard?) and they had produced a child.

No man who had served in the army in Africa was going to be an innocent in sexual matters, although Emile had only twice availed himself of the scores of local women who plied their trade at the garrison in Dahomey. And even then he was relieved not to have caught the venereal disease that was so rife among his comrades.

'Have you spoken to either Polly or Lydia about any of this?', he enquired once Walter had finished sorting his paints.

'No, but I did have a conversation with their mother, Mrs Middleton. The sea is of a most beautiful shade of green today, don't you agree?'

'And what was her opinion on the matter?'

'She agreed with me. Lydia is a flibbertigibbet whom her mother is considering sending to stay with a cousin of her age in England. She loves her dearly, of course, but understands her limitations. Oh, Christ…'

'What is it?'

'I knew we should have set up somewhere more distant from the golf course, said Walter, looking somewhere above Emile's right shoulder. 'Here comes that same English vicar who disturbed us last time.'

* * *

Despite having sworn to himself to never again play the wretched game, the Reverend Henry Gibson had immediately accepted Colonel Marsden's invitation to make up a four-ball at golf. The round was to be with himself, a certain Captain Woolacombe (a friend of the colonel visiting from Aldershot) and Mr Chapman, the British vice-consul in Dieppe.

Henry was desperate to learn any gossip about the ongoing investigation into Jeanne's murder and he knew that Mr Chapman, who took an interest in everything that happened in the town, would have the very latest tittle-tattle. A physically active, hard-drinking man in his late fifties, Chapman had little in common with bookish Henry, but their paths crossed at Sunday services and they were on cordial enough terms.

And it didn't take long for the subject to be broached, Colonel Marsden seemingly as eager as Henry to learn the latest news about a crime that was the talk of the delightedly scandalised English colony. Mr Chapman was however disappointingly vague in this respect, it becoming obvious that he knew little more than anyone else about the matter. The husband, he stated self-importantly, was still in custody and the police were not searching for alternative suspects.

'I heard the husband was overly fond of a drink,' remarked the colonel, instinctively fingering his hip flask before lining up his niblick for an approach shot.

'A terrible business,' said the vice-consul watching the colonel's half swing and then following the ball as it fell short of the green. 'I trust Jack the Ripper hasn't moved to Dieppe.'

The colonel and his friend laughed and shook their heads but Henry was chilled by the reference of the Whitechapel murders. To think that his poor Jeanne could have fallen foul to such a vile crime. Many were the times he confessed to God his morbid interest in those London killings. He secretly blamed Lucy, who had followed the newspaper reports with an unseemly fascination, even reading them aloud over the breakfast table. In the long-off days when they used to breakfast together.

'My sincerest apologies, vicar,' said the vice-consul, obviously noticing a look of distaste or disapproval on Henry's face. 'It is not seemly to jest about such matters.'

'I was just thinking of our poor victim here in Dieppe,' said Henry, who had been about to utter Jeanne's name before realising that this would speak of an unexpected intimacy. 'Is there anything known of the victim?'

'Your shot, vicar,' said the vice-consul, who was growing bored of a topic of which he knew disappointingly little. Lining up his niblick for a 50-yard pitch on to the green, Henry noticed the artist Walter Sickert and the young policeman standing at their easels, by the very cliff edge on which he'd encountered them the previous month.

Struck by the sudden desire to speak to the policeman, he returned the niblick to his bag and pulled out a baffie instead. Ignoring the colonel's warning of "Wrong club, surely, vicar", he sent the ball flying over the green and up towards the pair of painters.

'Fore!' he shouted by way of warning, the ball dropping in the long grass ten or so feet short of the men's easels. Walter and Emile turned towards the approaching figure, sweat dripping from his high forehead and the lank hair that was usually combed across his balding dome now hanging down one side of his face.

'Good afternoon, Mr Sickert, and, er, excuse me, young man I…'

'Emile Blanchet,' said Emile.

'Agent Blanchet, yes indeed. Uncommonly hot today, wouldn't you say?'

The two men looked at each other, obviously wondering at his business, especially as the other golfers were beckoning him with increasingly vexed shouts.

'I was wondering, Agent Blanchet, about the poor woman who was murdered in the Pollet. Jeanne was her name.'

'You know Jeanne?' asked Walter, surprised. 'Knew Jeanne,' he corrected himself.

'A very brief acquaintance,' said Henry, quickly adding after he noticed the two men again exchange glances: 'It was nothing like that…. I mean, it was the first of May and I saw her sitting on a doorstep and gave her a sprig of lily-of-the-valley.'

This sounded non-sensical and he needed to explain himself. The heat of the sun and his fellow golfers now bellowing at him from the green weren't helping him think clearly.

'She told me that her name was Jeanne. A pretty girl, I recall and such a pity.'

'Quite so,' said Emile. 'I'm afraid that I cannot be of any assistance since I am no longer attached to the case. Or indeed the Dieppe police.'

'Monsieur Blanchet has been temporarily suspended from duty,' explained Walter. 'A misunderstanding.'

'Oh, I see,' said Henry. 'But is it true what they say, Mr Sickert, that you discovered the poor woman?'

'It is so. But I wasn't aware that this was common knowledge.'

Henry had heard from Venetia Hall when he had handed her the sensational letter that morning and which she was no doubt currently devouring. Mrs Hall had apparently heard it spoken of at the casino by someone whose maid had heard it at the fish market where Mr Sickert's landlady had her stall.

'My apologies. I merely repeat some overheard gossip,' said Henry. 'I believe the young lady acted as an artist's model for you. It must have been very distressing. The husband, I believe…'

Henry's conjecture was drowned out by the shouts of his fellow golfers.

'Come on, vicar. Your shot,' bellowed the colonel.

'If you'll excuse me gentlemen, but perhaps we could meet up later,' he said hastily. 'I suspect I have something that might be pertinent to the case, but I'm unsure what to do about it. The police seem determined to charge the husband, but I believe… I think… there may be other agents involved.'

CHAPTER TWENTY-TWO

'Well,' said Venetia, addressing Tippet across the empty plate on which a pastry had sat a few moments earlier. The dog ran its tongue over the plate in search of remaining crumbs. 'Well, well, well. This is most extraordinary.'

Her eyes dropped again to the bottom of the letter whose words she had read and re-read numerous times.

I have it on the good authority of a mutual acquaintance (and who must remain anonymous here, in case this letter should fall into the wrong hands) that you are sympathetic to the plight of Monsieur Dreyfus. I sincerely hope and trust that you would be willing to assist in unmasking the real traitor in this most unfortunate case.

'This is most extraordinary,' she repeated, looking down from her perch above the Grande Rue. People had emerged from their lunches and were now parading up and down the busy shopping street, blithely unaware that the stout, middle-aged lady observing them might as well have been holding a stick of dynamite.

Venetia knew enough about the Dreyfus affair to understand that if the letter's contents were true, then she had in her hand what amounted to the scoop (that horrible American word again) of the century. Or it might be a hoax. The vicar had said that there was more – a folder of evidence to which the covering letter alluded – but not how he had come to be in its possession.

The Reverend Gibson, the poor man, had indeed seemed scared, and rightly so if this letter and its attendant evidence was genuine. He had said that the person who gave it to him had since been murdered and that he was uncertain whom to trust. Venetia shuddered, folded the letter and replaced it in her purse.

If the vicar was correct and the person to whom the letter had been originally entrusted had been murdered, then that would appear to be either the prostitute or the Arab soldier. Those where the only two unexplained deaths to which dear old Henry could be referring. Or was there another, so far undiscovered?

On this sultry late June afternoon, she, Venetia Hall, appeared to be in possession of evidence that could blow open the biggest scandal in French politics of the past ten years. Certainly, since the Panama Canal affair of '92 in which so many people had lost money. And while the enormity of the fact felt quite overwhelming, her novelist's mind was beginning to race. What a delicious book this would all make, although not quite in the style to which her readers were accustomed.

But what was such a sensational document doing in the possession of a common young strumpet in Dieppe? Unless, of course, it had been found on the body of the Arab found drowned in the port. But then surely the document would have been spoiled by immersion in the sea water, and the letter still clasped in her hand was in a good condition. She must quiz the vicar further.

* * *

With growing frustration, Commissaire Frossard sat looking at Pascal Déliquaire, his mute bulk slumped forwards over the table. Despite their best efforts - endeavours that had left the silent brute with yellow and purple bruises and swollen lips - he refused to sign the piece of paper that they repeatedly placed before him.

They had thrown the murdered tart's husband in a cell, waking him throughout the night so that he had slept only fitfully, if at all. They had chucked buckets of cold water over him and left him to shiver in his cellar prison, but all this seemed to make no difference. Indeed, the only time they had been able to instil any sign of desperation in the creature had been when they had attempted to lure him into signing with a jug of cider. The wretch had been calling for strong drink for days and yet, by some act of brute will-power, the prisoner had managed not to weaken and sign.

The examining magistrate, Maitre Toussaint, had always been cowed by Frossard and been only too willing to give the commissaire considerable latitude in his interrogation. But even the pliable Toussaint had grown restless about the fisherman's unwillingness to confess to killing his wife, and had given Frossard until the following morning to either break the man or find sufficient evidence against him.

Part of the commissaire's exasperation was with the shadowy emissaries from Rouen. Why had they found it necessary to kill the girl when surely a degree of coercion would have sufficed? If she had possessed this valuable document then a stiff beating would have revealed its whereabouts. And to murder her in such a grisly manner as to get tongues wagging and promote a scandal. There had even been talk that the infamous Jack the Ripper had moved from London to Dieppe!

But then without her demise, the existence of the document would have no doubt been revealed and its continued concealment was evidently worth more than the life of a wretched prostitute.

At least Frossard no longer had Agent Blanchet to contend with. What on earth had the police authorities been thinking by hiring the son of Nathalie Levallois, the Red Maid of Montmartre herself? It was a question he had asked of his superiors in Paris, but as yet no reply had been received. Knowing the top brass as he did, they would probably prefer the Dieppe police to be staffed by the offspring of priest-hating socialist scum than by patriots such as himself.

Frossard's thoughts once again drifted back to those far-off spring days in Paris. How he had learned to kill other men, as well as women and children, without regret or revulsion. And there had been so many, too many to remember. But the memory of the first man he had executed still lingered - still managed to infiltrate his dreams. The scene had been played out so often in his head that Frossard felt that it would follow him to his deathbed.

He had only been seventeen years of age, having joined the government army for the lack of work in his village. Entering Paris under strict orders to eradicate Communard vermin without mercy, he had pursued a rebel into an alleyway behind a smart boulevard. The rodent-like man with plaster-caked hair and eyes glaring white against his soot-darkened face had thrown up his hands in surrender. The wretch had seemed to grin at Frossard as if complicit in an obscure game, and Frossard had been initially confused by the man's apparent good humour. Later he supposed that perhaps this strange creature had simply been gritting his teeth.

Forcing the man to face the wall, Frossard had fired his Chassepot rifle, thankful for the bolt action so much quicker than the ancient muzzle loader with which he had once poached rabbits and hares. The first bullet had opened a large hole in the seam of the back of the man's tunic and thrown him against the wall. Frossard had come closer for his second shot but wished he hadn't as blood and brains splattered over his own tunic. In future he would use his bayonet for what he heard being called a "coup de grace".

What he would also remember was looking up and noticing that he was being watched from an upper-storey window by a smartly dressed woman and her young daughter. The little girl had turned away in horror, but the woman had shouted 'Bravo!' and clapped her hands, as if she had been watching a play from the box at the theatre. 'Kill them all!'

Frossard had raised an arm as if to acknowledge the woman's applause, before a sudden urge to be sick made him turn and stumble out of sight. The vomit had spilt on his well-polished toecaps. But he had steeled himself. Pierre Frossard would never again bring shame on himself by feeling queasy for killing the enemy. For those priest and king haters, those so-called communards, were less than vermin. And vermin must be destroyed.

Nowadays there were those who would separate the Christian faith from the state, would excise its functions so that the holy Roman Catholic church had no say in the running of the nation. What sort of moral decay would that bring about? That is the disintegration that occurs when you first abolish the monarchy. If every man is born equal, then who is to set the standards for others to follow? Anarchy, in a word, and hadn't we seen what these anarchists do with their bombs?

Which reminded him. He must call on Madame Remy and her delightful daughter. No more being brushed off by surly maids just because he slipped a friendly arm around their waists or ran an appraising hand across their rears. None of those wretches compared to the ripe and sumptuous Marie-Hélène. Promoted, married and redeemed, Frossard viewed his future with an optimism he hadn't felt in over ten years.

The prisoner jerked, as if awakening from a nap, and rolled his bruised face in the direction of Frossard. The man's eyes were swollen shut so that the commissaire couldn't tell whether the brute could see him or not. With a smacking sound from his parched lips, he said.

'A drink. A drink. A cup of apple jack and I will sign.'

Frossard leapt from his chair and shouted for Bastin.

'Do we have any apple brandy in the station?' he asked his subordinate.

'Why, yes, I believe so,' replied Bastin, who had been sipping from the flagon that very morning.

'Fetch it at once as the prisoner will sign in exchange for a cup.'

As Bastin lumbered off as fast as his ungainly bulk would carry him, Frossard all but rubbed his hands with glee. He could already imagine the gratitude of the officers in Rouen at a job well done. All he had to do now was to locate the documents and a posting to Rouen, or perhaps even Paris, was within his grasp.

No more the long years of being overlooked and despised, just because he held views different to those who had decided that they had the right to govern others. Small men and not a patriot among them. *Dieu, le Roi*, as it says beneath the sacred heart of the Vendée. God, the king. Long live the King, Long live the good priests!

Bastin returned with an earthenware flagon, having surreptitiously taken a swig before entering the room.

'Good. Now pour some into a cup for our prisoner,' said Frossard as Pascal's swollen eyes followed the sound of brandy being poured into a tin mug.

With the mug placed before him, Pascal clenched the vessel clumsily between his palms, his fingers, following the interrogation, little more than useless appendages. He lifted the vessel to his lips and swallowed the contents in one go, letting the empty cup fall onto the floor.

'Now sign,' said Frossard, handing Pascal a fountain pen.

By way of an answer, Pascal merely swept the piece of paper off the table, his unsigned confession floating gently onto the floorboards, where it came to rest next to the empty mug.

As Bastin raised a hand to strike the impertinent prisoner across the back of his head, there was a knock at the door, swiftly followed by Renard's face.

'Apologies, commissaire, but there is a man claiming to have important information about the murder. An Englishman. Says his name is Walter Sickert, or something to that effect.'

CHAPTER TWENTY-THREE

The painting expedition to the clifftops had proved a failure. The oppressive heat, albeit tempered slightly by a soft sea breeze, followed by the interruption by the English vicar, had mitigated against the steady concentration necessary for artistic endeavour. Besides, Walter could tell that his companion's thoughts were occupied elsewhere.

Having stored their paints away and folded their easels and reached the welcome shade of the deep lanes that wound their way back into Dieppe, Emile finally broke a long silence.

'So, what do you propose I *do* about the Middleton sisters?' he asked.

'Do? I don't propose you *do* anything for the time being,' replied Walter. 'I believe that Lydia is taking the boat to England with her dear mama sometime in the next week or two. They are visiting Mrs Middleton's sister to arrange a longer stay for Lydia with her cousin in the autumn. No doubt she didn't mention any of this to you.'

'She did not,' confirmed Emile with a tinge of bitterness.

Walter nodded, his suspicion that Lydia was not entertaining serious intentions towards his young friend validated. For her, it was a mere holiday flirtation, the sort of summer romance that Venetia Hall wrote about. To his amusement, La Villain liked having these tales of love amongst Dieppe's English visitors being read aloud to her, Walter simultaneously translating and enjoying himself enormously in the performance.

'Lydia's absence will be your opportunity to call upon Polly, for you both to become more intimately acquainted,' he said. 'It needn't be the sort of occasion to be apprehended, one that might make you both self-conscious.

A light supper in my studio, perhaps, arranged as if by chance. I won't even state a date beforehand.

'In the meantime, I suggest you busy yourself somehow, and allow your friendship with Lydia to slip away as naturally as the turning tide.'

'A poetic image, indeed,' said Emile. 'But how am I to occupy myself while the tide turns. What am I to do when I am suspended from the job that keeps me occupied? Painting the landscape, whilst wholly enjoyable, leaves me too much space for contemplation.'

Walter was about to reply that if Emile had space to consider other matters whilst painting, then he was not properly focused on his subject. For how, if your mind is elsewhere, can you note the exact configuration of the cliffs as they fell away towards Pourville, or the way in which the north-facing chalk was stained brown with the rivulets of soil-stained rain water?

'I have a job for us both,' he said instead. 'I think we need to follow up the vicar's tantalising information about other agents being involved in Jeanne's murder. After all, you must recall the two men that the landlady mentioned to me before I visited Jeanne's home. We should undertake some private detective work, like the famous Sherlock Holmes?'

'Sherlock Holmes indeed!' laughed Emile.

It was the Rogersons who had sent Arthur Conan Doyle's detective stories to Emile, cut from a London magazine in which they were appearing at the time. "These will amuse you," Mr Rogerson had written across the top of one of them in his tiny handwriting. Indeed, they did brighten those long grey winters living with the mute, almost hostile strangers otherwise known as his grandparents.

The Rogersons had corresponded for a while after his mother's death, but regrettably lost touch after Emile was posted with the army to Africa. But when the collection of Sherlock Holmes short stories first appeared in French, Emile had purchased a copy, lending it to Walter. *Détective amateur* had been its French title and Walter had devoured it, returning from a trip to England with two full-length novels featuring the character.

'I think I am in enough trouble with my superiors without playing at being Sherlock Holmes,' said Emile.

'Quite so. I suggest you take a background role while I investigate. Be my Dr Watson, if you like. Involved without being noticeably involved.'

'We shall see,' he replied, putting the matter out of his mind as his thoughts had drifted irresistibly back to Polly. And the more he pondered the possibility of their being together, the more it appealed to him. But wouldn't she think him young and foolish? Then surely Walter wouldn't have raised the possibility if he didn't believe there to be some promise in the match.

And he found himself wondering what his mother would make of the Middleton sisters. Like Walter, she would probably have dismissed Lydia as a flibbertigibbet, although she might have enjoyed her high spirits. But he could imagine his mother being fond of Polly, sisterly almost. The thought was simultaneously comforting and discomforting.

And what would his mother have thought about Emile's treatment by Frossard and the rest of his cronies at the station? She would have been infuriated on his behalf and would perhaps have even intervened. She was afraid of nobody, especially not of self-important former army officers of the conservative persuasion. Hadn't Frossard actively campaigned on behalf of that monarchist Boulanger? Wasn't that why he had been exiled to this Normandy backwater?

'What will happen to Jeanne's husband?' asked Walter, interrupting his young friend's thoughts.

'They'll probably get him to sign a confession and then the court will wave it through. Then they'll transport the guillotine from Rouen and park it outside the prison gates here in Dieppe. There will be quite a crowd, no doubt, even early in the morning. Do you think the husband, this brute Pascal, did it?'

Walter shook his head. 'Not for a minute,' he said.

'Then we must do something. I must do something.'

They carried on in silence, now approaching the outskirts of the town. The afternoon heat shimmered atop the cobbled streets that led to the Grande Rue. Other side roads were in deep shadow, Walter stopping to observe one. Once his eyes had adjusted to the relative dark, Emile noticed that the narrow street contained nothing but a laundry and a butcher advertising horse meat. He tried but failed to see the interest aroused in his friend by such a humble alleyway.

They carried on down the Grande Rue, observed from the first floor-balcony of Maison Grisch by Venetia Hall. Past the Café Suisse they emerged by the fish market, with its tall arched windows in front of which a line of about a dozen carriages awaited the arrival of the afternoon boat from England.

'It's so damnedly hot,' said Walter. 'I have an idea. Follow me.'

Retracing their steps to the fish market, which was now closed, Walter approached La Villain's stall.

'Give me your easel and your pochard,' he commanded, thrusting them beneath his landlady's stall, along with his own. 'I think we should go and bathe. Follow me.'

Criss-crossing their way through the streets between the Grande Rue and the promenade, he led Emile towards the casino.

'We can hire bathing suits here for 50 centimes,' he said. 'A changing hut for a further 75.'

It was only after they stood in their navy-blue striped one-piece bathing suits, wading through the gentle waves of low tide, that Emile was able to share his dreadful secret.

'But Walter,' he said. 'I cannot swim.'

* * *

Venetia and Tippet, the latter panting wildly, had made their way to the casino by the time that Walter and Emile arrived for their sea dip. Seating herself on the terrace among the brightly clothed ladies who sat chatting or reading beneath the awning, she took out her notebook and pencil and began to jot down her observations. These mostly concerned the bathers as they emerged from the little bathing boxes that stood just beneath the terrace wall.

"*The fashionable thing for ladies this season is to bathe in costumes, black knickerbockers and tunic,*" she scribbled, also noting the broad red sash tied around the bathers' waists and the black caps secured with a broad red ribbon and huge coquettish bows on top.

She enjoyed watching the bathers go down in pairs along the line of planks called, rather grandly, the *Estacade*. This translated as the 'pier' ("*Not to be confused with our own grand piers at Eastbourne and Bournemouth,*" she wrote). The Casino's more rudimentary structure led out to the deeper water, into which they could gently lower themselves by way of some steps. For a modest price, it saved them picking their way painfully across the pebbles on the beach.

The baking hot afternoon had flushed out half of the town's English colony, she noted, including the artist Walter Sickert and his policeman friend, who were standing waist deep directly below where Venetia was seated. Sickert appeared to giving the younger man a swimming lesson to judge by the manner in which he was demonstrating the breaststroke action.

If the young policeman really was learning to swim, then he had better beware, she thought. Bathing at Dieppe can be tricky, as she had often informed her readers (and now repeated in her florid longhand), "*because of the sudden shelving of the shingle beach, so that at one moment one is walking on level ground and the next, one is out of one's depth*".

Venetia herself hadn't intended to take to the water, but the oppressive *chaleur* of the afternoon was fast making this a tempting option. Tippet was still panting in the shade beside her seat, which decided her on a different course of action. She pulled herself from her chair, took the little dog in her arms and sought the cool of the casino's interior.

Some wonderful piano music was emanating from the Salle des Fetes and once Venetia's eyes had grown accustomed to the relative gloom, she noticed it was being played by a young man with regrettably long hair. The audience was sparse and the young man, having finished his piece with a dramatic flourish, stood up, bowed and walked off, frowning. Clapping rather too loudly was Colonel Marsden, propped as usual against a pillar and clutching an empty glass.

'Bravo!' he exclaimed. And then noticing Venetia, he added: 'Ah, dear lady, will you join me for a peg of something? A whisky and soda perhaps?'

'No thank you, Colonel, although I might take an ice,' she replied. 'Are you not tempted to bathe on such a gloriously hot afternoon?'

'Pish posh,' he replied. 'Can't understand the idiot fashion. Don't suppose you've come across that Miss Barclay, by any chance. She bathes in a man's rig-out instead of the usual get-up.'

'How do you mean?'

'In striped tights.'

'Is she English?' asked Venetia, itching to take out her notebook and record this amusing anecdote for her readers back home.

'Very much so. Young and pretty and the chief occupation of a certain class of man is to try and get a snapshot of Miss Barclay as she comes down the Estacade.'

Venetia might have taken her leave at this point, except that she had a sudden notion to ask the old sot about the matter that had been darkening her throughout this otherwise serene and cloudless day.

'Tell me, Colonel,' she said. 'Have you been following what is known as the Dreyfus Affair?'

'Dreyfus? The Alsatian Jew? The spy, you mean?'

'The very one,' replied Venetia.

'Well, in strictest confidence, I prefer Germans to the French. I know that's queer, what with living here and everything, but then I don't really mingle with the locals. Be that as it may, one's country is one's country and one shouldn't sell secrets to the enemy.'

'So, you think this Dreyfus was guilty as charged?'

'Why, yes, don't you? He had a fair trial and it was proven that his handwriting was on the secret documents sold to the Germans. Personally, I believe such treason should be met with the death penalty. *La guillotine*!' he added with an almost lascivious flourish, as if describing a particularly attractive lady.

'I don't suppose solitary confinement on a disease-ridden tropical island is much short of a death penalty,' said Venetia.

'Is that where he is now?' asked the colonel, eyeing his empty glass meaningfully. 'May he rot there forever.'

'But there are those who claim he is innocent,' persisted Venetia, eager to gauge what she might call the "public opinion" on the matter. 'They say that the army has become so invested in his guilt that they won't brook any evidence to the contrary.'

'The honour of the army must be upheld,' said the colonel, almost standing to attention as he did so. 'Come and have your ice, dear lady, and I will take another peg of whisky soda. It's the only thing on an insufferably hot afternoon like this. What can we get for your poor doggie, panting so?'

They walked in silence down the corridor that led to the buffet, Tippett trotting obediently at their heels. Venetia wondered whether she should share the contents of the letter with a man who was so convinced of Dreyfus's guilt and so blind to the army's shortcomings.

'What do you think of France being a republic, colonel?' she asked, once he had taken a gulp of his replenished whisky soda. He swilled the glass around in his hand and looked into the liquid as if the answer might be found there.

'I have to say that I prefer our system. That's to say with a queen at the top to guide and advise our ministers. Politicians need something higher than themselves, don't you think?'

'Quite so,' replied Venetia, who was a great admirer of Queen Victoria, but worried what would happen when the day came that her dissolute son would inherit the throne. Waiting so long to inherit the throne could not be good for the man.

'And the Prince of Wales, is he a good thing?'

'Ah, yes, the prince. On which subject, I believe our future king is in Dieppe at the moment,' said Colonel Marsden. 'Visiting the duchess so-and-so…'

'The Duchesse Caracciolo,' said Venetia.

'That's the one. The lady hasn't been seen in the casino since last week and there are private detectives lounging around the harbour. My money says that the prince's yacht is moored somewhere off Dieppe. She's a Jew too, you know, the duchess. Just like the spy Dreyfus. They're everywhere, you know, especially in places you least expect them.'

CHAPTER TWENTY-FOUR

'Walter Sickert?' echoed Frossard. 'The Englishman who's being teaching Agent Blanchet to paint? What a laughing stock that young man has made of himself. The sooner he's permanently out of the way, the better. And what does this Monsieur Sickert want?'

'He claims to have some vital information that might assist in our case,' replied Renard. 'It's Sickert, sir, who discovered the victim.'

These words roused Pascal, who had hitherto been slumped forward on the table. He now reared up and bellowed: 'That's the man who killed my wife! He was in our bedroom, standing over my poor dead Jeanne, her blood all over him.'

Bastin, standing behind Pascal's chair, answered him with slap to the back of his head.

'Keep quiet, you,' he snarled.

'Well, I suppose we ought to hear what the Englishman has to say,' growled Frossard, staring forlornly at the unsigned confession that lay between him and the prisoner. 'Does he speak French?'

'Fluently so,' said Renard, his head around the door. 'He lives with a Polletais fishwife and can even speak their patois.'

'He's a brothel-creeper,' said Pascal, swiftly followed by another slap from Bastin.

'He knows everybody in Dieppe, from the highest to the lowest,' said Renard. 'Lived here, on and off, since he was a lad.'

'What was he doing in the victim's bedroom again?' asked Frossard.

'Looking for the girl. Apparently, he likes to paint her in her room at the *maison close*, but she hadn't turned up for work as usual. The door was open and he went upstairs.'

'The cheek,' blurted Pascal, followed by the inevitable slap. It seemed to make no difference. Bastin was possibly hurting his hand more than he was inflicting pain on the prisoner.

This Englishman was a terrible nuisance, thought Frossard. If only Pascal could have discovered his dead wife, then everything would have been so much simpler. Well, he would let this Sickert make a statement and then the Englishman could go away satisfied in the knowledge that he had done his duty. And they, the police, could continue to persuade Pascal to own up to his crime.

The circumstantial evidence was all there with the history of brutality and the drunken rages. And if they needed to measure his head and the length of his middle finger (or whatever the new Bertillon system advocated) then so be it. He was so obviously the criminal type.

'While I go and speak to the Englishman, clean up the prisoner's face,' he told Bastin. 'Then photograph him, face on and sideways... you know the score. *Un photo d'identité judiciare*,' he added, just in case Bastin hadn't understood. 'Make him look even more savage than he is.'

Standing in the reception area was a tall, bearded man in his mid-thirties, Frossard guessed, with golden hair and a strong jawline. He was wearing a loose, ill-fitting linen suit and stood with his hands behind his back, twiddling with a boater. He watched the commissaire approach with a look that suggested a wary amusement.

'*Bonjour*,' said Sickert, and continued to speak in fluent French. 'I am the man who discovered the dead woman. I am an artist and Jeanne was one of my models. Usually I would paint her – fully clothed, I might add – in her place of work. That's to say the *maison close* run by Madame Marchand just across the Pont Colbert.'

'Wait,' said Frossard, raising a hand. 'Renard, fetch your notebook and write down Monsieur Sickert's testimony.'

Once Renard had done as instructed, Walter resumed his tale.

'On calling on the Maison Marchand, Madame Marchand herself answered the door and informed me that Jeanne had not come to work that lunchtime as usual. It was after midday by this time. She added that two gentlemen had earlier called for Jeanne and when informed that she wasn't at work yet, they asked where she lived.'

'And you naturally went to her house to see if she was there,' said Frossard.

'That's correct. I knocked but the door was open. I then went inside to call her name, but noticed that the living room and kitchen were in complete disarray. A dresser had been pulled forward on to its front, drawers pulled out of chests and contents strewn all over the place... a similar scene in the kitchen. Smashed crockery, copper pots and pans and other cooking utensils lay among cushions that had been ripped apart. Fearing something had happened to Jeanne I called out and then went upstairs...'

'Which is when you found her?'

'Yes.'

'Naked?'

'Naked and dead. Very dead.'

'What did you think had happened?'

'Why of course, like you, I suspected the husband,' said Walter, noticing how Frossard looked at his colleague to make sure he had written down those words. 'I've seen with my own eyes the bruises he has left on that poor woman.'

'The whole of Le Pollet knows how badly he treated her,' said Frossard. 'How did Pascal... the husband... seem to you when he arrived on the scene.'

'Well, he had been drinking. You could smell that at 20 paces. But...'

Walter was going to say that he had seemed genuinely shocked to find his wife dead and had sincerely believed that Walter was the killer. But Frossard had raised his hand again and signalled to his colleague to stop writing.

'Thank you Monsieur Sickert. I believe that you are a permanent resident of Dieppe and that I might find you at the lodgings of a Madame…'

'Villain. Augustine Villain.'

'Oh, yes, of course. She has a stall in the fish market, I believe. Very well thought of and I wish my landlady would buy her fish there. We will be in touch if necessary.'

'The important thing here, in my opinion, is the presence of the two gentlemen callers….'

'Quite so, thank you…'

'They were unlikely to have been customers of Jeanne's professional services,' Walter persisted. 'Surely not two of them together, and at that time of day.'

'Well, you never know. A man of the world like yourself will understand anything can happen in these… these circumstances. But I will speak to Madame Marchand and get her description of these mysterious gentlemen. Now, if you don't mind, I have more immediate business to attend to.'

Frossard clicked his heels and turned, Walter catching a sly, insolent smile on his colleague's face.

* * *

'You have a caller, sir,' announced Clotilde. It was one of the few sentences that the maid had learned to deliver in English. Even then she delivered it with a look that suggested she didn't quite believe the words would be understood.

Henry, sitting rigidly at his study desk, had heard the forceful knocking and feared the worse. Had Mrs Hall taken the letter to the police and now the gendarmes were coming to arrest Henry for being in possession of such a seditious document? In anticipation of an official visit, he had placed the bundle of papers in his desk drawer, ready to be meekly handed over on request. Better to be rid of the things if they are the reason why Jeanne had been murdered. But then he heard his wife's voice in the hall.

'Why Mrs Hall. How good of you to call. Is it Henry you're wishing to see?'

Henry doubted whether Venetia would ever have reason to call on Lucy. He had often detected a coolness in his visitor's demeanour when the subject of Lucy had arisen. A barely veiled sarcasm directed at Lucy's lack of wifely virtues. "Does she not want to help arrange the flowers?", Venetia would ask with a look that wanted to add: "Or is she too busy playing in the casino with her lady companion?"

Henry pulled himself out of his chair – the effort seemed considerable, as if his legs were weighed down– and walked over to the now opened study door. Mrs Hall, her little dog in one hand and passing one of her colourful hats to the waiting Clotilde with the other, looked up as Henry's appeared in the open doorway.

'Excuse my intrusion, vicar. I was passing and thought I might discuss the upcoming flower rota with you. And apologies for having brought Tippet with me but he finds this heat intolerable.'

Ignoring the non-sensical reason for bringing her dog, Henry made a sweeping action with his arm that beckoned Venetia into the study. He noticed Lucy roll her eyes and turn sharply on her heels as he closed the door behind them.

They stood waiting silently as they listened to Lucy clump up the staircase and then Clotilde descend the steps into the kitchen. Lowering the dog on to the carpet, Venetia rummaged inside a capacious bag, retrieving the letter and placing in on Henry's desk.

'I have read this so often that I feel I know every word of it by heart,' she said. 'I am at a loss as to what should be done and rather wish you had never shared it with me.'

'I know, dear lady. I am so dreadfully sorry. It had become an intolerable burden for me to carry alone and I thought…'

'You thought that I was a broad-minded woman with worldly connections who might be able to assist in this dilemma. And I don't entirely blame you for your estimation, but this…'

She pointed at the letter, which had now become somewhat crumpled. 'I feel certain that I am going to regret this request, but may I see the documents that came with it? In for a penny, in for a pound.'

Henry retreated behind his desk and pulled open the drawer. Retrieving the bundle, he pushed it across the desk towards his visitor.

'I haven't investigated further, beyond noting that everything was written in French,' he said. 'There appears to be some scraps of handwriting. Difficult to decipher. And another covering letter, this one written on a typewriter.'

Henry pulled out this letter and handed it to Venetia.

Le Testament de Georges Picquart Avril 1897
En cas de décès du soussigné, remettre ce pli au Président de la République, qui seul devra en prendre connaissance.
G. Picquart
Lieutenant-colonel au 4e tirailleurs.
Sousse, 2 Avril 1897.

'In the event of the death of the undersigned, deliver this letter to the President of the Republic, who alone must take note,' said Venetia, translating the letter heading. 'Dear Lord. What does that mean?'

'For the eyes only of the President of the Republic', supposed Henry.

'Extraordinary. And if it was the president's eyes only, what was it doing in the possession of a cheap tart from the fisherman's quarter of Dieppe?'

Henry winced at the description of his angelic Jeanne as a "cheap tart", but realised that this is how she was seen by everyone, even the enlightened Mrs Hall.

'Presumably it was the messenger that left it with her,' he said.

'Well, I can I hardly believe it was Monsieur Faure,' said Venetia, trying to imagine the president of France frequenting a back-street brothel in Le Pollet. 'Mind you, Dieppe does have more than its fair share of illustrious visitors. I wonder if Monsieur Faure has been here this summer.

'In any case,' she continued, shaking off this whimsical thought. 'I am not sure I wish to read any more of this letter.'

Venetia nevertheless let her eyes run down the page.

Au mois de mai 1896, mon attention avait été attire sur le commandant Walsin-Esterhazy, du 74e d'infanterie…

'Oh, it goes on to name names,' she said. 'I most definitely don't want to be party to this.'

'No,' said Henry, walking over to the study door. Opening it he was relieved to see that the hallway was empty and that Lucy hadn't been eavesdropping. But then why should she have been? Her husband's activities were not of the slightest interest to her. He could hear Clotilde clattering about in the kitchen, otherwise the house was quiet. He closed the door again.

'Who then was carrying these documents and why?' asked Venetia, picking up her little dog, which had begun to whine. 'It's a true mystery.'

The dog made an attempt at licking Venetia's face and she placed him back on the carpet. Henry began to leaf through the folder, much of which was illegible to him, written in a scrawling script in a French language that he anyway struggled to understand.

'Wasn't there talk of that poor man discovered drowned in the port being of Arabic origin?' said Venetia, almost to herself And this covering letter by Picquart, or whatever his name is, was written in Tunisia. Here, let me see again. Yes, Sousse. That's in North Africa, I am certain.'

'Maybe he fell off a passing boat,' suggested Henry. 'But that doesn't explain how the letters came into Jeanne's possession.'

'Jeanne?'

'That was the cheap tart's name,' replied Henry sharply.

'I am sorry, vicar,' said Venetia, after giving him a long, appraising look. 'We are all God's creatures.'

'The last shall be first, and the first last.'

'A most Christian attitude. But we're no nearer understanding how these documents came to be in the tart's… in Jeanne's possession. Oh, just a moment…'

Venetia gave a cry of triumph. She had turned over the covering letter and discovered some words scrawled in ink at the end of the type-written document. 'We have our intended recipient.'

She handed Henry the letter. Scrawled in ink along the bottom were the words 'D.C. Villa Olga'. Henry stared blankly at the signature and shrugged.

'Why, the Villa Olga is the house belonging to the Duchesse Caracciolo. The initials D.C. The villa is down on the old Napoleonic gun battery beside the casino. The black-beamed Norman style manor house named after the duchess's daughter Olga Alberta.'

'The Duchesse Caracciolo? Can you be sure?' asked Henry, who knew that the duchess regularly managed to scandalise the English colony. She was thought to have several gentleman admirers, while her daughter, Olga, was rumoured to be the goddaughter of no less than the Prince of Wales. At the very least, the Prince of Wales regularly visited the villa and the girl's middle name Alberta was said to be in his honour.

'No, but it makes sense,' said Venetia. 'The duchess is thought to be sympathetic to the Dreyfus cause. She has connections with very important people. Who knows? Possibly even with the president of the Republic?'

CHAPTER TWENTY-FIVE

'Astonishing,' said Louis Leblois, not for the first time since Lieutenant-Colonel Marie-Georges Picquart had arrived at his lawyer's office in the 4th arrondissement of Paris. 'Quite astonishing,' he repeated, inspecting the papers through his pince-nez.

The two men had been friends since their schooldays in Strasbourg. The telegram had taken Leblois by surprise, with its announcement that Georges would soon be returning to the city from North Africa and was urgently seeking an audience. He had known that there had been some contretemps with the war ministry that had led to his friend being stationed in Tunis. Not disgraced but seemingly exiled. But Georges had hitherto been tight-lipped about the nature of this disagreement.

But now everything was clear. The dossier that Georges had handed Leblois immediately on entering his office appeared to prove without doubt that the man responsible for passing military secrets to the Germans was not the unfortunate Jew now languishing in solitary confinement on a former leper colony in South America.

'Who else knows about this?' he inquired.

'Apart from the chiefs of staff of the French army?' said Georges with undisguised asperity. 'They are all scared for their positions. I have been spied upon, exiled to the colonies and told in no uncertain terms not to reopen what they call a "dangerous debate". Dangerous for them, I needn't hasten to add.'

Leblois removed his pince-nez and inspected his old friend. He was tanned and healthy-looking after his posting beneath the African sun, and didn't appear to be in the grip of an unhealthy mania. In fact, he seemed to be the same old level-headed, scrupulous Georges towards whom he had been drawn in their first term at the lycée in Strasbourg.

'What would you like me to do with this?' he asked, indicating the pile of papers that lay across his desk, every bit as explosive as a jar of nitro-glycerine.

'Firstly and most importantly, we must *not* inform the Dreyfus family about all that we know – or indeed to give them the slightest suggestion of it. They will run around shouting from the rooftops and agitating for an immediate re-trial. We need to move more carefully in the matter, trusting only those who believe in the cause and who can be trusted to act with prudence.'

'Given the powerful forces aligned against Dreyfus, I think that might be wise,' agreed Leblois. 'The name of one potential ally in this matter has already come to mind. Auguste Scheurer- Kestner.'

Picquart nodded. Scheurer- Kestner was vice-president of the Senate and widely considered the moral conscience of the Republic. Moreover, like Leblois, Picquart and Dreyfus, he was from Alsace and thought of Dreyfus as more of an Alsatian than an Israelite.

'Very good. And Clemenceau? What of him?'

'I think for the moment that would be unwise,' said Picquart after some thought. 'These days Georges Clemenceau is no longer a politician but a journalist and he will almost certainly choose to publicise the matter. In any case, he is a close friend of Scheurer-Kestener, and if Scheurer-Kestener chooses to confide in Clemenceau, then so be it. But we must emphasise the need for caution and discretion in this matter. Not a word of it must reach the ears of the Dreyfus family.'

'On that we are agreed,' said Picquart.

'You look perturbed,' said Leblois, noticing a shadow cross his friend's face.

'I have not told you everything,' he said. 'I believe I might have acted foolishly.'

'How so?'

'There are two copies of this dossier. I thought it best to have some form of insurance against its loss. My experiences last year, when I discovered that my own staff were spying on me and that forgers were at work trying to discredit the evidence I had disclosed, has made me perhaps excessively wary.'

'And this second dossier?'

'I sent it with one of my most trusted subordinates, a native captain with my regiment in Tunis. He was to convey it to a sympathetic newspaper editor in London, by way of another supporter based in Normandy. This person has excellent contacts on the other side of the water.'

'And did he succeed in this mission?' asked Leblois, fearing that he already knew the answer.

'I believe not. The man was supposed to telegraph me as soon as he had made the delivery, but I have heard no more from him. The contact was a lady in Dieppe, a member of European aristocracy and a long-time sympathiser with Dreyfus's cause. If I might have expected to hear from her, then sadly that is not so either.'

Leblois walked over to the window and looked down on the bustling street below. Men, women and children gaily going about their business and their pleasure on this brilliant summer's day in Paris, while Dreyfus sat alone in that tiny hut in the steamy heat of the tropics, denied any fellowship and his every movement observed and recorded by mute prison guards.

'That is most unfortunate,' he said, turning to face Picquart. 'But then *nulla nuova, buona nuova*, as the Italians say. Or no news is good news, as we say.'

'But I also believe that there might be some news. Bad news. I received reports that police in Normandy had been inquiring about a certain military insignia. Insignia that belonged to my regiment. They were trying to identify a dead man.'

'I see,' said Leblois, followed by a long silence as his gaze was directed to a corner of his desk.

'I think that some discreet investigating is in order,' the lawyer said eventually. 'Indeed, I myself could do with some sea air. This heat is making Paris quite unbearable. I believe I have a railway timetable somewhere about the office. Which station do I need for Dieppe?'

* * *

They had arranged to meet at two o'clock outside the casino, Mrs Hall having first scoured the gaming rooms to ascertain whether or not the duchess was in attendance at one of the tables. Since the lady in question hadn't been seen in the casino since the arrival of the Prince of Wales's yacht earlier in the week, Henry agreed that it was unlikely that she would be there now.

After Clotilde had shown his visitor out, he had sat forward in his study chair, put his head in his hands and began to pray. Lord, give me the wisdom to know what to do with these papers, he began. In the silence that followed, he heard footfall on the staircase and then Lucy shouting something at the maid. The door slamming shut had been followed by a deeper silence as Henry attempted to reconnect with his maker.

No obvious answer relaying itself to him, he sat back – determined more than ever that they would deliver the dossier to the duchess and let that be the end of it. Was this renewed resolve by way of the Holy Spirit? Henry would have liked to think so, but he was also aware that he just wanted rid of these papers for which other men seemed willing to commit murder. To wash his hands of the things. Just like Pontius Pilate. No, that wasn't helpful.

The clock on the mantlepiece told him that it was half part twelve. Cooking smells were seeping out of the kitchen and Henry's mouth began to salivate. Such were his jangled nerves that he had failed to eat that morning, foregoing breakfast for a pot of coffee.

* * *

Lunch had been one of Clotilde's better efforts – some well-cooked fish in a creamy sauce with new season turnips and potatoes. He ate furiously, wiping the plate with a piece of bread before tucking into a fruit jelly that had first made an appearance at the previous evening's supper.

He would usually have returned to his study for a nap, but such was his determination to hand over the dossier that he scooped it up and folded the incriminating papers into a satchel. Shouting his thanks for lunch to an unseen Clotilde, he let himself out of the front door and strolled down the side streets that led to the promenade and the beach.

The Duchesse Caracciolo's house was at the far end of the beach, beyond the casino and under the cliff dominated by Dieppe's castle. Recently built in the fashionable ("regrettable", Venetia had called it) black-beamed style of a Norman manor, the Villa Olga was shunned by the ladies of the English colony. The duchess was said to live in sin with two gentlemen admirers beside the Prince of Wales.

Henry had no idea as to the truth of the matter. The duchess's daughter, a renowned beauty after whom the villa had been named, was forever being sought as a model by visiting artists. Musing thus, he noticed Venetia emerging from the casino terrace and, checking his fob watch, noted that it was a little past two.

The importance of their mission was underlined by the fact that Venetia didn't have her dog with her. She must have left the little creature at home – the rarest of occurrences (Henry was quite sure that she would bring the animal to church services if wouldn't have been frowned upon). Noticing Henry, she waved her unopened parasol and began bustling along the promenade.

'You have the thing?' she asked, as if the dossier had become an object of such horror that it was no longer possible to specify its true nature. Henry nodded in reply and they both looked along the beach to where the Villa Olga lay beyond a heat haze.

'This is a civilised time to call,' said Venetia, as if trying to convince herself.

'By all means,' said Henry. 'And we're only delivering a parcel, just like a postman.'

'An excellent analogy. Shall we?'

Together they set off, passing the front of the casino, and then the home of the artist Jacques-Émile Blanche, and finally to the gate leading towards their desired destination. Two men, who were lolling by the entrance to a short front path and smoking cigarettes, unfurled themselves as Henry and Venetia approached.

'Private detectives,' whispered Venetia. 'The prince is in residence.'

'*Bonjour*,' the larger and older of the two men said in an English accent, throwing his cigarette on the ground and grinding it beneath a well-polished boot.

'Good afternoon,' replied Venetia, taking the initiative. 'Is the duchess at home?'

'She cannot entertain callers today, I regret to inform you madam,' the man said in a voice that was straining unsuccessfully not to betray its natural cockney cadences.

'But I have something of utmost importance to give to the duchess,' said Venetia as Henry struggled to retrieve the dossier from his satchel.

'Again, I must tell you that her ladyship is indisposed.'

'That is regrettable,' said Venetia.

'Can I give whatever it is you have to her ladyship?' asked the younger detective, throwing his cigarette to the ground.

Henry and Venetia looked at each other, Henry then nodding his assent. 'I think it probably best to divest ourselves,' he murmured.

'Very good,' replied Venetia, before addressing the younger man. 'But do make sure she receives it personally. Don't hand it to a maid or a butler, but make sure it arrives safely in the duchess's own hands.'

Henry had a sensation of lightness as he handed the dossier over to the younger man. A feeling of relief.

'I promise I will personally hand deliver this,' said the detective, frowning at the pile of papers untidily bundled together.

'Well, good day then,' said Henry tipping his hat. The older man did likewise, while the younger one stared dumbly at the papers.

'What is this rubbish?' asked the older man once the callers were out of earshot.

'Darned if I know, Charlie.'

'Give me a look then.'

'It's all in Froggie language, Charlie.'

'What time are we off?'

'Four o'clock sharp, to catch the tide.'

'Give me those then, Albert.'

The younger man handed over the bundle. Charlie leafed through the top copies and made a sour face. 'A load of old Frog language.' And with this he walked over to the sea wall. The high tide was lapping against the promenade at this point, and with a grunt he threw the bundle into the water. Both men stood and stared as it bobbed about on the surface, slowly bloating and intermittently divesting itself of individual pages like petals falling from a blown rose.

'Bon voyage,' said Charlie, hit with a sudden concern that his action had been foolishly impetuous. What if those papers had been important and it was later ascertained that he had been handed to them with the express desire that they be personally delivered? But recalling the pasty-faced vicar and the blowsy woman, he reassured himself that they couldn't have been of such import to disturb the lady when she was entertaining such a prestigious visitor.

Probably some nonsense to do with the church. He'd never seen any reason to darken those doors, except when he married his Iris. No, he'd done the right thing in dispatching those papers to a soggy grave. And besides, their boat sailed in two hours. By nightfall he'd be safely home with his Iris in Putney, far away from this smelly Froggie port.

CHAPTER TWENTY-SIX

Emile was unsure as to what sort of reception he would receive when he returned to his lodgings. Madame Remy had seemed rather shame-faced when he had confronted her about the anarchist pamphlet being left in his room, but perhaps he had over-reacted.

After all, the poor woman was not knowledgeable about the greater world beyond Dieppe. Beyond her doorstep, if he was to be honest, which is where she claimed to have discovered the pamphlet. And he had never seen her read anything, not a newspaper or a magazine let alone a book. So perhaps all writing was as one to her, just meaningless symbols as mysterious as the hieroglyphics of Ancient Egyptians were to Emile.

Neither Madame Remy nor Marie Hélène were at home when he let himself in, however, which was unusual. The little maid who did most of the scrubbing and polishing appeared in the hallway, evidently on her way home to wherever she lived. She bobbed her head shyly, eyes averted, and pulled on her overcoat.

He made his way to his bedroom, behind which door the uniform now hung like a sloughed skin. He had been ordered to surrender the kepi to Frossard, as if the headpiece was somehow symbolic. Throwing himself backwards on to the hard little mattress, he thought again where else he might live.

Several disturbing undercurrents in Emile's life were beginning to converge. No, worse than that; they were coming together at pace. The likely inroads on his savings, now that he was suspended without pay, was the least of those matters troubling him.

Much more disturbing was the case of the twin murders. And Emile had no doubt that the killings were allied. He had only dimly made the connection before, but he was now guiltily certain that he had been the unwitting agent of Jeanne's demise.

Walter had told him about the fez in Jeanne's boudoir and Emile had relayed the information to Frossard. Naturally he would not have suspected his police boss of involvement in the prostitute's murder, but this was a coincidence so strong as to be persuasive. After all, Frossard had been unnaturally interested in the dead Arab sailor and seemingly obsessed with finding something that might have been in the drowned man's possession.

It was the way in which he had had his men ransack the cave dwelling of the brothers who discovered the drowned Arab. How he'd pulled the wretches in for some forceful questioning that had left each man black and blue. Frossard was being driven beyond the normal bounds of police conduct – or human morality, it appeared – by a mysterious object of desire.

Emile's first thoughts were that it must be treasure of some sort – gold or diamonds, perhaps. Frossard had never struck him as a particularly greedy man. Embittered and not a little vain, but not avaricious. But then perhaps everybody has their price, and his boss was getting on in years with very little material security to show for them.

That Frossard was somehow involved, he now had little doubt, apparently abetted by these two strangers who had approached Jeanne's employer on the morning of her murder. Perhaps there was a way of flushing out these killers, of luring them to self-exposure. Walter had compared themselves to Sherlock Holmes and Dr Watson. What would Holmes have done?

He would have done something. And Emile was aware of being at a crossroads. To act or not to act. To be or not to be. The Rogersons had encouraged him to read Shakespeare. So many great sayings. What was the one that he really liked? Something about there being a tide in the affairs of man, which, if taken at the full, led to something good. And if not taken, then led to disappointment. He'd have to ask Walter. His friend had often spoken of being an actor in his younger days and would surely know his Shakespeare.

Walter had tried to tried to sooth the feelings of guilt that had overcome Emile, telling him that any proficient police officer would have passed on to his superiors the information about the fez. After all, it was a vital clue. And then he thought of the poor girl whose life had been lost, her naked corpse carted off to the morgue in a bundle of blood-soaked sheets and blankets.

Lying there, staring up at the white-beamed ceiling, Emile's thoughts drifted unexpectedly to his parents. Because of their physical likeness, he had always believed (feared, more like) that he took after his father. The drunken armchair revolutionary Ludovic. 'Ludo' for short, like the new board game from England that Lydia liked to play with Polly and Walter and anybody else who came within her orbit. Strangely she had never asked Emile to play – another sign, perhaps, of their incompatibility. Or did she sense his aversion to such games?

Was he fated to be like his father? Or might he learn to become more like his mother, the woman of action? She never failed to do the right thing, even when the right thing was so detrimental to her own well-being. Whether leaving home at 15 to support herself as a seamstress in Paris, and therefore not burdening her parents with a useless mouth to feed, or dutifully sacrificing a more profitable future in England by returning to these same parents in their old age, she always took what she saw as the correct path.

No, he must try and follow her example and not fatalistically submit to becoming like his father. Ludo the children's board game… how apt! His mother had said how her father liked to sit in London taverns and play draughts with fellow exiles. Emile had never had a fondness for such games, even when living with the Rogerson children. They had preferred dressing up and inventing plays to amuse each other.

His eyes fell upon the uniform hanging from the back of his bedroom door. It's blue colouring was brilliantly illuminated by sunlight pouring in through an adjacent open window, through which he could hear some sparrows arguing in the eaves. The scarlet piping on the trouser legs also looked especially radiant in this light.

Despite what his father might have thought of his son wearing the costume of state authority, Emile had always been proud of this uniform. People called him a *mouche*, or a fly, the old word for police informers or spies that still lingered among the population at large. But he believed that he served a purpose in protecting these very same people from murderers and thieves. But what if these very thieves and murderers wore this uniform?

Emile swung his legs over the side of the bed and pulled himself to his feet. Stopping only to run his hand down the disembodied tunic, he opened the door and ran downstairs, without even acknowledging Madame Remy and Marie-Hélène who had seemingly returned from an errand, their mouths hanging open as he pushed by. And out of the door. The late afternoon heat that hit him like a purge. He had a plan.

* * *

Frossard sat behind the table, clenching and unclenching his fists. The victim's husband, Pascal Déliquaire, was no longer seated opposite him, having been freed on the orders of Maître Toussaint. The magistrate had finally reached the end of his considerable latitude in the matter.

'Don't worry, Commissaire,' Toussaint had said obsequiously. 'You can always pull him in again at a later date, when you have more evidence. A witness would be better. Could this English artist be persuaded perhaps… no, pretend I never said that.'

'Well, I suppose Pascal's not going to run away,' Frossard had replied with a wink. 'He hasn't got the wit. Or the sobriety.'

If only the man would fall drunk from the jetty and drown. How convenient that would be for everybody, he thought, as he sat waiting for Bastin and Renard. They had been sent to fetch Madame Marchand, the owner of the *maison close* where Jeanne Déliquaire had worked.

A long-ago former prostitute herself, Madame Marchand had run the little brothel in Le Pollet for more than two decades without any reported problems. Her licence was renewed each year without hesitation. She obeyed all the regulations, including the requirement to shine a red light during business hours.

Unlike some of the establishments that Frossard had visited during his posting in Paris - sometimes on police business, at other times for his private pleasure – the three licensed brothels in Dieppe had no garish names such as Miss Betty's or (one of his favourites) Temple of Peeping Toms. The number of prostitutes in Dieppe were augmented by women who hung around in the port's bars waiting for visiting sailors, while Parisian courtesans pursued their wealthier clients to the town during the summer season, installing themselves in the sea-front hotels.

Frossard had never had any luck with women, something he put down to his small stature. This in turn he blamed on the food shortages and almost perpetual hunger of his childhood in the Vendée – although both his parents had been short, perhaps for the same reasons. He was glad that Agent Blanchet was no longer around to tower over him; the differences in their heights always put Frossard at an immediate disadvantage.

He had thought that maybe his commissaire's uniform, along with the sword that a man of his rank was expected to carry, might impress some of the ladies. But they seemed to find something almost comical about the way he strutted around Dieppe. Urchins would sometimes openly laugh at him, Frossard thinking that if they knew what he had done to children in Paris all those years ago, they wouldn't be so cheeky.

He occasionally made a drunken grab at his maids but nothing ever came of that, the young women fleeing his employ soon afterwards. Word seemed to have spread because he had increasing difficulty in finding anyone to keep house for him. His current cook was too ugly to lunge at, perhaps the reason why she had stayed longer than most. But her cooking was terrible and she didn't clean properly.

But the young Remy daughter – Marie-Hélène – there was a different prospect! She was ample of bosom and clear of complexion and seemed the obedient sort. She was used to cooking and housework and was youthful and strong. Frossard could already imagine her looking after him in old age. Perhaps they might even have a child or two. He had never imagined becoming a father, but a pair of dutiful daughters might be rather pleasant.

His musings were cut short by footsteps clattering across the floorboards of the main office, swiftly followed by Renard's face appearing around the opening door.

'Madame Marchard, sir,' he announced, swinging the door wide. A dignified woman in her late fifties stepped into the room, the visitor removing a feathered hat to reveal faded auburn hair piled in ringlets on top of her head. Frossard's eyes followed the generous curve of her breasts, down her green satin dress, and around her tightly corseted waist.

'Madame,' said Frossard, standing up and giving an extravagantly deep bow. She merely nodded in acknowledgement and sat down on the chair recently occupied by Pascal Déliquaire. Her posture was upright and her expression defiant, and Frossard knew that he would have to tread carefully with his mission. After all, she had lived her whole life in Dieppe, and who knew what important personages she could list as current or former clients?

'What is the meaning of this?' she demanded. 'I run a clean and honest establishment.'

'You are in no trouble, madame' said Frossard, raising his hands defensively. 'It is merely to ask you a favour. We renew your licence each year without hesitation and would very much like to continue doing so.'

'A favour with a veiled threat attached,' replied Madame Marchand, staring unflinchingly at Frossard through flint-grey eyes.

The commissaire laughed uneasily. He had handled himself clumsily, having hoped to make himself understood without his methods being thrown back in his face.

'If you like,' he said. She didn't reply, but a faint smile had appeared on her lips, which reassured him.

'You see,' continued Frossard. 'A witness has come forward to say that on the morning of Madame Déliquaire's murder, you told him that you had received a visit from two gentlemen inquiring about Madame Déliquaire's whereabouts.'

'By this witness, I take it you are referring to the English artist Walter Sickert. That is what I told him because that is exactly what happened. Two rather unpleasant-looking gentlemen, in my books. And believe me, I've seen a few.'

'They were policemen.'

'I see,' said Madame Marchand, frowning. 'And why were they asking for my Jeanne?'

'It's a delicate matter and I'm afraid I can't give you any details. In fact, it was a highly secret matter of state importance. A matter of state. The government…'

Frossard realised that he was making a bad fist of his explanation, his visitor frowning ever more deeply.

'My Jeanne was of interest to the government?'

'Well, not her precisely, but something that might have come into her possession.'

'And did they find what they were looking for?'

'I am not at liberty to say, madame.'

'Did they kill Jeanne?'

The bluntness of her question took Frossard aback. He blustered: 'No, certainly not. Why ever should they do that?'

'To find what they were looking for,' said Madame Marchand, her gaze level and the complicit smile vanished from her lips.

'I can assure you not. I believe they spoke to Madame Déliquaire, who denied having the thing that they were looking for. And then they left.'

'You believe they spoke to her?'

'Madame Marchand,' blustered Frossard, attempting to rediscover his footing but realising that the ground on which he was standing was shifting and treacherous. He must attempt to give some halfway plausible explanation for the men's visit. 'These are gentlemen of the utmost probity and would never think of raising a hand to a woman. Unlike the poor woman's husband, of course…'

'Then why have you released Pascal? By the look of his face, you have no compunction against raising a hand against a man.'

'Please Madame Marchand, I must ask you not to make such wild accusations. We did not exceed the usual force required in such important police work. The simple fact is that, for the moment, we lack the requisite evidence to convict Monsieur Déliquaire. But fear not, we will find it. Perhaps while you are here, you may give me the names of any other of Jeanne's customers who might, shall we say, be of a suspicious type.'

'I'm sorry *monsieur le commissaire* but the privacy of our services is much valued by our clients. Besides,' she added with a stage whisper, looking towards the door. "There's one or two here that might like not to be named.'

Bastin or Renard, Frossard asked himself? He could imagine both of them availing themselves of a prostitute's services. For the first time, he felt a spasm of pity for the dead woman.

'Mind you, there was one,' said Madame Marchand. 'He didn't look dangerous but he was an odd one alright. An Englishman. A priest, I think Jeanne said. Didn't want any of the usual services to speak of, more like he wanted to save Jeanne's soul.'

'Very interesting,' said Frossard, suddenly alert.

'Henri,' I believe. 'Pronounced the English way.'

'That's very useful indeed Madame. In the meantime, I must ask you remain silent about these two gentlemen callers. I cannot over-state the need for secrecy on this matter. You must forget all about these men. They never existed. Your continued livelihood depends on your compliance in this matter. Do I make myself clear?'

Madame Marchand stood up and, fixing him with a contemptuous glare, said: 'Perfectly clear, Commissaire Frossard. Perfectly clear.'

CHAPTER TWENTY-SEVEN

*'There is a tide in the affairs of men
Which, taken at the flood, leads on to fortune;
Omitted, all the voyage of their life
Is bound in shallows and in
miseries...* Now, how does it go from there?'

Emile watched his friend with a growing sense of wonder. Standing at his full height and striking a dramatic pose in the middle of the faded Persian rug, Walter, whom Emile thought of as a much older brother or an uncle, was transformed into a youth of Emile's age. His hair seemed that much more golden, his complexion clearer.

'Oh yes. That's right. Here goes:
"*On such a full sea are we now afloat;
And we must take the current when
It serves,
Or lose our ventures.*'

Walter gave a deep bow to signal the end of his performance. Emile began to applaud.

'Brutus in *Julius Caesar*,' continued Walter. 'He's urging his fellow conspirator Cassius to do something or other nefarious... the exact details elude me. You know I was once the envy of my fellow actors for my ability to learn great swathes of Shakespeare off by heart. Ah, yes, my 'salad days' - to quote again from Shakespeare. *Antony and Cleopatra*. I believe Cleopatra was referring to her youthful infatuation with Julius Caesar as her "salad days" ...'

Emile realised that Walter, his gaze fixed somewhere above Emile's head, was now deep in a reverie. In fact, his friend was remembering his time as a 'general utility player' in George Rignold's touring production of *Henry V*. That time in Manchester when Rignold, taking the title role, appeared in full armour and mounted on a real horse, until the unfortunate animal fell through the stage. Walter, whose job it was to hold the horse's bridle, just managed to let go in time before the beast crashed through the boards.

His most prized memory of those far-off days was however his association with Henry Irving, and with Walter's puppyish infatuation with Irving's protégé Ellen Terry. He would never forget the enchanted morning that had been spent escorting this goddess of the stage around Regent Street, seeking out suitable gowns for her Desdemona.

'Do you ever regret foregoing acting for painting?' asked Emile. The question seemed to snap Walter out of his reverie.

'One has to choose, you know,' he replied. 'I enjoyed the company of actors. Even the ones who'd started out in the circus and had difficulty getting sober by time of the evening performance. How they drank! And the applause… there's nothing quite like it. But you, young Emile, what brought this famous Shakespearean oration to mind? Have you reached a full tide in your own affairs? Perhaps you have realised that the time is ripe to court Polly?'

Walter retreated to the battered little leather armchair in one corner of the studio, his turn now to play the audience.

'No, not that. Although I was indeed most interested in your thoughts about the differences between Polly and Lydia…'

'Do you know the biggest difference,' interrupted Walter. 'The biggest difference is that Polly is here in Dieppe while Lydia is no longer present. She took the morning boat to England, accompanied by her mother and Little Lil.'

'Gone?' said Emile, a little forlornly.

'Gone. I believe she said she would write once she had settled at her cousin's. But now - don't you see? - the coast is clear.'

'But Walter, that was not on my mind. It seems however that you were correct in your assessment of Lydia's fondness for me. A passing flirtation… a holiday plaything…'

'Please, stop, Emile. Lydia was genuinely fond of you. But she is immature. But what was this other matter?'

It took a few moments for Emile to collect himself. A few weeks earlier and he would have felt perplexed and deeply wounded by the news of Lydia's sudden departure. Now, however, his abandonment felt like a sharp but sudden jab, painful in the instant but leaving no lasting discomfort. On later reflection he would feel relieved that the matter had not been drawn out with lingering, repeated farewells and increasingly insincere expressions of amity. No doubt Lydia felt the same. For now, however, he must return to the reason for his visit.

'I came today because I've been thinking about what you said about us playing at being detectives. You as Sherlock Holmes and me as your Dr Watson. But I must be Holmes in this matter. That's to say I must take the lead. I am after all still nominally a policeman because I'm not entirely sure how far Commissaire Frossard has taken the matter of my suspension. Is it indeed official? He seems to be acting as a mini republic within the Republic and I don't trust him.'

Walter pressed the fingers of both hands together and looked up at his young friend, his expression taking on a new intensity.

'What has been troubling me, 'continued Emile, 'Is the connection between the dead Arab and Jeanne. Now, you told me you'd seen a fez in Jeanne's bedroom when you painted her, and I passed that information to Frossard, thinking that there might be a possible connection. After all, the dead Arab was seemingly a soldier or sailor – uniformed at least. And Jeanne, was, well…'

'A strumpet,' said Walter. 'A dollymop. A piece of mutton…. The English language is rich in such metaphors. The fact is that she was a lovely girl.'

'I never had the privilege,' said Emile, realising that he sounded prim. 'But anyway, the next thing we know is that Jeanne has been murdered.'

Emile picked up the train of his thoughts, suddenly aware that he was standing in the exact same spot on the Persian rug from which Walter had earlier recited the Shakespearean speech, and in almost the exact same posture. The painter continued to view him over the top of his conjoined hands.

'And then there are the two men who called on the *maison close* that morning and who were redirected to Jeanne's home address. Just hours later you discover Jeanne's ransacked house and Jeanne lying dead upstairs. Who were these two men and what were they looking for?'

'I have reported that matter to Frossard,' revealed Walter. 'He didn't appear to think these two men of any importance. Or perhaps he simply had a convenient suspect in this wretched Pascal, Jeanne's husband. In my opinion, brute that he may be, Pascal is not our man. Even when severely inebriated, why would he wreck his own home and murder his wife in such a vile fashion? A black eye here, a smashed plate there. But murder? Even in a drunken rage, I don't think him capable.'

Emile's attention was taken by a movement outside of the windowed studio door. Polly was emerging from the cottage across the courtyard, a shopping basket in her hand. She didn't look towards the studio but opened her parasol and set off on her errands.

'Polly is to become a mademoiselle again,' said Walter, following his gaze. 'Or rather, she is to obtain a divorce. Unlike my own unfortunate casting asunder, in France it can be completed in a matter of weeks instead of years. The English are so backward in such matters. *Vive la revolution!*'

'Back to the matter at hand,' said Emile sternly. He had no wish to contemplate Polly's marital status at the moment. Walter seemed to think that Emile was able to switch his affections between the sisters with the facility of a circus rider changing horses in mid gallop. He said: 'The fact is, I have a plan. A plan to flush out the real killers.'

* * *

'What in heaven's name were you doing visiting a prostitute?'

In heaven's name, indeed, thought Henry. Lucy stood in front of his desk while Alice, he knew, was listening from the other side of the closed study door. Three policemen had come knocking shortly after breakfast. None of them spoke English so that Clotilde had had to translate, much to her difficulty and his humiliation. "They want to know if you have meeting with the *prostituée assassinée*," the maid had said, her eyes unable to meet Henry's. Lucy appeared in the hallway at that moment, providing a more spontaneous translation.

'I had gone to save her soul,' he said now, standing up from behind his desk so that he now towered over his wife instead of vice versa. Lucy gave a short bitter laugh and said: 'Oh please, Henry. Don't be so pathetic. There's only one reason why men visit women like that and it's not for their spiritual welfare.'

'That's where you're very much mistaken,' he replied, making an effort to restrain his quickening temper. 'You'll recall our good friend in London, the Reverend Stimspon, and the way he rescued many fallen women and led them to the convent where their lives were subsequently transformed…'

'You are telling me,' Lucy interrupted, grinning at Henry in a most hostile manner. 'You are telling me that you had taken it upon yourself to do such work among the fallen women of Dieppe?'

'No, not exactly,' replied Henry, suddenly aware that he and Lucy were currently engaged in their longest verbal exchange in months. Was Alice enjoying the conversation from her listening post in the hallway? Or did she for once feel excluded?

'It's just that I have had something of a crisis of faith,' he continued. 'Now that you are pressing me to explain, I am not sure that I can in simple terms. Or rather, I will attempt to explain, but you might have to offer some forbearance…'

'Forbearance? I'll offer you forbearance as soon as you explain exactly what you were doing visiting a fallen woman who has subsequently been murdered. And what was this object that the policemen seemed so desperate to retrieve?'

'Oh that. I know not,' Henry lied, relieved to be able to glide over the matter of the dossier. At least that was no longer sitting on his bookshelf like a guilty conscience. 'As I was attempting to say, I have experienced something of a crisis – not of faith perhaps, but of how I spread the Lord's words and do His work.'

'Please don't be sanctimonious with me, Henry. I'm not in your congregation now. Exactly why did you visit this… forgive me if I must use the word… this prostitute?'

'I am simply trying to explain, my dear,' Henry said, noticing Lucy flinch at his use of an endearment. 'I have been growing increasingly weary of facing the same flock each Sunday and delivering sermons to a sea of blank faces. You should view the congregation from where I stand. Their expressions are so vacant, each and every one of them hoping that I do not drone on for too long.'

'Then you probably need to write some more challenging sermons,' said Lucy. 'I must say that you've seemed off your game of late.'

'I'm glad you noticed. But I am often of the impression that I could recite *The Owl and the Pussycat* each Sunday and it would make no difference to the mute reaction of my listeners. Perhaps they would prefer it. Increasingly of late, I feel as if they are either in church out of a sense of duty or it's to see and be seen by the town's English community.'

'That is also undeniably true. But they also come to replenish their souls.'

'And their souls probably need replenishing. Forgive me, that was not Christian of me. Or perhaps it was Christian of me. There. You can see what a muddle I am in. The truth is that they probably think that their souls are hale and hearty and require no attending to.'

'How can you be sure of that? It seems most presumptuous.'

'Well, my point is this. Shouldn't I be administering to those who have truly fallen by the wayside? The thieves and the fallen women?'

'And the murderers too? The one that murdered your little friend in Le Pollet?'

Lucy glared at him with a look of triumph. Henry slumped back down onto his chair, resting his elbows on the edge of the desk with his face in his hands. 'Poor sweet Jeanne,' he murmured.

'Poor sweet Jeanne, did you say? *Jeanne*? How well did you know this girl?'

'Oh, hardly at all,' answered Henry with a dismissive wave of his hand. He looked up and stared at his wife's frozen countenance. 'Twenty minutes, perhaps less and maybe more. We talked about her soul and she prayed with me. But the fact is that she showed me more love, or more compassion, than you have in the last 20 years of our marriage.'

There was an audible gasp from behind the study door, followed by the sounds of footsteps running up the staircase. Lucy's initial instinct seemed to be to race after Alice, but then she obviously thought better of thereby admitting that her companion had been listening in to their conversation.

'How dare you?' she said now, turning on him with blazing eyes.

'And how dare you assume that the only reason to consort with fallen women is to avail yourself of their services? If you spent as much time reading the scriptures as you do frittering away your inheritance at the casino, you would know what the Lord said. "Truly, I say to you, the tax collectors and the prostitutes enter the kingdom of God before you".'

'You have quite lost your mind,' Lucy said, turning and striding to the door. She looked back at him as if to speak again but seemed to decide against it. Henry closed his eyes, listening to the study door slamming shut and Lucy running upstairs as fast as her little legs would carry her.

CHAPTER TWENTY-EIGHT

Emile had been feeling apprehensive about his first time alone with Polly, rehearsing potential scenarios in his head. Should he acknowledge that fact that Walter had been encouraging a match, perhaps even make a joke about it? No, that would be tasteless and open to misunderstanding. He couldn't quite shake off the sense that Polly was older than him in years, despite being the same age, and he worried that she might find him callow. But then why should she? As Mrs Middleton had observed during that first evening together, Emile had experienced much for one so young.

After Walter had put the idea of her being more suitable a match than Lydia, and with Lydia decamping to England without even a word, the realisation that he found Polly the more attractive sister – that his eyes were indeed drawn more to her – was becoming ever clearer.

But how would these nascent feelings stand up to reality? After all, he hardly knew Polly beyond the bare outline of her life: that she was the mother of a three-year-old girl, and that she was currently divorcing a husband who no longer cared for her (if he ever had done). That she was clearly devoted to her mother and was bound to her in their quixotic odyssey around the more affordable corners of Europe.

Polly was as quiet as Lydia was talkative, and seemed worldly wise in equal measure to Lydia's immature frivolity. It was a hard-won wisdom, of that Emile had little doubt, but also innate. There was a dignity to her that he recognised, a dignity that his own mother had carried throughout her tragically fore-shortened life. But since Walter had planted the seed in his mind, and the seed had sprouted, he was afraid that he might be running ahead of himself.

In the event, their first meeting alone had a force of circumstance that overcame his initial trepidation. He had been hatching a plan with Walter to flush out Jeanne's killers.

Emile would go to the police station and inform Frossard that he knew the whereabouts of the dossier. The English artist Walter Sickert had it in his possession, he would say, and was intending to take it back to Great Britain on the morning sailing. Frossard must act quickly to retrieve it. Emile would tell him that it was currently stored in Walter's studio.

This was all too plausible since Walter had discovered Jeanne's body and clearly been in her confidence. And on reflection, Emile was surprised that Frossard hadn't already made a search of Walter's studio. But then perhaps it was easier for his henchemen to rough up a poor prostitute than an eminent English artist.

For the execution of his plan, the location was unsurpassable. The Tour aux Crabes, being a dead-end at the top of a long steep flight of steps, would provide no easy means of escape for the killers. They would be trapped.

To provide muscular back-up, Walter would ask La Villain to approach some suitably burly friends among the fishing community. They were horrified by the manner of Jeanne's murder. The dead woman was one of their own and much liked despite her feckless husband. The plan was that they would be secreted in the Middletons' cottage across the little courtyard, ready to emerge once the killers entered Walter's studio and no doubt started ransacking the place. Given the brutality meted out to Jeanne, they would need to be armed.

Walter reacted to the plan with undisguised glee. First, he added with a knowing look, Emile ought to pay a visit to Polly to obtain her permission for the use of her home as a hiding place for the fishermen.

Polly answered the door with a fleeting but warm smile and beckoned Emile to follow her inside. With her standing before him and silently searching his face, Emile realised that he had never before noticed the colour of her eyes. They were an unusual blue flecked with brown.

'Mrs Middleton,' he began.

'Polly,' she corrected.

'Polly. Walter and I have been devising a possibly foolhardy plot to try and catch the killers of the poor fallen woman in Le Pollet.'

'Jeanne, yes. Walter has told me all about it. Terrible… quite terrible. Tell me about your plot.'

Emile explained his idea, gratified by how easy he found speaking to Polly. Oh, Lydia would no doubt have clapped her hands and exclaimed how exciting it all sounded, but her sister listened quietly, nodding occasionally, and only interrupting to ask salient questions.

'How would the fishermen know when to intervene? Would Walter be in his studio when these ruffians arrive?'

'We would need some sort of look-out,' said Emile, who had also pondered this aspect of his scheme. 'I think it might be too risky for Walter to be in residence when they arrive. And if the studio is locked, that would force them to break in, which would give us the signal we require. Even an excuse to intervene.'

'Or at least they would knock loudly,' said Polly. 'And the top of the steps would provide a good vantage point for a look-out.'

Emile was gratified that she seemed to be taking his plan seriously. She was now looking around the small vestibule to the cottage as if appraising likely hiding places for the fishermen.

'Polly, may I ask? Is this asking too much of you? After all, it's a risky business. These men, if they do fall for my ruse, are dangerous people.'

Polly smiled and said: 'I think it's a good plan, Emile. Any opportunity to catch these people red-handed has to be grasped. But what if it transpires that your commander…'

'Frossard.'

'If Frossard is behind it all? Where would that leave you? It would become apparent that you had tricked him into sending these characters to Walter's studio and that might land you in deep trouble.'

But Emile had already crossed the Rubicon, as his mother used to say. Mrs Rogerson had taught her that expression, which had something to do with Julius Caesar doing something from which there was no turning back. It was a river, he believed. His mother had crossed many a Rubicon in her life, unlike his father, who forever sat on the river bank, too fearful or just too plain lazy to cross.

In any case, Emile saw no future with Frossard still in command of his destiny. And if he could somehow prove that the commissaire was behind the murder of Jeanne, and possibly of the dead Arab, then at least he would have removed that particular obstacle.

'I am quite clear that now is the time to act,' he said.

'Good,' she said, lightly taking his hand in hers before letting it go and dropping her eyes towards the hallway floor. He stood there silently until she raised her eyes again, the blue eyes flecked with brown.

* * *

'You are sure to love Dieppe, my dear. It is the most extraordinary thing – such a simple place and yet people come here again and again, year after year. It is like Venice, you know, and Florence…'

Resisting a snort, Venetia reached inside her bag and retrieved her pencil and notebook. The English ladies at the next-door table to Venetia's regular perch on the terrace of Maison Grisch had been providing such amusing snippets of conversation that she felt duty bound to relay them to her readers.

'I don't mean to look at,' continued the woman, robed in a voluminous white dress, her white hat topped by a fluffy white goose feather. 'I mean in the affection it inspires in those that visit. It is quite a joke that people who once come to Dieppe always come back again.'

It was an observation Venetia had made many times to her readers back in England, and she wondered whether the lady was simply regurgitating one of her magazine articles. She slipped the notebook and pencil back into her bag and contemplated Tippet. The little dog, resigned to the fact that no more brioches were forthcoming, had settled down to slumber.

Venetia herself felt anything but restful. Having disposed of the damning dossier and therefore handed on any responsibility for its contents, so to speak, she had thought that she could put it out of her mind. But its revelations were so explosive that she could not simply forget them. And what if the Duchesse Caracciolo, instead of passing them to their intended recipient in London, the newspaper editor Rachel Beer, were to simply hand them in to the French authorities?

The two private detectives at the gate might also have inspected the documents before passing them to the duchess, although their contents, being mostly in French, would no doubt have mystified them. They didn't seem like the most educated of men. But they might have been able to identify the donors if asked, the English vicar and an English lady in a floral hat.

The women on the next table were now discussing the best addresses for summer lodgings and the delights of playing the 'little horses' at the casino.

'They don't attract me,' said the one who so far had done more than her fair share of listening. 'I think they are so stupid going round and round. I think the music is much preferable.'

Venetia was overcome with a violent and unexpected desire to stand up and leave. The dichotomy between her usual agreeably humdrum life in Dieppe and the explosive document she had recently witnessed, was becoming too much to bear. It was as if she was living two separate lives, one light and ordered the other dark and chaotic. She wondered how the vicar was taking it all. Dear old Henry had seemed positively cheerful at having been relieved of that sensitive bundle of papers. But perhaps now he was suffering similar after-effects to Venetia.

'We've opened Pandora's Box and can't seem to close it,' she said to herself under her breath, albeit loud enough for the two English ladies to look over at her with quizzical expressions.

'Dieppe really is a most engaging town,' Venetia said now, covering her verbal outage. 'I couldn't but not overhear your conversations, ladies. I must agree wholeheartedly.'

'Emily Partridge,' said the woman in white, introducing herself with a slight bow of the feathered head. 'And this is my friend Mrs Alfred Baker.'

'Venetia Hall,' said Venetia. 'Otherwise known as Edgar Stanton Lister.'

Emily Partridge looked non-plussed but Mrs Alfred Baker nearly flew out of her chair.

'Why, the author of tales of military valour?' she exclaimed. 'And I read all Venetia Hall's letters from Dieppe in *The Citizen*. To be perfectly frank, they are the reason that I am visiting. She... I mean you... make it sound such a magical place. What an honour.'

'The honour is all mine,' said Venetia, deeply gratified. 'It is always such a pleasure to meet a reader.'

'What excitements can we expect this season?' asked Mrs Alfred Baker, filling Venetia with an unexpected ennui. This was the sort of query she would normally pounce upon with delight.

'Why, people don't visit Dieppe for excitement,' she replied, trying to keep the weariness out of her voice. 'There are scarcely any "At Home" days, because everybody meets everybody else at the casino. And, instead of asking your friends to afternoon tea, you take them for a lemon squash, or a sherry-cobbler, or some other out-of-the-way drink, in the casino's great refreshment room.

'In any case,' she concluded. 'Dieppe is such a little place where everybody meets everybody else, morning, noon, and night. And on that note, I'm afraid I must leave you. But rest assured, we shall be reacquainted very soon. That is the charm of Dieppe for you.'

The ladies seemed taken aback by Venetia suddenly rising to depart, but she was so overtaken by a desire to curtail their company that she couldn't worry about social niceties. Taking Tippet in her arms, she bowed and attempted a smile, before descending the cool dark marble staircase that led back on to the Grande Rue.

It was only a short walk by the back streets that surrounded the great church of Saint-Rémy, with its confusion of Gothic and later additions, to the casino. As murderers were said to be compelled to revisit the scene of their crime, Venetia felt drawn to the gaming rooms where she hoped she might espy the Duchesse Caracciolo. Perhaps she may be able to discern from the duchess's demeanour whether or not she had received the documents.

A welcome sea breeze met her as she arrived on the sea front, but also the realisation that she was in full view of the Villa Olga and the private detectives, should they still be stationed outside its gates. Creeping like an assassin, she clung to the side of the casino wall, hoping the deep shadow might provide some disguise.

'What am I doing?' she said to Tippet, whose upturned face seemed to be asking the same question. 'I have done nothing wrong.'

And with this, Venetia returned to the shimmering afternoon sunlight and strode into the building. Her eyes adjusting to the relative gloom of the casino interior, she discerned Colonel Marsden at his usual post beside the entrance to the *Salle des Petits Chevaux*.

'Good afternoon colonel,' she boomed, perhaps a tad too effusively. The man looked more squiffy than usual, thought Venetia, noting that he could barely seem to focus his eyes upon the person greeting him.

Having finally managed to identify Venetia, the colonel half-bowed and half stumbled, pulling himself back to his full height with an exaggerated effort.

'My dear lady,' he said. 'Good afternoon.'

'Any excitements on the table. Is our illustrious Duchesse Caracciolo in today?'

But Venetia had already scanned the gaming tables and seen that she was absent.

'She's Jewish, you know,' slurred the colonel before draining a glass of what looked like neat whiskey or calvados.

'And so you have noted before, colonel. On numerous occasions.'

CHAPTER TWENTY-NINE

He was back in Africa. Back in the fierce wet heat of Dahomey, where the dense air smelt of vegetation and animal hides. It had been a massacre and the bodies of the female warriors – the Dahomey Amazons – lay scattered where they each met a French bayonet.

These brave, fierce women had been used to target French officers, but at the battle of Adégon that October, they had fought as a unit. French fire-power had been too great, along with the greater reach of their bayonets. But he saw no trepidation in their eyes as they engaged in close combat. Such fearlessness was unnerving.

His job now was to interrogate a prisoner, but this proud Amazon wouldn't answer the interpreter. A subordinate was urging him to shoot the woman, but he refused.

'Wait… wait… ask her again,' he cried.

Emile awoke, his damp body tangled in the sheet. Daylight and the shouts of the fishermen landing their catch drifted in through the open window. Kicking the sheet aside he sat on the edge of his bed and allowed the dream to evaporate. He retrieved his uniform from the wardrobe and now slowly – ceremoniously almost – began to dress. He squatted on his haunches to try and inspect himself in the little three-sided dressing mirror on the table opposite his bed.

Before his suspension, Emile would wait until he went downstairs for breakfast before looking in the full-length mirror in the entrance hallway, straightening the uniform and brushing off any pieces of fluff that had attached themselves to it. But he had no wish to bump into his landlady and her daughter.

He opened the bedroom door and stood listening. Some seagulls were yelling from a nearby rooftop but all was silent within the house. Clumping downstairs in his regulation boots, Emile was startled to find Madame Remy standing at the kitchen door, a shopping basket in one hand. Seeing him dressed in his uniform she gave a short shrill cry of joy.

'Emile! You are no longer suspended from duty?'

'I should never have been suspended in the first place, madame,' he replied curtly, walking to the front door without a further word and letting himself out into the blinding daylight.

They had timed his visit to the police station on the assumption that Frossard wouldn't wait long before he sent his henchmen to retrieve the phantom dossier from Walter's studio. That's if Frossard didn't lead the raid himself, which would be more of a risk. The fishing boats wouldn't be setting sail until that evening so the crew of burly men collected by Walter's landlady, La Villain, would be available to spring into action.

Walking along the side of the port towards the police station, Emile could see the fishing boats at rest on the harbour's edge, their bare masts reflected in the still water. It was in a herring boat like these that the Flemish fishermen had carried his mother to England after her escape from Paris, dropping her on the shore of Kent. Communards like his mother were randomly killed by royalist troops or sent to die in far-off tropical hellholes.

The true story of her escape from Paris to Belgium and then from Ostend to London was the family legend that he held closest to his heart, and he now saw the herring boats at rest here in Dieppe as a good omen.

Renard was seated at the front desk of the station, his surprise turning to a sly smile as he watched a uniformed Emile approach.

'Good afternoon, Blanchet,' he said warily, looking him up and down. 'Can I be of assistance?'

The door to the main office was ajar, and Emile could hear Frossard talking. He then heard him stomping over towards the door.

'Ah, Blanchet,' he said. 'You've saved Renard here an errand. I was about to send for you.'

'Why, sir?' asked Emile, suddenly confused. Was he about to be reinstated? Or perhaps a date had been set for a disciplinary hearing.

Frossard walked over to his desk, returning with the anarchist pamphlet that Madame Remy had left in his bedroom.

'This', said the commissaire, waving the pamphlet. 'Your landlady kindly informed me that she had found it in your possession.'

'But she put it there. She told me she put it there,' he blurted. 'Someone had posted it beneath her front door and she had assumed it was for my attention.'

'A likely story,' said Frossard. 'Blanchet, we all know your antecedents. We know who your parents were. Anarchists the pair. Are you telling me you don't share those allegiances?'

'I do not. And the pamphlet is nothing to do with me. I told Madame Remy as such and I am telling you now. Sir.'

Renard was looking at him with that sly smile of his, while Frossard stood with the pamphlet raised in the air – for all the world like a street preacher brandishing a bible.

'Your word against this blameless woman, Blanchet. The word of a man with anarchism and socialism and all those terrible words steeped in innocent blood.'

'I am neither an anarchist nor a socialist, but a guardian of the peace. A police officer who has sworn allegiance to the Republic.'

'No longer, I am afraid. I must ask you to remove your uniform and return it here. This latest outrage comes on top of last week's wilful disobedience and I feel it is no longer right and proper that you call yourself a police officer.'

'Can you do that?'

Renard covered his face with his hand, while Frossard's cheeks turned purple.

'I most certainly can, you impudent pup,' he shouted. 'Now get out. Leave your uniform with Madame Remy and she can bring it here. I don't want to see you again.'

Emile struggled to calm himself. After all, there was the plan.

'And I only came here today because I have a solemn duty to perform', he said.

'What *solemn duty*?' Frossard echoed sarcastically.

'The duty to inform on a good friend, sir. I feel horribly at war with myself over this matter, but my first obligation I believe to be towards the law. The bonds of friendship should not obscure one's moral duty.'

'What are you gibbering about?'

'I take no pleasure from what I am about to divulge.'

'Divulge what? Don't waste my time, Blanchet. Spit it out.'

'Very well, sir. It concerns certain documents that you may have been looking for.'

Now he had his undivided attention. Frossard's whole demeanour changed at once and he looked suddenly alert. Greedy almost.

'What do you know of any documents?'

'The cave dwellers,' replied Emile, who had been anticipating this question. 'I met the mother outside the station here while you were questioning her sons about the drowned Arab. She said you had been searching for some important papers.'

Frossard frowned at Emile, seemingly uncertain whether to admit to the object of his search. 'And these documents,' he said. 'You think you know of their whereabouts?'

'I believe I do sir.'

Frossard's eyes were now almost bulging out of their sockets. 'Come along then,' he said. 'Where are they?'

'Sir, before I do my duty and divulge their whereabouts, I would like to request that I be reinstated.'

'You choose to bargain with me, Blanchet?'

'It seems only fair, sir.'

Frossard remained silent, seemingly weighing up Emile's request.

'We will have to see,' he said eventually. 'It depends on the quality of your information.'

'Very well, sir. But it gives me no great pleasure to inform you that they are in the possession of my friend Walter Sickert. The English artist'.

'Sickert? The man who discovered the murdered prostitute?'

'The very same, sir.'

Emile waited for this information to sink in. He didn't want to say too much but to allow Frossard himself to make the connections between Walter and the missing papers. The commissaire was obviously aware that Jeanne's killers had been looking for the documents.

'Renard, close the door and man the outer desk and make sure that nobody disturbs us,' Frossard barked at his subordinate. A flash of anger passed across Renard's face at being denied further insights into this important piece of news.

'And how did your artist friend end up with these papers?' Frossard asked quietly after Renard had closed the door behind him. He obviously didn't trust his subordinate not to be listening from behind the door.

'He says that Jeanne… the murdered prostitute… entrusted them to him. She acted as a model for his paintings, sir, and they knew each other well enough. Apparently, the dead Arab sailor, who had been a different sort of client to the dead girl, had similarly entrusted her with the dossier, saying that he would return to retrieve it the following day. Of course, he never did come back.'

'And have you seen these documents?'

'Only briefly, when Mr Sickert showed me where he was hiding them. I have no idea as to their contents, but he seems to think they are important. So important, in fact, that he intends to take them to England with him on this evening's boat.'

'To England? This evening?' Frossard gasped. As Emile had hoped, he looked alarmed. 'What time is the boat?'

'I'm not certain but it's why I have come so urgently to inform you. There isn't a moment to lose. They are in his studio on the Tour aux Crabes.'

'Yes, yes,' said Frossard, looking flustered. And then he looked sly again. 'Why are you informing on your friend?'

'Sir, I am hoping by doing so that it proves my loyalty to the police. Despite what you may think of me, I am no anarchist. I am a loyal citizen and believe that my foremost duty is to the *patrie*.'

He had chosen the word *patrie* with care, knowing that it was one of Frossard's most sacred totems – this homeland to which everyone apparently owed their blind allegiance. He had heard the commissaire utter the word on countless occasions, each time accompanied by an almost comically dreamy expression. He had also noted how Bastin and Renard would drop the word into their conversation to curry favour with their boss.

Frossard seemed unsure how to respond, and had started pacing up and down the room. It was a risk, Emile knew, that he himself would lead the raid on Walter's studio. But he also suspected that the commissaire would pass the job to the two mysterious men who had killed Jeanne. Frossard certainly didn't appear eager to involve either Bastin or Renard in this business with the missing documents.

He stopped pacing now, nodding his head and obviously pleased with whatever decision he had arrived at.

'I think it best if you, Blanchet, stay out of this matter. Return to your lodgings and stay there until I send for you.'

'Yes, sir. Very good, sir'

Frossard seemed unwilling to say any more, so Emile clicked his heels, turned and left the room. Renard glared at him as he marched across the outer office and through the door. He had no intention of returning to the lodgings and his treacherous landlady. For why had she told Frossard that she had found the pamphlet in his bedroom, when she herself had placed it there?

He took a seat instead on the terrace of the Cafe Suisse, which offered a good view of the front of the police station while the deep shadow of the colonnades disguised his presence. And as Emile had suspected he would, Frossard soon emerged. With his head down he marched quickly along the quayside, passing within a few paces of Emile's table but taking no notice of those taking refreshments on the café terrace. Emile dropped a few coins on the table and followed the commissaire as he strode down Rue Dusquesne and towards the seafront.

He had to act quickly as Frossard seemed determined to reach wherever he was going in the shortest possible time. Emerging on the wide lawns that separated the town from the beach, Emile was just in time to see Frossard disappear into the foyer of the Hotel Royal.

By one of those coincidences that are strangely common in this life, not long before Emile had watched Frossard enter the Hotel Royal, Walter had been gazing at a sketch he had made of the same white-fronted establishment. It had been one of several preparatory sketches of the hotel that he had eventually worked up into a painting that he had exhibited three years earlier.

The critics made much of the greenish light on the building contrasted with the purple sky, along with the sun-reflecting windows. And his friend, Arthur Symons, had even been inspired to write a poem about the painting. Walter, despite his prodigious ability to learn Shakespearean texts, could only recall the opening lines of *At Dieppe*.

'The grey-green stretch of sandy grass,' he intoned dramatically to his empty studio. 'Infinitely desolate; A sea of lead, a sky of slate; Already autumn in the air, alas!"

Poor Arthur, he thought, never having a high regard for his friend's poetry. But so much better than these damn art critics. Walter had recently begun to pen another essay for *The Speaker*, this time on the role of these pernicious, self-appointed guardians of culture.

To the artist, criticism that furthers his business is good; criticism that hinders it is reprehensible, he had written. *The reader, on the other hand, is extremely inclined to hold that it is the duty of a critic simply to provide him with safe and reliable opinions. But the critic, poor fatuous man, is apt to fancy that he too is an artist.*

He lay the sketch of the Hotel Royal on top of a pile of canvases that he intended to move to the safety of the Middletons' cottage across the courtyard. If there were to be a fracas in his studio, he didn't want any of his precious artworks being damaged. He stacked several of his Venetian paintings near the door. These were going to be exhibited at the New English Art Club in the autumn. He had had some success at the NEAC with a similar Venetian theme the year before, the critic of the *Daily Telegraph* being surprised and delighted by his lighter, brighter tones.

The picture gladdens the eye with a brilliancy and sparkle of colour, the man had written (and Walter had memorised). *A frank play of light, for which we had not given Sickert credit.*

The only poor review had been for Walter's jocular title of this view of the canal running from the Ospedale Civile to the cemetery island of San Michele. He had called the picture *From the Hospital to the Grave*, prompting another critic to call it a "pseudo-romantic title, such as we associate with the provincial contributions to the Royal Academy."

The line had amused him. For, as he also informed the readers of *The Speaker* that morning: *We value the critic not so much for the opinions he may hold, as for his manner of expressing them.*

A knock at the door interrupted these thoughts, shortly followed by a flustered-looking Polly.

'Why, Walter, we need to make haste with moving your paintings,' she said. 'Emile will have visited the police station by now.'

'Yes, yes, my dear,' said Walter, momentarily regretting that he had agreed for his studio to become the scene of this entrapment.

'I think it best if we store your paintings in Mama's room. Then the men can gather in the hallway,' said Polly. 'They should be able to see out through the lace curtains on the door without being spotted from the outside.'

'And you must remain with my paintings. Your mother would never forgive me if you became involved in any unpleasantness.'

'But wouldn't it be better if I could act as a lookout? I could be hanging up some washing in the courtyard.'

Walter was impressed by Polly's courage and willingness to be involved so actively in their plan, but these men, should they arrive, had already shown that they had no compunction about roughing up or even killing a woman.

'I must insist that you do no such thing,' he said. 'Allow me to help you with those canvases by the door. They are very precious. I'm hoping to make a big sale with them in London this autumn.'

As they carefully lifted the pile of four pictures and edged towards the door, there was a movement in the courtyard. La Villain's face then appeared pressed up against the glass panes of the studio door. Behind her Walter could see four men of various shapes and sizes but each equally imposing, two of them brandishing wooden clubs.

'Augustine, thank you for coming,' said Walter, addressing her in the French patois of the Pollet, after opening the door and kissing her on both cheeks. The fishwife, with her russet tresses stacked high above her wide, pale face, eyed Polly suspiciously.

'This is my neighbour, Madame Middleton,' said Walter, stressing Polly's marital status. 'She is helping me move my painting to her home, which is where the men will hide.'

Walter's attention then turned to the fishermen that La Villain had brought with her. They each had such fascinating faces that he was gripped with a desire to fetch his sketch pad. One was of Normandy's ancient Viking stock, with dazzling clear blue eyes like cornflowers and hair the colour of ripened wheat. Walter could imagine him wearing a horned helmet and holding a double-headed axe instead of the sturdy lump of wood that he currently grasped.

Another appeared to have no nose and a face full of scar tissue, his visage a map of past accidents and fights, while another clasped his wooden club with the most enormous hands that Walter had ever seen. The last man was small and wiry but extremely tough looking, and with something of the gypsy troubadour about his countenance.

As Walter shook each man's hand, he noticed Emile, wearing his police uniform, had arrived at the entrance to the courtyard. The fishermen turned as one and seemed ready to launch themselves at his young friend.

'Steady, my braves,' he said in the patois of the Pollet. 'He is one of us. A good policeman.'

The short, wiry fisherman, spat – almost instinctively, it seemed – at the idea that there might be such a person as a good policeman. Then remembering that he was in the company of women he gave an apologetic shrug.

'Emile, how goes it?' asked Polly. 'How did Frossard respond?'

'He seemed most alarmed and set off immediately in search of the two men who we believe murdered Jeanne. He went once to the Hotel Royal, which is where I assume they must be lodged.'

'Emile, help Polly and I with my canvases, if you please,' interjected Walter. 'We're taking them next door to her cottage.'

Turning to La Villain, he added: 'Augustine, my dear one. We thought that the men could hide in the hallway opposite. We will have a good view of the studio when the thugs arrive.'

La Villain stared silently at Walter for a moment, a tinge of amusement on her face, before saying with grave solemnity.

'We were all horrified by what happened to poor Jeanne. She was one of us and we have known her since birth. If these men truly are the culprits, then they will pay for it.'

On La Villain's advice, Walter had bought a bottle of Calvados for the fishermen, and they had brought playing cards. If it was going to be a long wait, she said that she would keep an eye on them to make sure they didn't drink too much. In any case, they would have to leave at five o'clock to catch the evening tide. It was currently just before midday

CHAPTER THIRTY

Henry sat in the deep afternoon quiet of his church, alternately praying for guidance and catching the thoughts tumbling from his confused mind. The stillness here amidst the empty pews was of a different order to the charged silence that had overtaken the house once his confrontation with Lucy had concluded, and which had made remaining at home feel unsupportable.

There was relief that he had finally spoken of what had been on his mind for so long, but also a line had been crossed. That there was no going back. There could be no more pretence, no more hiding behind daily habits and convention. But how could they continue living under the same roof now that they stood exposed to each other, as naked as Adam and Eve and just as ashamed?

And then he found himself amused by the analogy. Their home together had never been a Garden of Eden. Not even in the early days of their marriage, when the children had been young. Heaven! When they had even shared the marital bed for long enough to beget babies.

His thoughts turned to these now long grown-up babies, Edward and Maggie. Edward still wrote the occasional dutiful letter, addressed more to Lucy than to himself. He had always been her favourite child. Henry's bond was more with Maggie, whose quaintness had a certain charm when she was a little girl. In a fully grown woman well past the marriageable age, her oddity was less becoming.

She had ceased writing after her last visit to Dieppe, three or four years ago, when she had taken a strong dislike to Alice. The way that Alice monopolised her mother. Henry had since heard through a mutual acquaintance that she had become a secretary to a wealthy widow in Chelsea, although

Edward presumed that this woman, in hiring Maggie, was as equally unhinged as his daughter.

Henry must leave Dieppe. He saw that clearly now. Perhaps he could have a quiet word with Lord Sailsbury the next time the prime minister attended Sunday service – although with the Prince of Wales in town, that might not be for a while. His lordship would surely have sufficient influence with the bishops and archbishops so that a more agreeable living could be had back in England. A market town not far from London, perhaps, from where he could keep an eye on Maggie.

He submitted his disquiet to the Holy Spirit and was surprised to be presented with a mental picture, not of Edward or Maggie or Lucy, but of Jeanne. Her upturned face, sitting on that doorstep on that bright clear May Day that seemed so long ago now. What was the Spirit telling him? That she was the true victim here and that her vile murder was more important than Henry's marital strife and career prospects? Was she even with God now? Why wouldn't she be, the poor innocent?

'Jeanne,' he sobbed. 'Jeanne.'

And then there was the terrible suspicion – more certainty, really - that the poor girl's murder was entangled with the dossier she had handed Henry for safe-keeping. Had he and Mrs Hall been cowardly by simply handing the papers over to the duchess's detectives? Shouldn't they have taken them to the police and voiced their suspicions? Hadn't they just washed their hands of their responsibility in the matter?

He had only skimmed the dossier, and anyway, his knowledge of the infamous case of Alfred Dreyfus was sketchy. Hadn't the man been a spy? But Mrs Hall had investigated its contents more thoroughly, and her panic over what she had discovered had transmitted itself to Henry.

Praying some more, the passage in the Gospel of Luke once again came to mind. He got up and went over to the vestry where he knew he could find a pen and paper, which were used primarily for the church accounts. He then climbed the steps to the lectern and opened the large Bible there, turning to the New Testament and the book of Luke.

'Yes, here we are,' Henry said to himself, marking a passage with his finger while writing down the chapter and verses that he was looking for. 'Luke 7, verses 36 onwards.' He then read:

"*And, behold, a woman in the city, which was a sinner, when she knew that Jesus sat at meat in the Pharisee's house, brought an alabaster box of ointment, and stood at his feet weeping, and began to wash his feet with tears, and did wipe them with the hairs of her head, and kissed his feet, and anointed them with the ointment.*"

'There,' said Henry. 'The text for Sunday's sermon.' And turning to the alter, he bowed deeply, a beatific smile on his face.

* * *

Frossard descended the front steps of the Hotel Royal with a self-satisfied smile upon his face. At last, he had located the documents that seemed so important to the army. Promotion and salvation would be his. And at long last he felt what it was to be a man of action again. To be at the centre of affairs.

As he passed along the quayside and towards the police station his thoughts drifted back to those glorious days in Paris. That victorious May week in '71. How his seventeen-year-old self, a poor little country boy from the provinces, was bloodied in battle as he helped put down the socialist rabble. He could still see the fires burning everywhere and rubble strewn across the streets of the capital.

His first taste of action had been when his troupe had come to a halt one hundred metres from a barricade that had been blocking the entrance to a wide boulevard. A red flag had been draped from a pole atop a great knitted pile of furniture, paving stones, omnibus carriages, mattresses and sandbags.

An officer, a proper gentleman at that, had ordered Frossard and about two dozen other men to follow him as he made a wide berth towards a side street adjacent to the barricade. Detailing four soldiers to each neighbouring house, the officer had kicked in a front door and, pushing past a terrified family group, had led the way upstairs until they reached the uppermost floor of the building. Frossard had followed him into this attic, which looked directly down upon the rebels defending their barricade.

The men and women below had seemed unaware of their presence, so keenly were their eyes focused to the front of them. Other attic windows had been opened across the boulevard and more rifle barrels had appeared. Frossard remembered taking aim at an Amazonian woman who had been shouting encouragement to the defenders, but his shot had missed. Another rifleman was luckier and the woman had flopped forward onto the barricade.

Frossard could still see the defenders casting around them in confusion, and then upwards at the troops now picking them off with deadly accuracy. In his haste to join in the massacre, he had unfortunately managed to jam his rifle. He had been pulled back by another soldier, who had taken his place in the firing gallery. And by the time Frossard had cleared the breech of his Chassepot, the fun was over; the barricade deserted but for a mound of bodies.

Cursing his rifle, he had followed the other troops back downstairs, only to find a commotion as the officer attempted to drag away the man of the house. An old grandfather type. 'He called me "*citoyen*", the damn fool,' the officer had barked to no one in particular, pointing his pistol into the old man's face and firing. The man had fallen back into the arms of his screaming family.

By the time he had reached the Jardins du Luxembourg, Frossard realised that he could afford to show no mercy. He had already seen one of his comrades executed for refusing to shoot women and children, along with a doctor who had attempted to treat a young boy wounded by the troops.

He had been able to hear the volleys of the firing squads as he approached the gardens, and at the park gates he was ordered to join a detachment to relieve these executioners.

He remembered being surprised to pass a small group of wealthy-looking onlookers, the ladies carrying jaunty parasols as if they were taking a springtime stroll in the park or attending the races. 'Kill them,' one of the ladies had shouted. 'Sabre them, without pity, my boys!'

'Pigs make a noise like these Parisians when you slaughter them,' he would later tell his fellow soldiers. 'The difference is that you can't eat a Parisian!' His joke had been met with such gratifying laughter that he would go on to repeat it endlessly that bloody May week. That bloody May week when the buildings shimmered in gold and red and those trees that had been spared were decked in their coats of springtime green

CHAPTER THIRTY-ONE

The men settled down upon the floor of the cottage hallway, backs against the walls playing successive rounds of Napoleon. They didn't gamble on the number of tricks won, seemingly content merely to emerge victorious in each round of the card game. La Villain stood in the corner of the room, counting the time passing by the level on the Calvados bottle. It was now half empty, she noted with concern.

Emile and Polly busied themselves in Polly's mother's bedroom, carefully sorting and stacking Walter's canvases and sketches. The room was up a short flight of steps, with a window that overlooked the port. From here, Emile found himself thinking, Polly's mother could have had a view of both the rocks where the drowned Arab was discovered and the brothel where Jeanne plied her trade.

The bedroom walls were not papered but the plaster painted a simple but cheerful yellow that Walter had apparently suggested. And among a number of Japanese prints decorating the walls, Emile noticed that Mrs Middleton had framed Walter's sketch of her daughters. It was the back view of Lydia and Polly whose creation Emile had witnessed when he first encountered the sisters.

'You remember that being sketched?' asked Polly, noticing Emile's gaze.

'Very much. I remember thinking that I had stumbled on a most unusual scene.'

'I only allow Walter to sketch me from behind,' said Polly. 'I disliked the ones he made from the front.'

'Why so?'

She didn't answer. Standing side by side in silence, they turned to each as if on an unspoken cue. And then they kissed. Only lightly on the lips, but neither pulled away abashed. They stood instead wordlessly contemplating each other, as if seeing each other for the first time. Eventually Polly spoke.

'I think you should leave before the police arrive. You can't be discovered here.'

'I can't leave now. I mean, I might encounter them on the way out.'

'Then stay here.'

He was about to speak again when they heard an uproar from below. Ignoring Polly's words, Emile rushed down the short flight of steps and into the now empty hallway. The door was open and beyond it in the courtyard a struggle was obviously coming to a conclusion. Two men lay prone on the flagstones beneath the cherry trees. A pair of fishermen sat on each of them, one straddling the man's back while the other pinned his legs as La Villain and Walter looked on from the side. Emile noticed that a pane of glass in Walter's studio door had been smashed.

'Here take this,' Walter said to Emile when he noticed him approach. 'It's some sort of identity card for one of the men. Keep it and hide it. But go back inside now, you can't be seen here.'

But it was too late because one of the men, his bald head raised from the ground as one of fisherman, the enormous blond Viking, grabbed him by the scruff his neck, looked over to where Emile stood, conspicuous in his police uniform.

'Help me, officer!' the main screamed. 'Can't you see I'm being attacked!'

Walter stepped in front of Emile, blocking him from the man's view while gesticulating behind his back for Emile to go back inside the Middletons' cottage.

'Why were you breaking into my studio, you thief?' shouted Walter as a distraction.

The blond Viking straddling the man's back and holding one of his arms, gave the limb a sharp yank. He gave a cry of pain and shouted through gritted teeth.

'Get off me! I am an officer with the army of France. I have been sent on urgent police business.'

'What business?' growled the Viking.

'Let go of me you oaf!'

This was followed by a scream as the Viking yanked his twisted arm again. Emile backed into the Middletons' cottage and examined the battered and somewhat soiled card that Walter had handed him. It appeared to be a military identity card made out to Jean Récamier of the 74th Regiment based in Rouen. No rank was specified.

Polly appeared on the staircase.

'My dear,' said Emile.

She smiled and descended the last few steps, taking the card from Emile's hand.

'What is this?'

'It is our man.'

'What does it mean?'

'I don't know, but at last we have a name for this killer.'

Emile then heard his own name being called, and with a chill recognised that the voice belonged to Frossard.

'Blanchet? Blanchet? Come out now. Make yourself known. What is the meaning of this?'

'Oh, my dear,' said Polly, grasping his arm.

'Keep that card safe,' said Emile. 'Don't worry about me.'

He held on to her hand for a moment, and turned to go.

'Please be safe, Emile.'

The scene in the courtyard had been utterly transformed. Now it was Walter and the fishermen who were on the ground, kneeling with their hands upon their heads as Renard and Bastin covered them with their revolvers and Frossard stood waving a sabre. Their former captives stood angrily brushing themselves down, turning to glare at Emile as he emerged from the cottage.

"You!' shouted the man who had been recently subjected to the Viking's arm twisting. He had replaced his hat, of the fashionable Homburg style.

'That man is a mutineer,' he cried, pointing at Emile but addressing Frossard.

'I cannot be a mutineer as, of two hours ago, I am no longer a police office,' said Emile.

'That is my friend and he is certainly no mutineer,' added Walter. 'He was merely assisting me in arresting these two burglars.'

'We are no burglars!' shouted the second man, who was short and thick-set with a cropped military haircut.

'Then why were you attempting to break into my studio?'

'We were acting on intelligence about stolen goods.'

'Who are you exactly?' asked Emile. 'You are not policemen as far as I can tell.'

There was no reply. Instead, Frossard pointed his sabre at Emile and said with a cold fury: 'Never mind your impertinent questions. You, Blanchet, are under arrest.'

CHAPTER THIRTY-TWO

If his hands hadn't been restrained behind his back with a length of whipcord that tightened if you struggled against it, then Emile would have fancied his chances against his captives. Bastin was lazy and sluggish and only liked to use his weight against the defenceless. Renard was as cunning as his name but also a coward who only owed his current position because of his obsequious loyalty to Frossard. And Frossard himself was old and increasingly frail, despite his proud military bearing.

Bastin had applied the whipcord at gunpoint, but he and Renard were no longer armed, having deposited the revolvers and Frossard's sabre before hauling him into Frossard's office. And Emile, stronger and fitter, would no longer have any compunction about defending himself against his fellow police officers. And his anger would have reinforced his strength. For now, he was absolutely convinced that they were corrupt. The precise nature of their corruption still eluded him, but not its manifestation.

The two men – the one identified as Jean Récamier and his accomplice, presumably also of the 74th Infantry Regiment based in Rouen – hadn't followed them to the station. Presumably they were currently ransacking Walter's studio, for which Emile felt a spasm of guilt. At least they had cleared it of anything of value. But he hoped they would not force an entry in the Middletons' cottage, for if that were to happen he would not be able to forgive himself.

But then hopefully they hadn't noticed that that was where the fishermen were hiding. And what of the fishermen? At least they didn't appear under arrest, since Frossard had singled out Emile for that fate. He suspected that, having realised they had been led into a trap, Récamier and his accomplice had made themselves scarce. Either back to the hotel or back to Rouen,

'You are telling me that you invented this story about the dossier in the hope that you could entrap the men you say killed the prostitute Jeanne Déliquaire?' the commissaire was saying. 'Even though you know that her husband Pascal Déliquaire had been arrested for that murder.'

Emile felt Bastin pressing down on his shoulder as Frossard was speaking. Having seen the battered and bruised faces of Pascal Déliquaire and the cave-dwelling brothers who had discovered the dead Arab, Emile knew that Bastin relished this part of his job.

'Is Pascal Déliquaire going to trial then? If not, why not?' asked Emile, knowing that his question would be answered by the hard slap that indeed swiftly followed. He briefly saw stars and his right ear was left ringing.

'Don't you worry about Pascal Déliquaire,' said Frossard, who was standing leaning across his desk, resting on his knuckles. Emile noted how his question had shaken the commissaire. He decided to press home his attack, even at the cost of another slap to the side of the head from Bastin's beefy paw.

'What exactly are these papers you are so desperate to retrieve? Papers that appear to have cost a poor girl her life.'

In the split second before the next slap came and the ringing in his ear became even more intense, Emile noticed the confusion in Frossard's eyes. In that moment he realised that the commissaire didn't know the precise nature of the documents he was so desperate to locate. He was a middle man.

'These documents are top secret,' Frossard blustered. 'Of national importance. They must be found before they fall into the hands of our enemies.'

'I still don't understand,' said Emile, trying to keep a conversational tone, as if they were friends confiding in each other. 'Why do you think that they are here in Dieppe, these secret papers? And why do think Jeanne had them in her possession?'

'Because you told me that your friend the painter… Sickert…had seen the dead Arab's fez in her room,' blurted Frossard before he had time to check himself.

'So, you think that the dead Arab had these documents?'

It all made sense to Emile now. The way in which he had had the cave dwellers' home searched so thoroughly and Frossard's growing desperation when he couldn't find anything hidden there. And the way the brothers had been roughed up, their only "crime" having been in discovering the drowned Arab's body and alerting the police.

Frossard sat down and studied Emile as if he was pondering what to do with him. Emile felt Bastin's hand pressing down again on his shoulders. Renard kept looking from the commissaire to Emile and back again as if wondering who was going to win a particularly tight game of chess.

'Who are the two soldiers who came to break into Walter Sickert's studio?' asked Emile

'I knew you were trouble from the beginning,' said Frossard, shaking his head and ignoring Emile's question. 'You know that I was in Paris at the same time as your mother, the so-called 'Red Maid of Montmartre'. We were on different sides, of course.'

'I did not know that,' said Emile, staring steadily at the commissaire and trying to imagine him as the young man he would have been in May 1871. During the *semaine sanglante*. Bloody week. It wasn't easy but he thought he could discern the small, under-nourished youth beneath Frossard's current mask-like countenance. Had he taken part in the terrible massacres that his mother wouldn't speak of, but which Emile had read about in first-testimonies of the Paris Commune?

'And no doubt you would have shot my mother out of hand, if you had had the opportunity.'

The slap he had been expecting did not arrive. Instead, a smile broke out on to Frossard's lips.

'Naturally I would have. Your mother and the vermin like her were enemies of *La Patrie*…'

'You have known all this time about my mother?' interrupted Emile, aghast. 'I have always detected an undeserved hostility towards me and now I know why.'

Frossard at first said nothing in reply. And then he had murmured, with a look of smug satisfaction: 'The apple never falls far from the tree, Blanchet.'

'Tell me about the women and children you murdered, Frossard'. Emile had surprised himself at his disrespectful tone, but had simultaneously felt liberated by it. He would no longer kowtow to this hated superior.

'Vermin, I said. Your mother and the rest of that Paris rabble were the enemies of good order. Of the *France éternelle*. Socialism for the masses... what a hideous idea.'

'My mother and others like her were not vermin, but I agree with you about the *France éternelle*,' said Emile, trying to hold a lid on his anger. 'The core of the nation. But the country itself evolves and must continue to evolve. We no longer have emperors or kings or the rule of the clergy...'

'More's the pity,' said Frossard. 'But we digress. I think we might have to take a ride. Somewhere discreet. Go and prepare the buggy, Renard.'

'What is the meaning of this?' exclaimed Emile, reflexively attempting to bring his hands up, only for the whipcord to tighten painfully around his wrists. He knew this type of restraint from his time in Africa. With its double running knot, it could swiftly be applied during an emergency and he had used it himself on native prisoners. Bastin slapped him again, harder this time, catching him across his right eye. More stars.

'Are you sure commissaire?' asked Renard, discerning his boss's intention.

Frossard stood up and raised himself to his full height. Renard seemed to take this action for an answer and saluted sharply before leaving the room.

'How many men have you shot in the back?' asked Emile. 'Paris during the Commune must have been open season for someone like you. And women and children...'

'Those as well,' said Frossard quietly before the back of Bastin's hand landed on Emile's face. It would be the last for now, as the commissaire told his henchman to go and fetch the revolvers. What did they intend? To shoot *him* in the back and then claim he was attempting to flee? Well, Frossard had had plenty of practice in that cowardly art.

'I despise you.' Frossard spat the words, now that they were alone. 'And all those like you. You've had an easy life, never having to worry about anything.'

'What do you know of my life?'

'Only that you can speak two languages. That you associate with artists and intellectuals, that you seem to know so many people. That you seem to have a charmed existence here in Dieppe when I know no one.'

'This is not my idea of a charmed existence,' said Emile, who could feel his right eye closing up.

At that moment Bastin returned, looking alarmed. Behind him through the open door, Emile noticed a group of smartly dressed men, along with some uniformed officers.

'We have visitors, commissaire' he said. 'They want to speak to you urgently.'

* * *

The fishermen had dispersed to catch the tide, seemingly in good humour as if they had engaged in some entertaining sport. Rough but fun. Only the blond Viking had suffered any injury but merely a bloody nose. Walter, La Villain and Polly now stood in the courtyard, the latter suddenly beginning to sob.

'I'm sorry,' she said.

La Villain put an arm around her shoulder and murmured something soothing in the patois of Le Pollet. She smelt, not unpleasantly of fresh fish, thought Polly as Walter then stepped forward to take her hand.

'Emile will be fine. We'll make sure of that,' he said. But could they? Could he? Walter didn't put anything past those men. Looking up, he noticed that the cherries hanging from the branches like drop earrings were nearly ripe enough to eat. In normal times this would have made him stupidly happy. He loved nature and its rhythms.

'I'm sure he will,' said Polly, dabbing her eyes with a lace handkerchief on which Walter noticed drops of blood. Presumably from the Viking's nose after she had ministered to him.

'Be careful,' he said, gently taking hold of the handkerchief. Polly emitted a short laugh at the blood-splattered state of the thing.

'It's the fisherman with the bloody nose,' she said. 'I forgot I used this to stem the bleeding. I….'

But she was interrupted by a figure who appeared, breathless, at the top of the steps. She had long flaxen hair, eyes the colour of forget-me-nots and cheeks red with exertion.

'Why. It's Emile's admirer,' said Walter. '*Bonjour Marie-Hélène.*'

CHAPTER THIRTY-THREE

Emile's right eye had all but closed up, but through the other one he saw Frossard blanche, stiffen and then stumble to his feet. Painfully craning his neck, which felt as if that too had been injured by Bastin's meaty blows, Emile was also just about able to discern these visitors who had managed to put Frossard on high alert.

There were three of them and they were all staring straight back at Emile. Each wore the same concerned expression. The examining magistrate, Maitre Toussaint, stood between a distinguished looking older gentleman in a frock coat and a uniformed military officer.

'Frossard. What is the meaning of this?' Toussaint asked in a brisk, businesslike voice so unlike the chummy and often obsequious attitude he usually adopted with the commissaire. It seemed he had more important people to impress now.

'I… we…', stuttered Frossard, trying but failing to stand to full attention. He seemed suddenly to have lost the use of his legs and Emile wondered whether the commissaire was about to faint. Putting a hand upon his desk to steady himself, he quickly regained his composure however.

'We arrested Agent Blanchet this morning for perverting the course of justice.'

'How so? And why wasn't I informed?'

'I had only just begun to question the prisoner, maitre. It was more a question of internal discipline than a criminal matter.'

'I wouldn't like to see the state of his face *after* you'd finished questioning him', interjected the older, distinguished looking gentlemen.

'Commissaire Frossard,' said Toussaint. 'May I introduce Senator Scheurer-Kestner. Our distinguished visitor from Paris has taken a personal interest in one of our cases.'

The name meant nothing to Emile, but Frossard obviously recognised it, noticeably bristling as, without acknowledging the introduction, he asked: 'Indeed. Which case?'

'We'll get to that in a moment,' said Toussaint. 'Before that I would like you to untie Agent Blanchet and tell me exactly in what manner he has been perverting the course of justice.'

As Bastin, who had been lurking guiltily by the doorway, went off to fetch a knife with which to cut the whipcord that was now digging into Emile's flesh and stinging fiercely, Frossard cleared his throat. He seemed unsettled by the change in attitude from his old crony Toussaint and unsure of how much he should divulge to his visitors.

'Firstly, Blanchet came in here wearing his uniform when he was suspended from duty...'

'Why was he suspended from duty?' asked the magistrate. Sharp and direct, this was Toussaint as Emile had never witnessed him before. 'You seem to have been consistently failing to keep me informed, commissaire.'

Emile stifled his amusement at this about-turn from the examining magistrate, who was usually more than happy to give Frossard a free rein with his investigations.

'I suspended him for insubordination and failure to follow simple orders, *monsieur le Procureur*', said Frossard, the first time that Emile had heard him to address Toussaint formally. 'I asked him to do one thing and he does another.'

Bastin reappeared at that moment brandishing a knife with which he cut Emile free. After flexing his fingers, which had grown white and numb, Emile gently touched the side of his face. A sharp pain warned him not to go there again.

'You. Go and fetch a doctor at once,' the magistrate barked at Bastin, who saluted and rushed off. 'Try Dr. Painlevé.'

'How are you feeling?' asked the senator, addressing Emile.

'Thank you, sir. I think I'll live.'

The senator smiled kindly and turned to Frossard.

'You were telling Maitre Toussaint about this officer perverting the course of justice. Can you continue, commissaire?'

'Very good, *monsiuer le sénateur*. If you so wish.'

'I do so wish.'

'Very well. Agent Blanchet came here with false information about a crime, which caused a considerable waste of police time.'

'What sort of crime?'

'About some missing goods.'

'What sort of goods?'

'Some papers. Some top-secret papers of national importance.'

At these words, the senator and the army officer turned to each other, seemingly in amazement. The officer raised his eyebrows as if acknowledging some deeper meaning. Toussaint also observed this unspoken exchange.

'What are these top-secret papers?' he continued.

'I don't know their exact nature, *monsieur le Procureur*. But I do know that they are of utmost importance to *la patrie*.'

'If you don't know the nature of the papers, how can you judge their importance to *la patrie*, as you call it.'

'Because that's what I've been told.'

'By whom?'

'By the army.'

The senator and the officer exchanged another look, as if Frossard's words had confirmed something they had hitherto only suspected. The bewildered magistrate threw his hands in the air and shook his head.

'The army? What does all this mean Frossard?'

'I have been requested by the army to find some missing documents.'

'Would you mind telling us who in the army made this request, commissaire?' asked the senator.

'Maybe I could answer that question,' said Emile, four sets of eyes swivelling in his direction.'

'You, Blanchet? How so?' demanded Frossard.

'Quite simply because the men who were also so desperate to find these secret documents murdered a young woman. And one of these men also happened to be carrying a military identity card.'

The senator turned to him: 'Murder? What young woman?'

'Jeanne Déliquaire,' replied Emile. 'She was a local prostitute who happened to have been unfortunate enough to have been entrusted with these documents by one of her customers. A customer who was discovered drowned in the port. An Arab gentleman.'

The senator and the army officer exchanged another look, the officer this time offering a pained expression.

'This is all nonsense,' interjected Frossard angrily and turning to the army officer. 'You, sir, must understand that no soldier would go around murdering innocent French women, even if the dignity of France herself was threatened.'

'Murder? I don't know,' said the officer. 'But I do know that there are great lengths that the French army would go to in order to maintain its own dignity.'

'Apologies,' said the senator. 'May I introduce Lieutenant Colonel Picquart of the 4th Tunisian Tiralleurs. If we are not very much mistaken, the dead Arab of whom you speak was one of his trusted subordinates. Now, Agent Blanchet, you were about to identify the army officer who seems to have been issuing the commissaire with his instructions.'

'This is all highly irregular,' blustered Frossard. 'I will be making a report to my superiors.'

'And so shall we,' said the senator. 'Now Blanchet. Give us the name of this soldier.'

Emile, who had been repeating the name to himself throughout his interrogation, lest he should forget it or Polly somehow mislay the card that he had entrusted her with, now spoke.

'Jean Récamier of the 74th Regiment based in Rouen. No mention of rank.'

'The 74th,' the senator and Picquart echoed in unison, this time without exchanging a glance.

The sound of feet signalled Renard's return; his reddened face soaked in sweat. He now stood gaping at the scene that greeted him. Turning to each of the visitors, his eyes alighted on the now untethered Emile and finally, questioningly, on Frossard.

'The carriage is ready, commissaire,' he said, dimly aware that his mission had been superseded by events.

CHAPTER THIRTY-FOUR

Emile spent the next hour or so being attended to by Dr. Painlevé, a fussy older gentleman who inspected his wounds through a pince-nez and whose clothes smelt of mothballs. He dabbed the area around Emile's swollen eye with carbolic acid before applying surgical gauze. He repeated the treatment for the detective's wrists and neck and reported no serious damage; some broken skin and bruising at most.

Not that Emile was really listening to the elderly medic, being more consumed in digesting the amazing scene that had just unfolded and the revelations contained therein.

Matters had taken a turn when Frossard had seemed to lose his temper with the senator, suddenly snarling at him like a rabid dog. And just like a mad beast, flecks of spittle emerged from his mouth as he rounded on this august gentleman with a shocking lack of decorum.

'I won't take any lessons on policing from you, Monsieur Scheurer-Kestner,' he had shouted, the cloddish Vendéen accent that he usually attempted to mask now fully pronounced. 'You who have no love of France. All your life you have done nothing but chip away at the pillars that have made this country great – the monarchy, the army and the church. Why, you are not even a Catholic. You Protestants and your Jewish allies would destroy everything that is great about France…'

'May I remind you that *you* are a representative of the Republic,' interjected a horrified Toussaint. 'Excuse me, senator.'

But Frossard had continued his tirade, having seemingly lost all control of his feelings.

'Why, senator, you even spent time in prison for your seditious ideas…'

'As you were lucky not to have done during the attempted coup by General Boulanger,' Scheurer-Kestner had replied, finding his voice at last. 'The Republic survived Boulanger and it will easily survive you, Frossard. Didn't you sate your hatred during the Paris Commune? According to your own military record, you were responsible for murdering innocent men, women and children during that terrible uprising.'

'Murder? My military record? Where does my military record say anything about murdering anybody?'

'But you did, didn't you? I know in which regiment you served during May 1871 and just what that regiment did during the *semaine sanglante*... the Bloody Week.

'If I killed anybody then I was following orders. I have always followed orders, unlike Blanchet here. The Parisians were traitors. Worse than sewer rats.'

Emile leapt from his chair. 'Tell me about the women and children you murdered, Frossard. Did you count them, like a poacher counts dead rabbits?'

But Frossard was no longer listening. 'Look. Look at this,' he said, opening his desk drawer and producing a pamphlet which Emile recognised as the one that Madame Remy had placed in his bedroom.

He handed the pamphlet to Toussaint who, frowning, inspected it. The magistrate in turn handed it to Scheurer-Kestner.

'What is the meaning of this?' asked the senator.

'This seditious document was discovered in Blanchet's bedroom by his landlady. The poor woman did not know what to do and handed it to me. In strictest confidence, you understand.'

'My landlady put that thing in my bedroom in the first place,' shouted Emile, shocked at this complicity between Madame Remy and Frossard. How had they even met? 'I had never seen it before until it suddenly appeared on my bedside table,' he continued. 'Madame Remy – that's my landlady - said it had been posted under her front door and she had assumed it was for me. But I put her right, so I can't understand why she would want to come to Frossard with this... this lie.'

'You are the liar, Blanchet, and the good lady rightly didn't believe you.'

'Okay, gentlemen, that is enough.'

It was a new voice, softly spoken yet commanding, and it belonged to a short, portly man whom Emile had recognised as Juge d'Instruction (examining magistrate) Eric Poisson. Behind him stood a phalanx of five or six uniformed gendarmes and behind them, Emile, noticed, Walter, Polly and Marie-Hélène. What on earth was Marie-Hélène doing there?

'Commissaire Aubert from the Yvetot police will be arriving later today and will take over all ongoing investigations.'

As the meaning of the words sunk in, Frossard had looked at first bewildered and then angry.

'But *Monsieur le Juge...*'

'Commissaire Frossard, I would like a word with you... alone. In the meantime, if you could clear your desk for Commissaire Aubert, that would be greatly appreciated.'

* * *

'There,' said Dr. Painlevé, clipping shut his leather valise and bringing Emile's thoughts back to the present. 'No serious damage to report, I am happy to say. Your wrists might sting for a day or two, but keep them bandaged.'

'Thank you, doctor,' said Emile. He was seated on the bed - little more than a wooden bench really - in one of the vacant cells in the basement of the police station. The doctor grunted as if dismissing the need for gratitude in such a small matter, stood up and left the cell.

As he himself was preparing to leave, he was met by Frossard, his face grimly set and his arms restrained on each side by a gendarme. On seeing Emile, the commissaire made a futile effort to free himself from their grip.

'This is an outrage… and absolute outrage,' he shouted. 'This man here is the one who should be under arrest.'

One of the gendarmes meanwhile signalled with a tilt of his head that Emile should vacate the cell. They threw Frossard forward and shut the door behind him, locking it with a heavy key.

'What happened?' asked Emile.

'He tried to strike the senator.'

'Tried?'

'He missed.'

Climbing the stairs into the main office, Emile noticed Renard and Bastin. They were seated at their desks, apparently engaged with some paperwork, or at least trying to look busy. Bastin didn't look up as he walked past – purposively thought Emile – but Renard gave him a fleeting conspiratorial smile. Emile didn't return it.

CHAPTER THIRTY-FIVE

'And one of the Pharisees desired him that he would eat with him. And he went into the Pharisee's house, and sat down to meat.

'And, behold, a woman in the city, which was a sinner, when she knew that Jesus sat at meat in the Pharisee's house, brought an alabaster box of ointment.'

It was the turn of Mr Chapman, the British vice consul, to read the lesson. He spoke as usual as if reciting the railway timetable, without any sense of the punctuation or dramatic rhythm or even seemingly of understanding the passage that Henry had chosen for him. Chapman was a regular churchgoer only in the sense that he religiously attended All Saints on those Sundays when Lord Salisbury and his family were also expected.

'And stood at his feet behind him weeping, and began to wash his feet with tears, and did wipe them with the hairs of her head, and kissed his feet, and anointed them with the ointment.'

The beautiful words fell like dust from his mouth. At this point the only stirrings of unease that Henry noticed among the congregation came from the second row, where Lucy was seated in her customary position huddled against Alice. She had understood that this reading from Luke, the one about Jesus forgiving the prostitute her sins, would form the basis of Henry's sermon.

Mr Chapman concluded the passage, forgetting to bow to the cross but executing a curious bobbing genuflection in the direction of Lord Salisbury's pew, as if his performance had been solely for the prime minister's benefit. The organist struck up the opening chords of *Praise, My Soul, the King of Heaven*.

As the congregation gratefully seated themselves at the end of the final verse and Henry mounted the pulpit, he caught Lucy's eye. Almost shielding herself behind Alice, she looked terrified, as if her husband were an anarchist smuggling a bomb into their midst. Which, in a way, he was.

He began with the passage from Luke, about how Christ's Pharisee host had been scandalised by his guest forgiving the woman her sins. The faces in front of him varied from polite interest to those resigned to yet another of Henry's interminable sermons. There was a noticeable surge of attentiveness however when he said:

'Now imagine that our Lord was here in Dieppe today.'

Lord Salisbury looked curious, his wife frowned and, behind them, Henry noticed Lucy shaking her head.

'For we have sinful women in this town. Yes! Prostitutes to give them that unattractive name.'

Three or four fans were simultaneously opened and flourished, their lady owners brushing them in front of their faces as if being orchestrated by an unseen conductor. Lord Salisbury leant forward in his pew as if to obtain a clearer view of Henry.

'I want to talk today about one of these sinful women. Her name was Jeanne. And if I use the past tense, it is because Jeanne was foully murdered some weeks past.'

Lucy had now buried her face in her hands. Lady Salisbury appeared to be comforting her younger daughter, while her husband was now frowning.

'I came to know Jeanne, very briefly.'

There was a gasp from the back of the church.

'I first encountered her last May Day, while out walking in the fishermen's quarter. Le Pollet. She was sitting on a doorstep, her faced raised towards the spring sunshine.'

People were fidgeting and coughing now.

'Jeanne… as I later discovered to be her name… handed me a sprig of lily of the valley as I believe is customary on that day of the year in France.'

Henry thought he heard a man laugh, but he might have imagined it. He could see Jeanne clearly now, the freckles across the bridge of her nose. Those lovely eyes, clear like spring water. Her miraculous likeness to his lost love Florence.

'It was only later that I discovered what this sweet girl did by way of occupation.'

There was definitely laughter now. Supressed laughter. Henry raised a hand as if about to give a blessing. The congregation stilled.

'At first of course I was horrified. The poor girl. That wretched sinful profession. But then I remembered the example of our dear Lord, who spurned not the sinful women of Judea. I thought… I thought…'

What had he thought? That he might save the girl's soul? That he might bring the light of God's love into her pitiful, fallen life? Or was it simply to gaze at her again, this ghostly mirage of his lost love. To look into the past, at the life he might have lived instead of the empty meaningless years.

Henry glanced at Lucy, but she had slumped forward so that the only the top of her head was visible above the back of the pew where Lord and Lady Salisbury sat rigidly staring back at him. Behind them he could make out Alice, a look of utter hatred on her long, pinched face.

'I thought that I could bring God's grace to this dark corner of Dieppe. To this fallen woman. Instead, to my consternation, I discovered that Jeanne, poor sweet Jeanne, had no need of God's grace. It was I, the Pharisee, who required salvation.'

The first people stood up to leave at this point. Lord Salisbury turned to watch, and then nodded to his wife, the whole family rising as one at this signal. They filed out down the aisle without a backwards look, other members of the congregation standing as they passed. It was all very orderly, Henry thought, as if they were processing to take Communion.

* * *

'What will happen now?'

Walter, Polly and Emile had retired to the Café Suisse, where they sat in front of three glasses of absinthe and a pitcher of water. It was Walter who had spoken but Polly had been asking herself the same question.

'The judge told me to take the rest of the week off and to report to Commissaire Aubert next Monday.'

'A holiday? Perhaps we can do some painting together,' said Walter, pouring water through the perforated sugar spoon that lay across the rim of the absinthe glasses. He watched the green liquid turn a cloudy white, before looking up to see Emile and Polly smiling at each other. At least he thought that Emile was smiling, although the bruised state of his face, with one eye swollen shut and taped over with gauze, made it hard to judge.

'Or perhaps you have better things to do,' he added. 'Anyway, down the hatch. This will help counter the pain.'

'I must go and thank Marie-Hélène', said Emile, almost to himself. 'But I don't know how I can see her without encountering her mother.'

'I don't think that Marie-Hélène was being entirely altruistic coming forward to tell the truth about that pamphlet,' said Walter, holding his absinthe glass up to the light. 'Her mother was planning to marry her off to Frossard. They had come to some sort of bargain involving that anarchist pamphlet. Luckily Marie-Hélène overheard it all. Can you imagine being married to Frossard?'

'I think I almost can,' said Emile with a bitter laugh.

'Poor Marie-Hélène,' said Polly.

'But what happened to this mysterious bundle of documents that provoked so much trouble in the first place? Did you ask that Colonel Picquart fellow about their exact nature?'

'I did, and he wouldn't say.'

'Well, I'm sure that the truth will out eventually,' said Walter before draining his absinthe glass. 'Now, the weather is pleasantly overcast and I must make some sketches before that wretched sun decides to come out again.'

CHAPTER THIRTY-SIX

Dieppe, March 1898.

Lying beside and above him on the bed, she cradled him in her arms. It was a pleasurable sensation that simultaneously made him feel uneasy. Surely Emile should be holding Polly in his arms and not vice versa. Was she mothering him? Had his own mother held him like this? Surely, once, but he couldn't remember.

On the whole however he had grown surer of himself – surer of them both – in the months they had now spent together in the cottage at the top of the Tour aux Crabes. A nest of sorts, perched on the old town battlements as the winter gales battered Dieppe from the sea. But there still lingered a small insecurity. Polly was already a mother after all, and soon to be divorced. Although they were the same age, she had experienced so much more in the field of human relationships.

'You did a good job Commissaire Blanchet,' she said now, reaching out a hand for the glass of water on the bedside table.

'I know,' replied Emile.

He could feel Polly's laughter rather than hear it, a vibration of her rib cage. He turned and reached up to kiss her.

They had known for weeks that trouble was brewing. The police informers had been overhearing students discussing protests and which shops to target. Whether or not these paid informants had really gleaned this from overhearing conversations in cafes, as they claimed, Emile had doubted. They were paid off nonetheless.

More likely, like the rest of France, they had simply been reading the newspaper reports about the anti-Jewish riots that had erupted in Paris in January. The unrest began after the acquittal of Major Esterhazy – the alleged real traitor in the Dreyfus affair – and Emile Zola's sensational open letter with its inflammatory headline *J'Accuse…!*

Addressing the President of France, Félix Faure, the novelist had accused the government of antisemitism and the unlawful jailing of Alfred Dreyfus. The counter protests against Zola and "cosmopolitan Israelites" had started immediately afterwards.

Emile and his new team (Bastin and Renard having been posted elsewhere after Frossard's dismissal and Emile's promotion) had watched the riots spread across the country like a lit fuse making its way inexorably towards Normandy.

Nancy, Bordeaux, Lyon, Dijon and Avignon had already experienced the sacking of Jewish stores and the burning of synagogues. The fuse crept steadily northwards – first to Angers, then Dinan and finally Rouen. It arrived in Dieppe in late February.

The trouble began on the 24th with a group of students from the school of hydrography marching down the Grand Rue chanting "Out with Zola! Long live the army! Down with the Jews!". They were soon joined by a crowd of over one thousand people, many of them young. They gathered outside a clothing store owned by an Israelite named Blum, some of the protesters armed with stones gathered from the beach.

Emile and his team, working alongside a platoon of gendarmes, had acted quickly to prevent any damage being done to Blum's store, arresting ringleaders and dispersing the crowd. But the troublemakers had returned in their hundreds the very next day, shouting "France for the French!" and 'Long live Joan of Arc!" as this time they targeted a storefront belonging to a Monsieur Lévy. The arrival of mounted gendarmes quickly dispersed the troublemakers and any onlooking thrill-seekers.

There were a number of smaller demonstrations over the next two days, before petering out entirely. The fuse had finally reached Dieppe only to have met a depleted store of gunpowder. The moment had passed. The rarely excitable Norman population returned to their everyday concerns.

Emile felt Polly playing with his hair, idly curling it with her fingers. She had told him how she admired his thick, dark brown locks – an inherited trait from his despised father. Emile had grown to hate this man he never knew, this phantom who had bequeathed him his looks, and had therefore never considered himself handsome.

Polly's hair was fine and fair, through which her slightly protruding ears would poke. Along with everything about her, he had become uncommonly fond of what might be considered an aberration from the ideals of feminine beauty. And he liked to kiss those ears, which made Polly feign distaste but never recoil. Was this what true love felt like?

They had the cottage to themselves, but only until after Easter when Mrs Middleton would return with Little Lil. Polly missed her daughter, but understood that the company of her young cousins in England would be preferable to the mainly adult society in a wintry and politically volatile Dieppe.

Lydia had become engaged and would stay in England. Mrs Middleton's frequent long letters conveyed her concern that her flighty younger daughter was too young for such a permanent attachment. Emile, basking in the love he shared with Polly, looked back bemused at that fleeting passion he had felt for Lydia the previous summer.

"It had been a close shave", as Walter had remarked, before returning to London the previous autumn. He had some Dieppe scenes he wished to exhibit, while hoping to refresh his contacts within the London art world. Emile also suspected that the dramatic events of the previous summer, albeit happily resolved, had made a change of scene all for the more attractive. Walter too would return to Dieppe after Easter.

Before he left, Walter had sketched Emile in his new commissaire's uniform, the sabre of office worn proudly around his waist. He had since had the drawing framed and it now hung next to Walter's sketch of Lydia and Polly, the one with their backs turned towards the artist.

The cottage was cold and damp in the winter, despite the stove being permanently charged with coal and small logs from the local beech forest. Emile and Polly had decided to live without a maid, Polly cooking and cleaning while Emile eased into his position as head of the local police station. It was another good reason for Little Lil to live elsewhere.

With Polly's divorce going through the French courts at a speed and facility unknown in England, Emile would propose marriage as soon as possible. They would then look for a home of their own, with rooms for Mrs Middleton and Little Lil.

'What are you thinking about?' said Polly, shifting her weight for greater comfort.

'Just us, my love. The future.'

Emile looked up at Walter's sketch of himself in his new commissaire's uniform. He had been wearing it during the recent unrest, at the height of which he noticed an older man among the youthful faces of students and other troublemakers.

He had locked eyes with Frossard, so strange in his civilian wardrobe, the two of them suddenly insulated from the surrounding tumult by the strength of their mutual gaze. Frossard's mouth had opened as if to speak, but then he had turned his head towards the rest of the crowd and begun exhorting them with more slogans. Distracted momentarily, Emile had looked back but Frossard had vanished.

* * *

From her perch on the first floor of Mason Grisch, its balcony windows now closed against the cold winter air, Venetia watched the students marching up and down the

Grand Rue. She could hear their idiotic shouts of "Out with Zola!", "Down with the Jews!" and 'Long live the army!"

She felt relieved that she hadn't been the one whose revelations instigated this unrest. The one who possessed the letter identifying Major Esterhazy as the real traitor, rather than the wretched Dreyfus. That responsibility now rested with those who had finally recognised Esterhazy's handwriting and had alerted the supporters of the wrongfully imprisoned wretch.

She often wondered whether the private detectives guarding the gates to the Duchesse Caracciolo's residence had ever passed on the dossier. And if they had, had the duchess forwarded it to the ultimate addressee, the newspaper editor in London, Rachel Beer?

Venetia had closely observed the duchess in the casino in the weeks after she and Henry had passed on the papers. Nothing in her demeanour suggested that she was troubled or that she had read the momentous claims made in the dossier. But then would her habitually poised bearing ever betray any such inner turmoil?

Certainly, there had been no revelations in the English press, in Rachel Beer's newspapers or elsewhere. As for the Reverend Henry Gibson, the vicar had other matters to contend with following his controversial sermon about the murdered prostitute. Whether directly connected or not, Henry had received a new position not long afterwards. A parish in Lancashire – a mill town, she had heard - had become vacant and he had seemingly been persuaded to accept it.

How such matters were dealt with by the Church, Venetia had no idea. She imagined that Lord Salisbury, a man with deeply ingrained conservative values, might have had a hand. The prime minister had been personally affronted by Henry discussing his relationship with a Dieppe tart while his lordship's family were present in church.

Either way, Venetia had heard that Henry was no longer living with his wife. Lucy had, by all accounts, refused to move to Lancashire. A suitable excuse had been made about her remaining in Surrey for its more clement climate. Lucy's health was fragile and she wanted to be closer to her children. She would, it was said, join Henry at a later date.

No, Venetia and Henry had been wise to leave the momentous revelations about Major Esterhazy to more powerful individuals better placed to deal with the consequences. And yet the journalist in her felt ashamed at backing away from what would surely have been the scoop (that horrible American word again) of the century.

But then Venetia knew in her heart of hearts that she was not *that* type of journalist. The comings and goings of the English colony in Dieppe were her subject, not world-shaking affairs of state. Not revelations that threatened the very fabric of France. Leave that to such eminent public figures as Emile Zola.

And it suddenly seemed that these troubling events had reached the very doors of Maison Grisch. Venetia was just deciding how much of her brioche to share with Tippet when a fierce rapping noise could be heard directly below.

Craning to see as much as possible from the veranda windows, she could make out a small group striking their canes against the frontage of the patisserie. "Out with the yids… it's always the yids!" shouted one of the young men, who had just noticed Venetia peering down at him.

A discreet cough alerted Venetia to the presence of the patron, Monsieur Grisch, standing beside her table.

'Worry not Madame Hall. I have secured the front with an iron grill. They cannot enter. Unfortunately, you won't be able to leave until the police arrive. Unless you wish to depart from the service entrance at the back.'

'That won't be necessary, Monsieur Grisch,' said Venetia, who had no intention of missing this tumultuous scene. It wouldn't do for her readers, of course, spoiling her carefully cultivated image of Dieppe as a pleasurably invigorating destination full of society's most civilised individuals. These riots were the wrong sort of "invigorating".

'I'm so sorry for you, Monsieur Grisch.'

'And I am not even Jewish,' he said, throwing up his hands. 'I'm a Protestant from Alsace. Luxembourg originally.'

'I don't think this mob care for Protestants either, I'm afraid. You and I are in league, it seems with the Jews, to bring an end to Catholic rule in France.'

A sudden fracas alerted Venetia to the fact that the gendarmes had arrived and were now collaring the nearest youths.

'*Qu'ils mangent de la brioche*,' Venetia said.

Monsieur Grisch's furrowed brow told her that he hadn't caught reference to Marie Antionette's supposed remark about starving peasants. Let them eat cake. Tippet's ears had however pricked up. *Brioche* was one of the very few words, French or otherwise, that he understood.

POSTSCRIPT

Rachel Beer, the pioneering editor of the *Observer* and a staunch supporter of the wrongly accused Alfred Dreyfus, finally managed to interview the real traitor in the affair, Major Ferdinand Esterhazy.

Having fled France following his trial (in which he was controversially acquitted in January 1898) and shaved off his moustache, Esterhazy arrived in London in September of that year. The *Observer's* Paris correspondent Rowland Strong provided him with a bed in his own rooms on St James Street. It was there that he was interviewed at length by both Strong and Rachel Beer, receiving £500 for his services.

The resulting article, *Light Upon the Dreyfus Case*, prompted significant discussion in both England and France, where his confessions led eventually to Dreyfus's belated pardon. 'To pardon the innocent is an eccentric proceeding,' wrote Beer. 'Especially after a trial that was a mockery of justice.'

ACKNOWLEDGEMENTS

With enormous gratitude to Sally Harris and my sister, Harriett Gilbert, for their help and encouragement during the writing of this book.